CW00719937

Looking for Bluebirds

Looking for Bluebirds

MARK EVANS

Published by Finstall Press

A CIP catalogue record for this book is available from the British Library.

ISBN 978-1-9989957-0-7

Book layout and cover design by Clare Brayshaw

Prepared and printed by:

York Publishing Services Ltd
64 Hallfield Road
Layerthorpe
York YO31 7ZQ

Tel: 01904 431213

Website: www.yps-publishing.co.uk

To Tom, Jonno and Bee

Prologue

Every second passing. Another second lived.

They were exposed. Picked out by the searchlights and chased by anti-aircraft fire – an overture for the German night fighters, waiting for them over their target below.

From the rear turret Harry could see one now, tracking them. He opened up and was firing so fast that his gun jammed. Harry froze. Fuselage started splintering, fragments blown away. The radio-op's slumped. Flames licking like a slow burning fuse along the wing. One engine dead and the bomber's skewing. Pilot shouting, ordering them out. Winter, the mid-gunner, heading for the side door. Harry, the arse end charlie, grabbing a chute from the fuselage, turning the turret, squeezing through the gap and falling out, backwards. Into the dark. Through the darkness, black-cold, down, falling. Hearing his heart. Somersaulting. Downwards. Knowing there was always going to be 'his time'. This time, his time. Falling. Praying. Pulling the ripcord. Jerking upwards as the chute opened.

Going down through the darkness of night slowly, that black shroud to cover him now shredded by the barrage exploding around him; tracer bullets with colours making them look like bolts from a comic strip. Holding himself, trying to remember anything. Frightened of dying; of not dying. Bomber's gone. Friends dead. And he's falling. Nothing but fires below and the sound of whistling bombs somewhere behind and the whine of sirens getting louder as he falls. Not into water. Not water. The wind playing with him, as he comes down closer and closer. Using risers to guide him to the fields below. Down. But wind gusting, taking him towards trees. Stopping, then jerking up again. Canopy catching on branches and holding him. Heart still beating. One of the lucky ones. Looking down he could see that he wasn't far from the ground.

Pulled out his knife and started cutting through the suspension lines to get him away from the canopy that had him dangling. Trapped, but slashing and pulling to get away. The next thing he knew he was falling down onto the bank below. Not much of him to soften the blow and trying to remember anything he had learnt about protecting himself. This time he had a soft mossy bank to help him. Hurting, but breathing. Now he had to find a way to get rid of his chute.

Getting to his feet he moved towards the base of the tree. He was looking up at the branches and the chute blowing about when his head swung around and his hand dropped to his belt as he became aware of a movement behind him. No one was close, but he could only smile as he saw the billowing descent of another parachute lower down the field.

Winter?

Without thinking he left the remains of his chute blowing about in the wind and started running towards where he thought the chute had come down. By the time he had covered the distance, crouching and taking care over the ground because it was dark and the ground so uneven, taking the slope down towards a low stone wall, there was no sign of anyone.

For one moment he began to wonder if he might have been hallucinating when a figure appeared from behind the wall. Harry's hand dropped to his belt.

"Pretty dicey, eh?"

Harry moved up to the wall, saw Winter grinning as though his leave had just started and allowed himself to smile at the pilot's favourite phrase which Winter had managed to perfect.

"Telling me. Too close. Not sure if anyone else got out. We're down and alive and I can't see any reason to change that. Chute's tangled in a tree over there," Harry said pointing over his shoulder, "I need to get rid of it."

"I'm burying mine. I'll follow you."

Harry looked round him. Great big bloody field to land in and he has to pick the corner with a clump of trees. From here, he thought, his chute stuck up that tree looks like a bloomin' calling card if ever he saw one.

By the time Winter joined him, Harry was still struggling to get the parachute clear from the branches. What little moonlight there was seemed blanked by the canopy above.

"Forgot to say," started Harry, "it's good to see you Winter."

Harry was waiting for a reply and turned expecting to see Winter gathering the chute pieces together for burying. But Winter seemed to be looking behind him towards the trees that lined the field. Following Winter's gaze, Harry froze as he saw a group of men standing there staring at them. It was difficult to see if they were carrying weapons but Harry didn't want to risk it even though a couple were dressed in jeans and short sleeve shirts and looked like farmers. That's when Harry became aware of two lads who couldn't have been more than fourteen, coming out of the woods and surreptitiously joining the group. They had army caps on, wore small packs on their backs and carried sniper rifles. Harry feared the worst. He'd read somewhere about Hitler's 'werewolves'. He was about to say, "Don't move."

But feeling relieved to be alive, and perhaps hoping that the arm of friendship might have its uses, Winter, had put his hand in his pocket to find some cigarettes to offer the farmers. One of the boys opened fire on the gunner before the packet was out of his pocket.

"*Was ist das?*"[1] one of the farmers cried.

"*Ausführung!*"[2] the boy answered.

Harry froze, looking at the villagers as if pleading for his life and staring at the lifeless body of Winter on the ground ahead of him. He needn't have worried because the farmers were shaking their heads with looks of disbelief at such a gross act of cowardice.

"*Nein, nein,*"[3] he heard one of them say.

Two of the group of men then chased the boys back into the forest with the clubs and pistols that Harry could now see them brandishing. Tying Harry's hands behind his back so tightly he could feel the rope cutting into his wrists, they walked him to the nearest village. From there and a phone call later, a tortuous journey with nothing to hold onto in the back of a truck brought him bruised all over and crawling with tiredness, first to a transit camp and then onto a Stalag Luft.[4]

It was bad timing. Though Harry would never have known it.

---

1   What's that?
2   Execution
3   No, no
4   Luftwaffe-run prisoner of war camp for captured Western Allied air force personnel

1

Harry

At the end of April, 1945, on a bunk inside the camp, Harry was still trying to stop his wheezing and coughing. At that time he was aware of two things in particular: that the pains he'd been feeling in his chest were getting worse and time was still moving at a slug-like pace.

For Harry, like others, Monty was too far away. They all dismissed the Field-Marshal's caution that kept them waiting in limbo. Few of them were moved by the blood-red posters telling them that the Russians were the real enemy, and that *'England will find herself isolated against a Soviet Europe and a Soviet Asia from the Atlantic to the Pacific.'* As soon as they heard the heavy cannon fire getting closer and closer, they'd all start shouting, "Come on, Joe," even though there was as great a chance of explosions coming from the Germans blowing up bridges in their retreat.

Yesterday they all knew there had been room commander meetings, and bulletins were given out with the latest news. About ten in the morning Harry cursed when he heard the message that they were being ordered to dig slit trenches. "Not sure how much more of this I'm going to be good for," he said to himself. To be fair, he knew the SBO[1] did not want the POWs to be in the middle of a

---

1   Senior British Officer

battle between the Germans and the advancing Red Army. By evening the whole compound was slashed with endless foxholes. Because there were so few shovels, they had to dig with anything they could put their hands on. Harry had found yet another use for his Klim can. It wasn't fast work but Harry wasn't trying to compete with anyone.

As the sun came up, Harry gave a cursory glance through the barrack casement windows. Nothing had yet changed the dismal backdrop: other barracks, two fences, ten feet high, strung with horizontal and vertical savage barbed wire stretched around the perimeter to the front where Stalag Luft was inscribed above the main gate in gothic script; ten feet inside the fence was a double strand of barbed wire which acted as a warning wire. Anyone going over that wire would be shot. The compound was guarded by eight towers, one on each corner and one on the middle of each exterior side. From this compound, unlike many of the others, a walk along the much-trodden path inside the warning wire gave a view in the distance of the nearest village, dominated by the slightly tilting steeple of its church.

There was little that would have encouraged Harry or anyone from the huts to arise this early. Moving out of them into the yard when the siren for roll call went off was enough of an imposition and always accomplished with the lethargy and despondency of soldiers who had been in the camp for as long as they had, which in many cases stretched to years. For a while they had been shambolic, with POWs moving around to confuse the guards and catcalling back to annoy the Germans.

On this particular morning, the first man from Harry's hut to feel the need to gaze outside, as if needing to confirm that his incarceration was still as much of a nightmare as it had ever been, thought at first that he was dreaming.

"Who the hell is that?" he asked, in a tone more of surprise than shock, before repeating it as much to himself as anyone else.

The comment was almost lost in the ennui that had kept the men doing endlessly repetitive mindless tasks every day since their arrival at the camp. Though some were thought to be unstable on arrival at the camp and others to have been so ground down into states of confusion and depression by their treatment at the hands of brutal guards that their aberrant behaviour was tolerated as predictably unsettled, Harry and many inmates of the hut this morning recognised the voice as one that belonged to neither group.

Words for many of them had too often lost power and meaning, stripped of their usual associations. Often it seemed it was the tone of what was said that mattered more than the words themselves. Had it not been for this change of tone from the speaker, the fellow POW would not, despite the cold, have moved his scrawny frame off the mattress to join him at the window.

"Move over, will you?" the new onlooker said.

Crouching down so that he could see for himself through the grubby porthole of a window, it didn't take him long to reach his own opinion.

"Lads!" he shouted, "he's right! The bloody guards have gone."

"There's still one of them in the towers," someone shouted.

"Not Germans though," another answered, "they're wearing armbands!"

Harry, like the others, knew that the SBO's first duty was to ensure their safety. He later found out that in order to do so, he had hand-picked a group of men, called by him the 'Field Force', who would be in charge of camp order until Allied forces arrived. Each of these was wearing an armband with 'FF' on them.

Though the years incarcerated in pitiful conditions had blunted the appetite of even the strongest-willed amongst them, the movement that this comment generated from the hitherto prone figures was like a forgotten spark flickering into life again, hungry for oxygen.

Within seconds Harry and the others were getting out of their pits, still unsure whether they could let their minds accept the reality of what they had heard. Standing at the door someone pushed at the heavy panels gingerly, still expecting the retaliation of a clubbing from the stock of the guard's rifle. As the door swung back, the strange silence seemed to grow.

"Would you believe it?" someone said, looking at the deserted yard, "they've buggered off."

It didn't take Harry long to follow others from his hut outside. But he walked slowly with an uncertainty and shakiness that follows the shocked. With every unrestrained step taken, he became even more transfixed by the new world that now confronted him. Others were more than ready to take it in and accept the weird emptiness of the control towers, the absence of guards and their orders, so often barked at them through loudhailers. Amongst this group there was an explosion of shouting and laughter, hugging and crying as the reality of this morning's reveille seeped into their consciousness. And the greater the sound they generated, the easier it became for those like Harry who were still unable to accept that what they saw before them now was more than just a dream.

In the next few minutes, the rest of the camp joined in this sleep-walking exodus from their quarters, after being shaken awake by sounds that they had never heard before.

Inmates from huts all over the camp, curious at the strangely familiar sounds they could hear through their befuddled sleep, began to open up their own doors, just as cautiously, until there was a continuous flow of men walking out into the compound, each one looking as stunned as the next.

For much of the day, Harry joined others gathering in the southeast corner of the compound looking into the distance waiting for some sign. For some it had been months and for others years during which they had been forced to stay behind the warning line with the penalty of death for those who did not heed the warning. Now they were against the perimeter wire looking for any sign of the approaching Allies.

There were rumours flying about all over the camp about how far away they were and whether the Allied Forces might beat the Russians to it. After so long the excitement of the POWs was barely containable but gradually they got used to their first taste of relative freedom and the mood in the camp quietened. When it grew so dark that it made no sense to stay peering into the distance any longer, the men returned to the barracks. They had only just returned when the SBO came in and announced,

"This is the historic moment we have all been waiting for. American and British parachutists have been joined by their Russian allies."

Harry and the others didn't need to hear anymore. That was the time they began to properly believe they would survive and get home. Without waiting, they all ran outside, cheering, shouting and hugging each other. Later back in the barracks they couldn't stop the celebrations: shouting, singing, stamping their feet and using any metal they could find to bang against the pipes.

2

Martha

Hestor Street, a row of terraced houses darkened by age and the proximity of coke-fuelled industries on the eastern edge of Olthorp, had still managed to escape the ravages of bombing raids. Some called it the armpit of Olthorp because of the sulphurous smell that came from the munitions factory whenever there was a westerly blowing. This still couldn't dampen Martha's feeling for the place. Brought up among the hills and valleys that spread like a thorny spine away from the coast as it waved south, she would have nothing said against it. And over time, she had to admit, you even got used to the smell.

"It just lives with you," she'd say to those who complained about it, "and without the munitions factory we wouldn't be winning the war one and two I wouldn't have a job. It's a part of me now and I don't know what I'd do without it."

Built on a long strip of land, taken from farmers, which ran alongside the railway line, the factory was dug into an area which had steep sloping walls of earth around it so that any local blast went upwards and surrounded by several miles of fencing – high and sharp enough to deter any likely trespassers. To avoid detection from the air, it was covered by mounds of earth covered in grass. The inside, as Martha would testify, wasn't much more attractive. All the women worked in bays, dressed in their protective uniform, where the machines were mounted behind rails and safety instructions visible on the wall behind.

When she began to work there, she'd count the minutes til the end of the shift. After an early start, usually around six o'clock, they'd put on protective clothes and tie their hair back with snoods and spend much of the day working the machines where her hands felt constantly numb from the freezing oil that they used to keep the machines cool. It was a relief as much as anything when she was asked to move onto the section making bombs and checking high explosives fuses. But in the new section, the yellow dust from the cordite still found its way through every layer and when Martha got home and changed her clothes even her knickers were yellow. She and the other girls at the works used to make a joke of it, "Bloody regulations tell us we can only have knickers in white, pink or blue when we come to work, but there's nothing but yellow when we leave it," they'd quip. In the factory, they were known as the 'Yellow Canaries'.

On the other side of the town, heavy industry stretched all the way to the coast. Martha would admit that on a clear early summer's day, as she looked across the valley towards the sea, a coastline barely visible in any weather, she could still be moved by the sight of those stark proud chimneys billowing smoke from the steel mills, a patchwork of towers and pylons, like the playpen of some industrial beast.

When she remembered how the mills had managed to keep up their production despite Jerry's attempts to bomb them out of existence, she knew it made it all worthwhile. The thought of the mills being hit, she'd somehow never contemplated. How could she with her Billy working there? Though he knew the risks well enough, he'd never dreamed of working anywhere else.

"I got my papers," he'd told Martha, "and they told me where to go. That's enough for me."

But today, Martha knew, was different for everyone. Even though it was a public holiday and the sky was cloudless, Martha had been inside all day waiting for some end to the events that had begun so much earlier. She was taken by surprise at hearing Connie's voice screaming at her much earlier in the day, when she was about to walk out of the house, (she could have sworn that Connie had talked about a date at least a week away). But as the hours passed, surprise had given way to concern, worry and anxiety as she waited for the arrival of the midwife. Because she had taken her share of responsibility for the arrangements of the day's VE celebrations, she'd spent the day looking at the clock, worrying that time was running out and that she'd never be able to get to them before they ended.

Now as darkness was beginning to fall, Martha was still at home, listening for some sign that Connie's ordeal upstairs was coming to an end. She had taken herself into the kitchen and was trying to keep herself busy cleaning the larder cupboard, assembling on the counter the various opened, but not yet finished, packets of flour and sugar (with so little she need barely have bothered, though the thought of jam or jelly was still enough to keep it there), each one closed with a clothes peg, the large tins of dried egg and the Kilner jars, filled with the mouth-watering delights of deep-red Victoria plums. Looking at them, Martha wondered whether she had waited long enough for an occasion to feast on them.

In another jar on the shelf above the counter, she could see the ration coupons that she had been using to keep herself and Billy with a meal to eat every day and with a pair of shoes to wear as well. She knew that there was limited variety in what they ate, 'corned beef and tatties, again' she could hear herself saying, but Billy was too loyal by nature, too tired at the end of the day and too grateful for the offering in front of him to do anything but eat it with a certain hushed respect. As for shoes, so many points were needed to buy a pair that they'd both make do even when the soles of their shoes were so thin, it felt like they were walking barefoot.

She heard Connie again and couldn't believe she was in a different room. That's when she tried putting her hands over her ears and waiting for the next lull. It was during one of these short quiet all too brief spells, that she heard the midwife's voice calling for a bowl of cold water.

Martha was up in the bedroom as quick as she could. She'd never had visitors in her bedroom before, let alone two of them and for the first time she was worried about the state she and Billy had left it in. Knowing Billy, there was bound to be clutter about the room. She knew they were lucky to have got hold of bits of furniture – the wardrobe and chest of drawers (he had the bottom shelf, she had the top two) – because the news blamed the shortage of timber for the delays. For the two of them, it was hardly a matter of needing more space, because they had so few clothes anyway. Martha couldn't remember when she had bought any decent clothing for herself. They'd all listened to the advice to 'make do and mend'.

She put the bowl down next to the bed on the small bedside table where a candle had been left on a chipped plate and stepped back a little. It was hard to stop herself looking at Connie and trying to find her hazel eyes but that familiar face seemed to be locked in a grimace. Even when she whispered to her friend, "Connie, Connie, it's me Martha," the same grip of anxiety never left Connie's face and the sideways glance from the midwife was enough to persuade Martha to retreat downstairs as quietly as she could.

By the time she got there, all she wanted to do was to blank out the noise. She was so intent on trying to fill her head with the sound from the radio that she almost missed it. But then it was repeated and the shock of hearing the king saying that the war was over couldn't stop her. She ran up the stairs, shouting, "It's over, it's over. The king… I've just heard him… he's been on the radio. We've won the war!"

"That's the job," she heard the midwife say, in her slow singalong voice.

When news about the surrender on Lüneburg Heath came through, Martha had been at work at the munitions factory. The shouting and cheering was deafening, with everyone finding metal to clash against metal. Soon they all downed tools and went outside hugging each other and dancing. As soon as Martha got home that evening, she had turned on the radio.

It was still there in the front room, sitting on the sideboard next to the clock. There was little else in the room apart from the floral two-seater settee, an armchair with the antimacassar and a wooden table which they had put underneath the window sill. Though her mother had wanted to give the radio pride of place because it had been a gift to her, she knew it would be taken as a slight if she didn't use it. But Martha could still remember the look on her father's face as he came into the room when she and her mother and Robert had been listening to it. She wondered if it had been Vera Lynn singing – her mother's favourite. Without saying anything to any of them, her father strode across the room, turned the radio off, waited a few moments, put his hands inside the lapels of his jacket and looking at each of them in turn said, "God will speak to us in silence and we must be ready for Him," before leaving the room. He never relented.

But her mother had refused to throw it away, hidden it and only brought it out after her father's death. It couldn't have given her much joy, Martha realised, because her own funeral followed shortly afterwards. But for Martha now it was a godsend and she'd have it on all the time: 'Workers Play Time', 'Forces Favourites', 'Tommy Handley and ITMA' or the big American jazz bands – she'd come to love them all.

Earlier the previous week, a site had been chosen for the celebrations. Since then everyone had been preparing for the news that they knew couldn't be far away. Martha had helped to clean the site and there was no shortage of volunteers, including Billy, to feed the bonfire with crushed tables, discarded furniture and any item which they no longer had a use for or had been ravaged from the houses when buildings were destroyed by bombs.

Because everyone knew the moment was coming, they were savouring the anticipation of pleasure that they had been denied for so long. All that they had seen on the newsreels at the cinema in town gave them the same message – this war was nearly over!

Against the side wall of the house at the end of the terrace, trestle tables had been erected, lent by shops or the church. Shopkeepers had left sweets, jellies and fruits on them and neighbours had added their pooled meagre sweet rations. During the 'rumour days' they'd collected fat, sugar, and flour and made them into small cakes of all shapes and sizes for the children. Any spare jam jars had been offered and were now sitting on the tables, a small candle placed inside each one.

All through the week as the bonfire had been growing, men, women and children put bunting together, streamers and coloured towels, to drape across the street. Despite her condition, Connie had wanted to do her bit and she'd told Martha how that started everything off.

Connie

Connie said it was because she couldn't sleep – she'd been calling herself a walrus for ages and any movement seemed to wake her – that she had been up so bright and early that morning. After chatting to her neighbour across the street the previous evening, they'd agreed to hang a line between the houses. From the upstairs window, she had been trying to secure her end of the line. It was all fingers and thumbs with Connie and holding half a brick in her right hand she was about to bang in a nail that would hold it when she felt the first spasm. She shouted as the strange pain unfurled through her lower body. With the shock of it, her hand jerked forward and the brick fell, crashing onto the pavement below. The next moment she was on her haunches, her arms wrapped around her sides, resting on the swelling.

Connie told Martha that she'd packed a bag and left the house as soon as she could, taking the few things that she felt would be of any help. She realised that she needed to get to Hestor Street as soon as possible. But she thought Martha should be there and said a small prayer then when she remembered it was a public holiday. If not, Martha would probably have left for work already because Connie knew how proud Martha was over her recent promotion and realised that she'd never willingly be late for work. 'If it wasn't for the unions, we wouldn't be winning this war,' Martha had repeated to Connie many times.

So with one hand holding her bag and the other resting against her stomach, Connie had told Martha that she tried to walk as quickly as she could between the contractions. Each time she had another, she'd bend over and crouch. Only one person saw her slow stagger up the street – Mrs Granger whom Connie recognised. They'd worked together at the barrage balloon factory until it was too uncomfortable for Connie to spend so much time standing.

"You're in trouble aren't you, dear?" Mrs Granger said. "I can see that now. Hope the father's done the decent thing."

Breathing as slowly as she could Connie straightened up and walked away.

"Anyway, it's celebration time now, isn't it?" Mrs Granger had shouted after her. "But it looks as though you've got a double celebration on your hands, assuming it was intended."

Connie carried on up the street as fast as she was able, trying to forget the spite in Granger's words. By the time she turned the corner into Martha's street, she was exhausted and she watched, horrified, as she saw Martha close her front door, and then walk away towards the bus stop at the end of the street.

"Martha!" Connie screamed, bending over as another wave passed through her.

As soon as she heard the voice, Martha stopped and turned around. The next moment she came walking up the street towards Connie as fast as she could.

"Oh Connie, you've started," she said rushing up to her oldest friend and putting her arm around her for support, "come on, we need to get you inside."

Connie told Martha that she'd suddenly felt very weak, as though a valve had been released and the strength was suddenly sapping out of her. It was the shock of the pain and the realisation that the waiting was over, she said, that made her crumble.

"Oh, Martha, I don't think I can do this," she said.

"'Course you can. Here," Martha said, fluffing up the cushions at the back of the chair in the parlour, "sit yourself down there."

But no sooner had Connie lowered herself to the seat and begun to catch her breath, than she felt another surge starting.

"Oh God," she shouted, "it's getting worse."

Connie closed her eyes and tried to breathe in gasps though the contraction.

"We need to get the midwife for you," she heard Martha shout and then the sound of the door closing.

3

Martha

A little after tea time and desperate for air, Martha left the house.

Walking towards the noise that she was sure was coming from the site, she walked past the street lamps whose black and white stripes were looking tired and she wondered how much longer they would be necessary. She just wanted to savour the change, the warmth, the ordinariness of having street lights on again. At the next street she came to, she saw boys and girls racing. On a wooden table at this end of the street she saw a handful of eggs waiting for the winners. Eggs, she smiled! How many times had she dreamt of eggs! And as she heard the children laughing, unable to contain their excitement, she stopped and looked at them, as though they belonged to a species that had almost become extinct but was now free to live and grow again.

She looked up and saw a line suspended across the street. Gently swaying from it in the May breeze, there was an effigy of the most hated man in Europe. Down at the factory she'd heard that the dressmaker had been asked to help finish off the grey suit that would soon be burnt to cinders.

What a relief to be outside, she thought. Like a trapped animal, she'd gone from room to room, trying to find something to distract her but all the time followed by the waves of sound that were reverberating around her small house. Martha knew she'd make a hopeless midwife and had got herself into a real panic by the time the midwife eventually arrived. The hospital had talked about a change of shifts and asked Martha to leave a message for the midwife to come to her house as soon as she returned to the hospital. When the knock on the door did come, Martha burst into tears as she opened the door onto a middle-aged woman wearing a dark coat.

"I'm sorry," Martha blurted out, "please come in."

"I'm Ellen Price, but you can call me Mrs Price," the woman announced as she came into the house, untying the scarf from around her head as she did so.

By the time Martha had shown her into the parlour, she had taken off her coat and put it over the back of the chair, with her scarf.

"Well, where is she then?" Mrs Price asked.

At first Martha wasn't sure where Connie had gone, but then saw the kitchen door was ajar.

"Connie," she shouted.

Rushing through the kitchen and out into the back yard, she saw Connie panting and leaning against the door of the privy.

"The midwife's here, Connie," she said going up to her and putting her around Connie's shoulders.

Connie lifted her head and Martha was shocked at the look she saw on the face of her friend. It reminded her of the looks on people's faces as the doodlebugs came over and the motor had cut out.

"Come on," Mrs Price said, moving forward past Martha and up to Connie, "let's get you on a bed, shall we?"

Together they helped Connie to her feet and walked back with her through the parlour.

"She can use my bedroom," Martha said, "it's bigger. It's the one on the right."

"What? Do you mean this is not the mother's home?"

"No," explained Martha, "Billy and I live here."

Martha could see Mrs Price looking at her with those heavy eyebrows that seemed to meet in the middle.

"You see," continued Martha, trying to ignore the smell of mothballs that she thought must be coming from the midwife's coat, "she doesn't have family now and I'm her closest friend."

"And the father? Do we know who the father is?"

"Yes," Martha said quickly and then added, "but he's not back yet."

"Well, let's hope he does come back. There are too many without fathers already. Now let's just get – what's your name, dear?" Mrs Price asked.

Connie's chest was going up and down.

"Connie," she gasped.

"Good, Connie, because it's time we had a look to see what's happening down there."

As Mrs Price turned her head to indicate to Martha that she'd be better elsewhere, Connie took in a breath that seemed to turn into a cry as it went into her lungs and then she started gasping for air as if she was drowning.

"Slowly, slowly," Martha heard, as she watched the midwife putting her hand into the small of Connie's back, gently persuading Connie to climb the stairs.

The further Martha walked the more uncertain she became about leaving the house. For so long now, Connie had become used to whatever help and encouragement Martha could give her and Martha had never hesitated. As the days passed, Martha guessed how unforgiving people were likely to be towards Connie and how much harder she would find it. The least she could do was to offer support to Connie who was doing it all on her own and needed a friend, someone, anyone, to be there with her. That's when Martha turned back.

Billy

By the time Billy arrived at the site, there were bustling crowds around the bonfire, with Union Jacks everywhere. Some were hanging from windows and doors and others used them as dresses and smocks for children. Everyone was singing and shouting and there were children running between the tables and chairs that had been set up for the occasion. The bonfire was stacked up as high as a tram and was still waiting to be lit.

"Go and get Hitler," he heard someone shout.

As Billy moved forward, a young girl who couldn't have been more than seventeen threw her arms around his neck and kissed him.

"Ain't it beautiful, look," she said, before skipping onto the next person she came to.

He turned around to see a dozen or more children carrying candles in jars, walking slowly down the street. Darkness had been the only colour they'd lived with for so long. To see anything different now made him feel he was dreaming.

Billy might have had a heart of stone, he thought, hardened by the years of endless shifts at the steelworks, where the noise and the heat at the works made many workers feel as though they were already in hell, working such backbreaking hours that it took all his energy to find his way back home to bed, but looking at these lights now reminded him of seeing the fairy lights on the Christmas tree for the first time.

"You alright, Billy?"

He hadn't noticed where Robert came from, but as soon as he heard that voice with plums stuck deep down inside, it made him feel like puking.

"About as alright as you'd feel if you ever did a decent day's work."

"Don't start on that now. Anyway, I think I'm going to have to leave you to celebrate," Robert said.

"Not joining in the fun then? Don't think you've done your bit to deserve it, eh? Well, you'd be right there."

"No, it's the dancing on the grave of the dead I don't like, Billy. But at least this looks like the end."

"Well, it may be, but no thanks to you."

Billy pushed his hand through his dark hair and turned to look towards the crowds around the fire.

"Haven't seen Martha, have you?" Billy asked.

For a moment Robert stood there looking at Billy with a strange expression on his face, before asking,

"Why should I have seen her? She's hardly been talking to me as long as I can remember. Sometimes I even wonder whether she thinks she's got a brother."

"She thinks we all have a duty."

"And do you know she's right. Mine happens to be to my conscience. It's different that's all."

"And very bloody convenient," Billy said.

"Well, that puts us both in the same boat, doesn't it? I mean neither of us have seen the horrors of the front."

"That's a bit bloody cheap isn't it? I mean one of us goes down the steelworks days and nights, year after bloody year. You want to try it one of these days. Some days it's like hell down there, the heat and the smell with those furnaces.

And the other one refuses to fight and sits on his bloody arse instead. I don't see how these two could ever be the same."

"Listen," someone shouted behind them, "it's the king."

Billy and Robert were moved with the crowds closer to the radio.

"…we give thanks to Almighty God for a great deliverance. Speaking from our Empire's oldest capital city…"

The rest of the sentence was lost in a succession of fireworks that shot into the sky. As soon as the broadcast ended, someone put a gramophone on one of the tables and selected a record from the piles of records that people had left on the trestle table.

It was 'The White Cliffs of Dover'.

"Light the fire," roared the crowd.

Billy saw the firewatcher move forward, holding a long pole. At the end of it, an old cloth had been tied and soaked in paraffin. When he had moved the eager young bodies a safe distance from the centre, he bent forward, lit the end and pushed it towards the bottom of the mountain of the pile and then started walking slowly round, making sure that the fire was lit on all sides.

On top of the bonfire was the effigy which had been tied to a chair to make it more secure. It wasn't long before the fire was ablaze, sending sparks shooting into the evening sky.

The crowd standing around the fire weaved their arms together shouting for the hokey cokey and before he could step away, Billy found himself next to Robert and a few moments later he couldn't stop himself joining in with the singing and shouting "in out, in out and shake it all about," followed by the chorus. The more they sang they faster they went in and faster they came out again and the tighter he seemed to be holding onto Robert's arm. Each time they went towards the fire they threw up their arms together and screamed.

Billy looked across at Robert and could see him smiling and hear his laughter above the noise. Robert was barely able to stop himself doing the whole thing again when they'd all stopped singing and he started pulling Billy back towards the fire and out again.

"Like I said, Billy, everything's changed," Robert shouted.

Others had dropped off their arms and Billy was aware that there was no one else around them.

"It's time to celebrate, Billy," Robert said and as they moved together towards the fire Billy felt his arm being pulled back as Robert swung around in front of him. With his free arm Robert reached out for Billy's shoulder. But before he could do so Billy lifted Robert's arm from his shoulder and tossed it away.

"But what's done is not that easily forgotten, is it, Robert?" Billy said, as Robert turned to walk away.

A woman just beside Billy shouted,

"Soak it in water."

"Yeah, let the bugger burn for ages," Billy cheered, before walking away.

In front of the first pub Billy came to was a sign saying that they had run out of beer and the next was the same. He decided to stop there anyway and when he went inside he found someone in the corner was playing on the piano. All the drinkers were flinging their arms in the air, singing and shouting *God Save the King* and drinking as fast as they could. Billy recognised one or two from the steelworks and before he could get anywhere near the bar, someone grabbed hold of him and started to pour cider down his throat.

"Give us a hand, Billy, will yer? We want to get this old box outside," a man said slapping the piano with the side of his hand.

"Music by starlight," another cheered.

As soon as they had moved the piano onto the street and lodged it with wood to make it stable, everyone came outside asking for songs, promising the player drinks, if he'd play their favourite songs.

"'Lili Marlene' – 'There'll Always Be An England'" someone shouted.

With each song, there was dancing and singing and swapping of partners as no one knew who they were supposed to be with and no one really cared.

By the time he extricated himself from the conga that had weaved its way around the street and back to the pub again and again, Billy was walking with a stagger. From one street to the next he weaved his way and on every other corner he'd join another party, with bonfires fed from the rubble, each celebrating with fireworks and dancing.

Home seemed a long way to Billy that night. Blackouts still made the streets dark and difficult to navigate, and even though he lived here, it was still confusing. But all the way back, Billy couldn't stop thinking about Martha. He still couldn't understand why she hadn't been there, after she'd spent so much time clearing the site and then building it! Even though she'd told him she'd be there, no one he'd spoken to had seen her all day. How could she have missed it when they'd been waiting for this day, talking about it and planning for it for so long?

He slumped along the street. There were still so many fireworks and bangs going off in the neighbourhood that it wasn't until he was stopped outside his front door, underneath the window, that he heard it. Someone in his bedroom was screaming and it didn't sound like Martha. With his back to the house, he slid to the ground and waited. He didn't know how long he sat there before he realised that the noise had stopped. The window was open but the tattered black-out was still up.

"Martha," he called, getting to his feet and staggering a little, "what's going on? Haven't you heard? The bloody war's…"

The door opened.

"Over," Martha said, with a voice trembling in a way Billy hadn't heard before. "Hey, come here," he said, opening his arms to her. "It's over, it's over."

Before he had taken a step closer Martha threw herself at him and buried her head into his chest.

"Hold me," she sobbed, "tighter."

With his arms around her shaking body, he stood there breathing deeply, gently rocking her from side to side. The next minute there were huge explosions in the sky and for one moment he thought it was another barrage. Then he saw rockets shooting up, flare after flare lightening up the sky and the land around and the searchlights panning across the sky.

"Look Martha," he said turning her around with his arms around her waist so that she could see, "that's the end, isn't it?"

She put her hands to her face and started shaking her head,

"Can you not hear, Billy?"

And as the searchlights weaved their path across the sky, chasing each other in a playground of light above his head, he heard it for the first time. It was a cry that Billy had feared he might never hear in his own home.

4

Harry

The following morning the Russians arrived.

Outside, amongst the men waiting in the yard, Harry stood with the same sense of anticipation as the others. Not even the pain in his chest could take away the feeling of euphoria that had been spreading through the camp since yesterday morning. On his arm he was now wearing a white armband with 'English' written on it in Russian.

Like a dream, to many men like Harry, the first to arrive were on horseback.

Harry thought they looked like Cossacks. He could see they were armed with tommy-guns and that they were drunk. One of them held a clutch of gold watches hanging from his hand which he started throwing against a wall of the compound and laughing when the pieces began to fly in all directions.

Later, when this group was joined by other Russians, their commander told the SBO that they should be ready to leave within six hours. No sooner had the word evacuation been mentioned than the camp was spilling with rumours about where they would be going. The dreaded name of Odessa was spoken of with hushed breath because of the reports of so many casualties on the long march in such bitter conditions that other prisoners had suffered.

But as the two leaders were walking towards the edge of the camp, it was clear to Harry and the many POWS following them that the Russian colonel was drunk. The further they walked the more exasperated the Russian colonel became about how ungrateful the POWs were about their liberation. The SBO then turned to the group of men under his responsibility.

"Everyone in the camp has been under some strain for some time. Perhaps we can now show some celebration that the end of this terrible war is nearly with us."

They needed no second invitation. Within minutes, whatever semblance of discipline that had existed in the camp was gone. Thousands of POWs went wild with jubilation. Harry saw men pulling down the dreaded fences. It didn't take long for the towers to crash down outside the perimeter fence. If he'd been feeling up to it, Harry would have joined them. But he knew his chest wouldn't let him. Harry had to content himself with weighing up his possible options. Though he had a wiry build when he was brought to the camp and even with Red Cross parcels, meagre food rations had steadily reduced his physique since his arrival in the Stalag Luft to the waif-like body he now struggled to fill.

Walking about free in the compound in a dazed state, Harry started to feel that something of his luck had returned and a growing belief that he might still get out of it alive. He wandered slowly, not quite sure where to put his feet, emaciated, tired, hungry and sore as were the many other RAF servicemen who had been in the camp for far longer. He knew his service life had started late: so desperate to join up, he'd finished the training at the Officer Training Unit and then at the Lancaster training school as quickly as they could get him through.

They'd all considered themselves lucky to be in the camp, where morale had been good and relations with the guards generally fair. But recently there had been a terrible shortage of food supplies and they had been forced to live off a stew made of boiled grass and beets, with a few potatoes. There'd been days when Harry and others had even looked beyond the perimeter wire to the trees in the distance and wondered if there was any bark which they could pull off and chew. Had it not been for a delivery of Red Cross parcels, Harry wondered whether he'd still have been on his feet.

Harry had made up his mind on a plan of action given the circumstances. That's why he was walking in the direction of the officers' mess. Despite the possibility of going to the nearest village for sustenance as others had decided to do, or even try and reach the Allies front lines, his hunger and poor breathing had persuaded him to look for more immediate relief. Without breaking into a run, Harry moved as fast as he could towards the low squat building, constantly looking back over his shoulder.

Only when he reached the door did he notice two others coming found from the other side, whom he recognised as Dutch.

"Do you think there is food here?" one of them asked.

"No idea," answered Harry, "but there's only one way to find out, isn't there? What are you boys after? Seems to me this is an early Christmas for each of us."

"Bananas," the one said.

"Wine, maybe whisky!" added the other with a wide grin spreading over his sallow face.

"Well, let's see what the bastards have been living off while we've been starving," Harry said before adding, "and we're not going to be able to do that, until we've seen to this here problem."

Harry's miming of taking a wrench to the door was enough to send the Dutch into peals of laughter and have the two of them off scouting round the camp for something to give them a bit of leverage.

They returned a while later with a metal stake which they'd managed, with considerable effort, to lever away from one of the perimeter posts. One of the Dutch had bleeding hands from the wire which had been holding the stake in place. As soon as the other picked it up and used it to jamb the door open, the wood panel started to splinter and with a pistol crack the door gave way.

"Here we go."

Harry didn't need a second invitation.

Inside the mess there was a large wooden table under the window and chairs spread around the room. On a makeshift dresser against one wall, Harry could see piles of crockery and cutlery. Without hesitation he sprang across the room and pulled open the drawers and opened the lower doors of the dresser. Putting his hand inside the drawer he pulled out a number of checked tablecloths and threw them into the air like a magician pulling handkerchiefs from peoples' sleeves.

"Blimey," he said, opening the lower doors of the dresser and unable to stop himself sharing the secret with his fellow scroungers, "look at this."

Inside there were dozens of bottles of wine and others of champagne too.

The Dutchman whistled.

"It's party time now?" the Dutchman asked, unable to contain his laughter, and striding forward pulled as many bottles as he could carry from the dresser.

Within minutes the three of them had carried all the trestle tables outside into the yard. Over them, one of the

Dutch had spread the table cloths with bottles of wine laid out on top.

"What are we going to drink out of then?" Harry asked.

Looking around Harry saw the two Dutch were busy trying to drag out as many chairs as they could find.

"Leave it to me," Harry said, "I'll find some glasses."

Back in the mess it didn't take him long to find shelves of them in a tiny annex that was clearly not built for broad Germans. He laughed thinking how they had ever managed to use it. Alongside the heavy-duty glass tumblers, there were assorted wine glasses and fine cut glasses next to a decanter of the same style.

Putting his hands together he clasped as many glasses as he could and took them outside.

There were a great many more people gathering around the table, some singing, others holding a bottle above their head and dancing around the table.

"Look over there," someone shouted.

Harry put the glasses on the table and swivelled round. Walking towards them was a number of men, each of whom was laden with as much food as they could carry.

"Some bloody genius has found the food stores!" someone shouted.

Harry thought it happened so suddenly. From nowhere and everywhere men began approaching the food bearers, some stumbling, some walking with uneven steps and others even attempting to run, as the sight of food caught hold of their minds and gripped them with an intensity which they could do nothing to shake. What they had just seen had flipped a switch that had been off for as long as they could remember. No sooner had they caught up with those carrying the food than they started to snatch as much food as they could, stuffing whatever could be eaten into their mouths.

Harry and the two Dutch, driven both by their own hunger and by the wild reactions of their fellow POWs ran across and started to lunge for the food.

"Take yer bleeding hands off," one of the carriers said, "there's plenty for everyone where this came from."

But they couldn't listen. The food was there in front of them, food that they had dreamt about and hungered for so badly they couldn't take their eyes off it. One of the carriers was trying to fight off a pair of POWs but his miserable body couldn't withstand the ferocity of their hunger. As they tussled, they pulled him to the ground and the food he was carrying was thrown up in the air.

As soon as the food hit the ground, the nearest POWs dived forward and attacked it in a frenzy. Though others tried to stop them, they wouldn't listen, driven only by the pain in their stomachs and the possibility of finding some cure for it. The food never even reached the table. From every hut, men were now swarming towards the others holding the food and with no regard for their known rank of the carriers, began to fight them.

A few minutes later men were drinking from bottles that they had fought for and whose necks had been smashed on any concrete corner. By now the yard was filling up with men who'd heard there was food about and had followed the sound of shouting. Harry might have stayed even longer, filling his mouth with any scraps of food his clutching hands could hold. He couldn't remember when he had last eaten meat. Harry reckoned it was all about timing. Knowing he wasn't going to win that sort of free for all right now, he decided to go in search of his own booty. It didn't take him long.

By the time the message came through later that day that it wasn't necessary to leave, some order had been installed in the camp by the officer's Field Force. During the afternoon, Harry had watched while fires were lit, fuelled by burning pieces of wood from the punishment hut. As the hut was smashed to pieces using sledgehammers and other tools found in the works shed, then under the watchful eyes of the SBO, shouts of delight roared around the camp. Though few had felt the isolation and cruelty of the punishment hut at first hand, the stories of the survivors had been enough to warn off those tempted to fall foul of the regulations in the camp.

Wandering together with looks of quiet satisfaction on their faces, Harry recognised a group of all the national leaders in the camp. Within hours of the evacuation, they had established some authority amongst the POWs by ensuring that each nation was represented. For Harry, this was just a start after all. He wasn't going to put himself at risk of being shunted into some bleeding cell just when he was about to hear 'The White Cliffs of Dover' again. Still thinking about the bottle of wine he had found and buried in sand round the back of the mess, he saw the two Dutch being escorted roughly by a group of POWs. It didn't take him long to find out that the FF had their hands full, dealing with those POWs still out of control. He later learnt that the Dutch had been found carrying pistols which they had discovered in one of the Germans' quarters. A police squad had been formed by the commandant to look for and collect any firearms left by the fleeing Germans. The squad themselves were armed and walked about in pairs trying to cover as much of the camp as possible.

The more he thought about it the more Harry realised he couldn't take risks. He'd taken enough of those already just getting hold of the bottle. Even though the war might be ending, he thought, no one was going to treat it lightly.

He reckoned that left him with two options. Either the bottle stayed buried or he had to drink it fast. Put like that, maybe it wasn't so difficult to choose, he thought.

Though it was the sound of explosions that woke Harry up the next morning, he couldn't remember sleeping. As he tried to open his eyes and focus, all he could feel was a heavy throbbing at the back of his head and a sharp pain in his chest that he hadn't felt before. Trust you, he said to himself, first night of freedom and you still can't sleep.

Going outside, he was chilled by the sight of a Mosquito buzzing the camp. He prayed that the pilot would see the camp for what it was. The rolling of the wings was enough. Harry dragged himself back to the barracks and collapsed on a bunk.

Waking up today with a head that felt like a camp ball bladder that had been kicked around in the yard all day and a chest that was so tight he could barely breathe without wheezing, he struggled to get to his feet. Dragging himself from the ground, he looked up to see a sergeant come into the barracks and shout,

"Right the holiday's over! You lot'll be clearing mines today."

It didn't seem to matter now. Even though it was painful to do anything, the thought of the war coming to an end made him go through the exercise without complaining. All day he spent composing a telegram to Connie. He got his chance at the end of the day.

Dear Connie,

It's over! The Russians arrived today! We've been celebrating like there's no tomorrow.

Hope you got my last card because I haven't heard from you since.

I can't tell you how good it is to be writing to you and thinking I'll be seeing you soon. I just need to get my dicky chest sorted out. It's been OK but in the last few days it's been playing up and I may need to see the medic.

It's not long now.

Love from your

Harry xxx

P.S. I'm going to drink to you and to us as soon as I get the chance.

5

Extract from Robert's Diary

*A*s I moved closer to the crowd of people, I knew what would happen. I was still trying to get myself ready for the celebrations. Knowing that the same thing would be happening up and down the country didn't seem to make it any easier.

It came as no surprise. Each street party I saw, every bonfire smelt and every song cheered in the same gaudy celebration of war, stuck in my throat. I had named it the dance of death. If I hadn't been certain that Martha would be here, I'd never have come.

For so long, there seemed to have been one topic of conversation: how long would it take Germany to give in? But the newspaper headline which I'd seen someone reading at the hospital that morning confirmed what we'd all been waiting so long for: Nazi Germany Surrenders.

For everyone I came across while I was working for the FAU,[1] or prayed for and sometimes with – like the young sapper, just out of training, who'd lost a leg trying to defuse a bomb – the war couldn't end soon enough. And sometimes the accidents we dealt with seemed to me so shocking for being so pointless; one man became so disoriented in the fog

---

1   Friends Ambulance Unit

one evening, that he turned down the wrong track and ended in the canal. We were too late to stop him drowning.

Throughout my life I had been living with the legacy of being brought up a Quaker and affirming that allegiance with greater conviction with every passing day. As soon as the war started, I knew what I would have to do. When the time came, I went to the local employment exchange and on the form I was filling in, wrote in large capital letters: CONSCIENTIOUS OBJECTOR.

It wasn't long before I was brought up before the tribunal panel. Their fearsome reputation was well-known.

"Name?"

"Robert Chalmers."

"Age?"

"Twenty-four."

"Occupation?"

At the time it was common knowledge that there were various occupations – the reserved ones – which would make my decision to apply for an exemption a more reasonable one. It would have been easy, I knew, to acknowledge my Quaker faith as being the primary reason for my refusal to take up arms. But a part of me thought of it as a screen behind which I was not prepared to hide. Of course without such an admission, father would certainly have received call-up papers for the Great War and in all likelihood, would have been one of the millions who died. And now father surely expected his son to give an unequivocal answer, in much the same way that he had always done.

"Teacher."

"Of what?"

"Drawing, sir. Technical drawing."

"Important subject. Crucial at the moment I would have thought. Don't the services need men with such skills?"

I thought it would look foolish and sound absurd to avoid the truth.

"Yes," I replied.

"They need you, you say. I take it then you'll be going."

"No, sir."

"No, why ever not. You've just said how you're needed."

"I have an objection to fighting, sir."

"But no objection to others dying for you?"

There was a look of irritation in the judge's face that I didn't like. His eyes had narrowed and he peered over his glasses with a look of disdain.

"I don't believe that taking up arms is the right way to proceed, sir."

"I see," the judge said, "you consider another way to more efficient, is that it?"

"I think you have to explore every possible avenue of diplomacy first."

"And then when that fails, what do you do? Start again?"

Before I had a chance to reply, the judge continued, "And do you know something else, young man? In the long-run, we're all dead."

"I know sir, but I think while we're alive we all have our own choices to make. I respect those who have to make their own decisions."

"I'm sure you do. But I wonder if others would. Who do you know that's lost a member of the family recently?"

I could only think of the sapper and the stump of a leg that was left.

"Mrs Myrtle Hughes, sir. She lost a son. A sapper."

"Did she now? I wonder what she's feeling now every time she gets out an old photograph of her son, or sees his old boots in the garden shed. Do you think she'd prefer it if we each made our decision whether to fight or not? Sometimes *you have to forget what you yourself believe, think and fear and put the greater good first, Mr Chalmers."*

"Doesn't it depend on how you get there, sir?"

"No, Mr Chalmers. You're wrong because it's the end that is paramount. Defeating the enemy. How we do it is of little consequence."

"Yes, sir."

The judge leaned forward and put his two hands together.

"You are clearly an intelligent and thoughtful person who has decided to follow his conscience."

I gave a small sigh, wondering if this battle might not be turning my way.

"Mr Chalmers," he coughed into a small white handkerchief he pulled from his jacket. "This court is prepared to exempt you from military service on one condition."

I was looking straight at the judge, trying to remember who else had been given such a penalty clause.

"That you undertake a job at the local coalmine."

Coal Mining! As I saw the court recorder about to write the result into the court day book, I said,

"I must refute that possibility, sir. I was looking for full exemption."

"You may well have been," the judge said stroking his chin with the forefinger of his hand, "but you will be disappointed. And the court does not tolerate refusal lightly."

"I know, sir."

I spent the next month in prison.

Martha was still nowhere to be seen. Had I not wanted to talk to her, I'd never have approached this particular meeting-point. But I knew she'd be here and inevitably Billy would be with her.

Luckily he wasn't difficult to spot, tall, well-built and wearing a black woollen jacket that seemed to stay with him regardless of the weather. Laughing and playing the fool with those around him, he'd joined the crowds gathered around the bonfire. I knew he had it in for all COs[2] but needing to speak to Martha gave me no option.

I tried to be as light-hearted as I could but was ready for Billy to respond with his usual sarcasm. He didn't surprise me but I still needed to talk to my sister. I needed to share the shocking message that I had only received yesterday and it would stop me doing anything else until I did so. My hesitation gave Billy another chance to remind me that I didn't deserve to share the celebrations.

I thought that talking about each of us making our own decisions and how I couldn't enjoy dancing on the grave of the dead and wanting to share with him the celebration of the war ending might help but he didn't seem to see any part that I had played in it.

Even stranger was him asking about Martha. When I then made a joke about Martha not seeing a great deal of her 'brother', the word stuck in my throat and I barely heard Billy's response. But he repeated his line about duty and I about conscience.

He called it convenient but I wasn't prepared to tell him about the convenience of being locked up with people who'd tear you to shreds for a loaf. Billy had done his own war after all. It was when I tried to find some common ground about neither of us having seen the abattoirs of the front that Billy's reaction came as less of a surprise than a revelation. He seemed to find a real voice, comparing his harsh working life down at the steelworks with my own. As he talked and gestured, his beautiful eyes sparkled and I couldn't stop looking at them. I didn't hear what he said next. I just had this urge to put my hands to his face and hold them there,

---

2   Conscientious Objectors

feeling the roughness of his cheeks and inhaling his uneven breath upon my face.

That's when someone behind us shouted, "Listen, it's the king."

The fire was lit and we were moved towards it locking our arms together and singing. I wanted to try and close the gap between us and put my arm over his shoulder. But he tossed it away and I thought it was time to go.

When I finally moved off towards the centre of town, I still couldn't get the king's words out of my head. The war was over! But it was still Martha I needed to find.

I couldn't believe it was only yesterday evening. I can't think of what made me pick up the Bible that had lain collecting dust for so long. Father's death had surely come as a release for the family, though each was too loyal to admit. Mother had always cringed at the way his soft gentle encouraging words to his daughter became intolerant outbursts of bile towards his son, but would not hear of saying anything against him.

At the funeral, I had spoken to no one, wrapped up in my own guilt that for so long I had prayed for this deliverance. At home that evening, mother had pulled my sleeve after we'd eaten tea.

"Come upstairs a moment will you, Robert dear?"

They were the softest words I'd heard from her that I could remember.

"Here," she said opening the drawer in the side table that was next to the bed, "I found this when I was clearing up some of your father's things. I know he wanted you to have it. It just escaped my mind, it did. Anyway, you've got it now. That's the main thing, isn't it?"

There were so many things that had escaped her vacuous memory that I was pleased she could remember who it came from.

It was a Bible, **his** Bible. I took it from mother's hands and for a moment just enjoyed the leathery feel of the cover. Turning it over, I saw the pages were gold-edged. I couldn't remember a time when father didn't have this book. Ever since we were little, he had read to us from it, chastised us with words from it, and even expected us to remember passages from it.

So many times he'd sit there, with this book on his lap, and my eyes would fill at the prospect of father's latest sermon, which would typically be directed at my most recent failure. Martha would look at him, clench her teeth and shake her head. But she said nothing. If she had, she'd have been on the end of his tongue for weeks. They both knew it was worse than caning. At least that was over and forgotten when the pain subsided.

Mother had always been small. Now, I thought, as she stood waiting for my reaction to this gift, she seemed to be shrinking. As if she didn't want to take up as much space as she was doing. Her shoulders were hunched and her long brown hair looked speckled with salt.

"He–" she stopped as soon as she had started. Her head fell forward and behind the curtains of hair he could hear a soft sobbing.

"It's alright mother. I understand," I said coming towards her.

Her arms came up in front of her like a parrying gesture and I stopped.

"No, Robert. You can't," she said putting her hands up to her eyes. "He just wanted to say he was sorry."

That's all she said. Shortly afterwards, she left me standing there, Bible in hand, trying to shield the flood of questions that were drowning me. Father had never been one for gifts and never one to offer something to one child without *offering something to the other. Was this his redemptive gift? And why should he have waited?*

I looked at the Bible in my hand. There had never been a time when the black cover and gold-edged pages had not caused me to shiver with painful anticipation. That's why I decided to stow it away, amongst the papers and journals which I kept in an elaborate filing system of boxes of varying sizes.

If I hadn't been looking for a journal recently, I might never have discovered it. Frustrated at my inability to find the article, I pulled out drawers, overturned them on my bed and took down his box files from the top of the cupboard. I found it by mistake, hidden beneath piles of papers. Attending first to the reference in the journal for which I had been searching, I left the Bible there on the bed amongst the papers, at a safe distance from me. Though months after his death, I still hesitated before opening up wounds that still festered.

Perhaps it was because of the day, VE day, that I picked it up at all. Such a day, to end the monstrous months and years of carnage, marked an end for many of a time that needed to be forgotten and buried as far from consciousness as possible. No one knew what the next few years would bring. But for this brief period, things would be different. For me it would be like starting to learn a new poem.

I picked up the bulky tome and turned it on its side so that the gold edges faced me. Without thinking, my finger started to stroke the smooth glossy sheen of the pages. And I could see father doing it now, with a slow rhythmic movement, like a caress. Father used to say he was waiting for God to help him open the book at the right page.

"Christ will show me where to start," he'd say, "and he will speak to each of us."

His finger would stop its movement along the belly of the book and with his eyes closed, the finger would slide between two pages. Gently, he would open the Bible, rest it in front of him and start to read.

"Listen to the words," he would intone, "in the spirit in which they were written. Then the words will speak to our hearts. And we must listen," and he'd then wait for Martha and me to look up and find his eye, "and a way will open before you."

I'd come to hate these openings and the moment father had concluded with the words, "So help us Lord, amen," I'd leave the room and go upstairs.

Curling my fingers around the spine of the Bible, I hurled it towards the fireplace. The back of it hit the edge of the mantelpiece and fell to the floor with a heavy thud.

To me, there was something gratifying and yet demonic, about seeing it there spread-eagled, as if paralysed. Wanting now to hide from this image, I bent down to pick it up. When the spine hit the mantelpiece, the force of the blow must have loosened the binding because I could now see a leaf protruding from the golden edge. Unlike the other pages, this did not have the usual golden dappled edge. Leaving the book, my fingers took hold of the edge of the page. It came away in my hand and lifting it up, I saw that it was a small faded note of parchment colour which had been folded in half.

I stood up before opening up the paper. Looking at the writing was like receiving an uninvited visitor. It was unmistakable. Father had written with his writing arm arched so that each letter was folded over, as if someone had tried to flatten them. Written in black ink, some of the writing had faded and there were marks on the page which age alone had delivered.

Walking towards the window, I started to read.

Dear Robert,

Silence is a sin and I am guilty of it. I have carried this story to the grave and with it my remorse.

When my sister Agnes died in childbirth, with no one at her side, she left a child even more alone than she had been at her end. I promised her before God that I would care for the child.

I had just become a father with the birth of Martha. It was never the straightforward delivery that we had hoped and your mother had been told she would not be able to bear any more children.

We took it as a sign to us and she suckled both babies with God's grace and as much strength as her tired body would allow. You were twins before God. I hope that I regarded you with the same affection and love as I did Martha.

I have not spoken to you because somehow I could not find the right time or strength to share it with you. Though I have tried to regard you as my own, I know there have been times when I have failed.

I ask for God's forgiveness.

Your father

Howard

6

Connie

Connie could hardly remember the midwife leaving. Her body felt so tired it was all she could do to lean over and look at the baby in the basket on the floor next to the bed. But as she saw the downy dark hair, she could almost feel its glistening squirming body on her own as it was given to her by the midwife. The thought of it on her stomach with their two bodies still connected by a bloody cord, tripped that part of her that wanted to be strong for the baby. She couldn't stop them now and as the tears started to roll down her cheeks, Martha came over to the bed and kissed Connie again and again with her own wet face.

Connie didn't know what she'd have done without Martha. She'd had such plans to be organised but when the time came, the shock, fear and anxiety had made her stuff anything into a bag before leaving. That's why Martha had had to lend her so much. Even Martha's shopping basket had to be used as a makeshift cot for the baby. She was looking at it now, on the floor next to the bed. From the lighted candle she could see the face, poking between the folds of the shawl that surrounded it.

She had tried to get some sleep but lying in a strange bedroom with a new baby by her side was not the simple recipe for sleep that the midwife had encouraged. Connie was happy to lie back with her head propped by the pillow, letting herself adjust to the absence of tremors through her body. Every minute – or so it seemed to her – she'd stretch over to the basket, and just stare. Nothing had ever prepared her for this. Maybe nothing could, she thought. So full of the feeling that everything had been unbelievable and magical too, she just wanted to gaze at it forever. That way she could be absolutely certain that the baby was alive. She'd heard of new-born babies dying for no reason. Holding onto the basket, she pulled it up onto the bed beside her. There it was again – that slight movement of the shawl as the chest moved up and down. Connie thought the baby looked so fragile.

When a noise disturbed her, she looked up to see Martha standing by the door.

"I heard the bed moving," Martha said, coming into the room, "it never was the quietest."

"Sorry."

"Don't! There's nothing to be sorry about."

"I needed to see her."

"'Course you did. She's your baby!"

"To make sure she was still alive," Connie whispered.

"Hey," Martha said, moving round the bed so she could sit on it and comfort her oldest friend.

"Yes, just sit next to me Martha, will you, and look at her," Connie said pulling back the edges of the tartan shawl from the baby's head. "Isn't she beautiful. Look at her fingers."

"What are you going to call her?"

"Angela."

"That's a beautiful name. Any reason?"

"Well, at first I thought the whole thing was a bit of a miracle: first I got the telegram when they told me Harry's plane had taken off for the attack and nothing more had been heard. Then falling in love with a gorgeous GI and getting pregnant. And angels are sent by God aren't they?"

"That's right."

"But now, it's all different, Martha," Connie said grabbing hold of Martha's hand and clutching it, "it seemed ages later when I got another telegram telling me he was a prisoner of war. That's when he started writing to let me know how he was. And I don't know how I wrote back to him. How could I! And now it's just me and this angel waiting for him and I don't know what…"

She never finished and began to sob, her large breasts moving up and down with every intake of breath. Martha took her hand from Connie's and her arm reached out for Connie's shoulder which was swathed in Billy's cotton shirt.

"Shh! You're exhausted and you need to rest," Martha said.

"Oh, Martha," she said forcing herself to talk between the tears, "what's going to happen to it? What am I going to do?"

"No, stop that, Connie. When the baby sleeps, you need to sleep. Those are orders from the midwife, *ja*!" Martha picked up her right hand and gave a mock Nazi salute.

Connie tried to smile but she knew that no one else could feel that strange emptiness that she found inside herself now. As if that magical being which had been joined to her inside her body, for those many months, and which she'd spent so many hours dreaming about, had now been taken away from her. The baby was out there on her own in the world now with no one to look after her but Connie. After months of planning, it was as though she was now alone with the reality of what she had created for the first time. No, what they had both created.

But somewhere inside her, she supposed she'd always known that it might end this way. How could it be otherwise? Mitchell had left as quickly as he had arrived even though he whispered that he'd come back for Connie. But that was Connie alone he was expecting. There were still moments when she cursed herself for not seeing through him. She should have listened to the girls at the factory because they'd all been saying the same thing,

'They're lovely they are, those GI's, with their good looks and all that money they throw around. But it's like a reflection. It's only there while you're looking at it.'

Instead she'd gone with them to the dance at the Town Hall where there was a swing band playing. She couldn't wait for those evenings: the dressing-up, the makeup (the line down the legs always did smear in the rain), the music, lighting and the wish that you'd be asked to dance by the tall handsome stranger. There she was, sitting there tapping her feet and swaying to the rhythm when a young man with strong arms and smelling heavenly took her onto the dance floor. Wearing her green sequinned dress that she'd made herself, trying to copy one she'd seen a starlet wearing in a magazine, she'd felt in heaven and so flattered that she couldn't find a reason to resist his overwhelming charms. The gifts had followed, the stockings and cigarettes and sweets.

He never did come back after he found out about 'Connie's news' and she hadn't heard another word from him since. How could she worry about being on her own? From that moment on she knew what would happen and that she'd have to prepare herself for it.

"But I gave in Martha, didn't I?" Connie said.

"No, you were bloody mortal. Like anyone else would be who'd forgotten what it was like to be held by someone. Don't kid yourself you're any different."

"I just couldn't believe I could fall so easily."

"And were unlucky, that's all. I mean, didn't you tell Mitchell he needed to take precautions? They give johnnies out like chewing gum, don't they? That's what I heard."

Connie thought the silence that followed was like an empty pit, waiting to be filled.

"Oh my God, Connie, you told him it was safe, didn't you?"

"But it didn't matter then, Martha."

Connie looked at Martha wanting to make contact with her, looking for the friend that had been on her side through all those months, wondering why she had never told Martha before.

"You see I was his GI bride, wasn't I?"

"Does he know anything about this? That he got you in the sack?" Martha asked.

"Yeah, don't you remember? He saw me when he was last here on leave and that's when I told him."

There was a silence.

"Well, what did he say?" Martha asked.

"It was all Mitchell. I can hear it now. *'There's my girl. Always thought I was the quickest lighter in the house.'* Something like that."

"He said that to you after you'd just told him you were pregnant? Hell, Connie, where did you get him from?"

"Well it's alright for you, isn't it? You and Billy, I mean. How long have you been together? And you've got each other, every night."

"Don't start, Connie."

"Yeah, but it's true isn't it? Feeling his body next to yours, listening to his heart beat and hearing it quicken as he's getting close –"

"Shut up, will you. You know damn well he wouldn't be here if he had his way. They needed him here."

"Oh yeah, not like someone else I could mention."

Even as she said it, Connie held her breath, knowing that she'd crossed a line and taken a side in a way that they had sworn they wouldn't. As Martha's open hand caught her face, Connie was shocked more than hurt. Putting her hand to her cheek, she looked up to see Martha shaking her head.

"I didn't choose my family," Martha said, turning round and closing the bedroom door behind her.

Connie lay back, holding her hands to her face feeling the tears dribble through her fingers. How could she say that to Martha, she asked herself? Whose side was she on anyway? Robert had followed his conscience like others in his family. Who was she to judge him?

If it hadn't been for Martha, Connie didn't know who would have been able to help her. She remembered those long months leading up to the birth. How many times had she felt the withering look of others as her body grew larger and had to rely on Martha to stay positive, always encouraging Connie to believe that she could manage on her own?

Now she felt like collapsing into sleep which her body yearned for but which her mind still tried to fight. At first it seemed impossible for her to separate from the overwhelming reality in the basket at her side, but in the end she must have given in.

Perhaps it was the tenor of the voice that woke her – it was like a deep growl which she realised must be Billy. She was staying in his house after all, even though she hadn't yet seen him. In the night she had been aware of noises coming from the bedroom next door because she had heard the bed shudder and creak.

Billy! She could see him so clearly with his deep-set eyes and that dark hair of his which he always seemed to be brushing away with his hand. During the last terrible war years, there'd always been something permanent about Billy, as if he'd always be here. Like a lucky charm. That's how Martha once referred to him. Brought up the northern side of the valley, he'd never considered leaving and he'd been working at the steel mill for as long as Connie could remember.

She heard a rattle from the plumbing, like sluice gates opening and shutting and then silence. Holding onto the headboard, Connie moved her weight towards the side of the bed closest to the window, putting her feet onto the floor. Just standing there, wearing Billy's frayed shirt which hung down to her knees, was all she wanted to do. It was lucky for her that Martha managed to find some old shirts of Billy's that she could use. The one she'd had on earlier was a mess.

"Don't be embarrassed," Martha had said, trying her best to comfort Connie as she eased her out of one shirt and into another. "A baby deserves the best."

But now she couldn't stop herself thinking about what had happened. How could she have been so unprepared? Maybe she had her days wrong, because she certainly wasn't expecting it til next Friday. She didn't want to think about what she would have done if she hadn't caught Martha as she was leaving the house.

More than a minute passed with her relishing the touch of the grainy woollen rug under her feet. She so wanted to lunge forward and tear back the blackout now that it was light outside, and let the warmth of the new day come spreading onto the tiny body beside her.

Instead she pulled back the curtain so that light could just chink into the room. Her eyes shut because it seemed so bright. Another May morning! Yes, it was May, she thought. There, outside, it was the same as it always was. Why should it be different?

Because everything inside the room had changed, she thought. It was like being caught between two worlds: one had the comfort of familiarity; the other the fear of uncertainty. Even her body felt strange: the protruding stomach replaced by ever-so swollen breasts that felt painful, ready to be emptied. With her feet close to the ground, she walked around the bed and stood over the basket gazing at the small nose and the deep-set eyes. In these features, she wanted to see something of herself, but the longer she peered down at the baby, the clearer her memory of Mitchell became.

As she looked up she caught herself in the mirror: still the same curly hair dropping to her shoulders and that dimple on her chin that he used to tease her about. But with a jerk of her head she blanked out the image. It was only the two of us now she said to herself.

Mitchell had always said that he would come back for Connie and take her home. The whole idea of starting somewhere new had filled her with such excitement and she dreamed about sailing for America as soon as it was safe to do so. That's what he'd said she should do.

A noise, no more than a whimper, brought her back to the baby in her makeshift cot. Before she had taken two steps towards the basket, she heard something behind her. Martha was at the door.

"Connie, I'm so –"

"Don't bother! I don't know what got into me."

Connie saw Martha's shoulders drop.

"I thought I heard the baby," Martha said coming forward. "Is there anything I can do?"

Connie went to the basket, lifted the baby out of its mobile cradle and walked with it in her arms towards the small chair in the corner of the room. Laying the baby on her lap, she undid the top two buttons of the shirt. The nipple was dark brown and swollen.

"I'm going to try and feed her," she said, picking up the baby and turning its face so that the nipple was next to the baby's mouth. Connie could see Martha watching as the baby moved its head and brushed the tip of the nipple. Its head seemed to turn again, rooting it out.

"Come on my angel," Connie cooed, "time to drink."

"I'll leave you to it," Martha said.

"There's no need," Connie told her.

Martha sat on the edge of the bed, and waited until Connie had put the baby down before asking.

"How was it?"

"Sore," she said.

The next moment Connie couldn't stop herself and the tears began to stream down her face.

"There now, Connie, it's early days, isn't it? Bound to be slow to start with," Martha said.

"Not sure I gave her anything, Martha. Look at me," she said pulling apart her shirt, "I'm dripping."

As Connie pulled back her thin nightie, there was a liquid slowly oozing from one of her nipples.

"Pass me a cloth will you, Martha or I'll be soaked through."

When Martha came back giving her the muslin cloth, Martha seemed to hover at the end of the bed.

"Anything the matter?" Connie asked.

"Look, Connie, I feel terrible talking about this now, but Billy and I were wondering if you'd thought–"

"What? About how long I'm going to be here?"

"No, it's not like that. It's just that Billy and–"

"Yes," she cut in, "you and Billy are feeling very put out by the baby and me. That's it, isn't it?"

"For God's sake, Connie, I was only asking what your plans were."

"Plans! Sleep, that's my plan. Strength, that's what I want. God, I knew I shouldn't have come."

Connie started moving to the side of the bed.

"And I'm only saying that I'll be–"

Connie never finished. As soon as she put some weight on her legs, they seemed to give way and reaching out to the bed for support, her hand only caught the eiderdown, with her own weight and failing sense of balance, it slid away from the blanket and she fell backwards until she was lying prone against the wall.

"Connie," Martha screamed, "Connie, are you alright?"

Connie was groaning and she could feel the tears filling her eyes. With her head turned to the bed, she was holding Billy's shirt with both hands between her legs. Even in the dim light, she could see a red stain spreading.

7

Martha

"Connie," Martha said as gently as she could, "we need to get you back on this bed."

Martha was a size or two smaller than Connie and with Connie still carrying weight that she had been building up during the last months, it was all Martha could do to lift her shoulders from the floor. When Connie was sitting upright, her hands pressing on her lower abdomen, Martha told her that she would get Billy to help. Martha had gone before Connie had time to argue.

She found Billy in the bathroom, splashing cold water into his face.

"Billy," she said with a voice on the edge of breaking that Billy rarely heard, "we need you."

It was clear from the look on his face that he wasn't used to seeing Martha in such a state.

"What's up," he asked, pulling his straps over his shoulders.

"Oh God, Billy, she's had a fall and it's all my fault."

There was something about Billy at times like these that Martha had fallen in love with. Going at his own pace, he was always ready to do what he could to help without hesitation. Such a gentle giant.

As she came back into the bedroom with Billy, she asked him if they could lift Connie together onto the bed.

"She's been bleeding, Billy," she added.

"I think I'd be better on me own."

Though he was a big man, six foot and more, to Martha he seemed to have the suppleness to squeeze into places others half his size couldn't find. Standing with his back to the bed, he crouched down and put one huge arm under Connie's neck and the other under her knees.

"Nice and steady, Connie," he said and like a weightlifter, he pushed from his ankles, straightening up, taking the strain in the lower part of his back. No sooner was he standing than he started shuffling sideways until the end of the bed, turned half right and then half left at the other side. Now he was carrying her so that he could lay her down as gently as he could against the pillows which Martha had puffed up for her.

As he turned to leave, Martha reached out for his hand and squeezed it. That's when he looked towards the basket and the tiny face peering out of the shawl.

There was a silence in the room. Connie was lying there with her eyes closed and her jaw locked, as if she was trying to ready herself. Martha stood watching her, aware of the baby's rhythmical breathing and hoping it would stay like that while she helped to sort out the mess she knew she had caused Connie.

"I'm just going to get a bowl of warm water, Connie," she said, following Billy down the stairs.

How could she have done that to her friend? Hours after she'd given birth to a beautiful baby girl! She put her hand up to her face, shaking her head in disbelief. In the kitchen she found the bottle of disinfectant she kept under the sink and put a couple of drops into a bowl of warmish water. From the top of the sideboard, she pulled a white soft linen cloth.

Connie hadn't moved by the time Martha returned and Martha thought she looked stunned, vacant almost.

"Connie," she said in a voice that quivered, "Connie, you've been bleeding. I may have to clear it up. "Here," she went on holding out one of the towels which she had brought up with her, "let's fold it and put it under you. Try and keep you dry."

There was a grimace on Connie's face as Martha put the small plastic bowl on the bed next to Connie's feet.

"Help me up, will yer? I'm still a bloody whale," Connie said, trying to squeeze her mouth into a smile.

It was all Martha could do to take the strain off Connie's back as she raised herself up. The towel slid underneath her and stretched down to her knees. Undoing the last three buttons, she pulled apart Billy's shirt. Connie was wearing a pair of bloomers that she'd given Connie last night.

"Those will need some washing," Connie whispered, as Martha took them, folded them and put them on the floor at the end of the bed.

"Better get you another pair just as soon as we've cleaned you up."

"Not a pretty sight, is it?"

"Don't be silly, Connie. It's one of the stitches probably. Look, I've put a couple of drops of disinfectant in the water. You can't risk getting an infection."

Using the pinking scissors from her mother's old sewing box, she'd cut the linen into smaller squares. Holding her hand in the water she let the cloth get infused with the water.

"Here we are, Connie. Tell me to stop if you need to."

As Connie screwed her eyes shut, Martha took the cloth pad and held it against Connie without applying any pressure.

"No," groaned Connie, "not again."

"Give me your hand," Martha said and reached out with her other hand for Connie's tight fist. "There," she said putting Connie's hand against the pad, "you hold it and then you can decide how much pressure you can put on it. You've been doing it all by yourself so far. Why stop now?"

As Connie held the pad against her, Martha could hear Connie whimpering and see her shaking hands.

"Right, let's dry you and get you into a new pair of bloomers, shall we?"

Martha went to the chest of drawers and pulled out a large white pair.

"Can't say much for the size, Connie. Won't be doing to let Mrs Price see you in a bloody pair, would it?"

It took some time for Connie to relax, but then Martha saw Connie turn her head towards the basket on the floor. Connie's gaze had been lowered but now she looked up to find Martha's eyes.

"Come here, Martha," she said, holding her hand out on the tartan blanket next to her.

Confusion made Martha hesitate for a moment. But then she slid her body along the bed towards Connie and picked up Connie's hand, and fearing that it might be pulled away, started stroking the long fingers with her other hand.

There was a sniffle at first and then Connie's whole body seemed to be shaking in waves of grief. Martha inched closer and put her arms around Connie.

"I'm so sorry. I'm so sorry," Martha began, before bursting into tears herself, "you must have caught me on the end of a nerve."

The two clung to each other and both bodies locked in an embrace.

"I feel I could cry all day long," Connie whimpered.

"It's alright. You're allowed to. And anyway it wasn't fair of me to say that."

"And I've never known when to keep my mouth shut, old big mouth Morris."

"It's Robert."

"I know Martha."

"You know, sometimes I feel him like an open sore. The comments – I'm so tired of them. It's the same people all the time with their snide remarks. At first I tried to defend him, but I don't bother now."

Martha pulled away and looked at her friend.

"Before your treasure wakes, I've got a plan."

"I'm not sure what I'd trust you with Martha Hilton."

"Let me wash your hair and brush it. You need to look beautiful for your girl."

It was a little later Martha heard the front door bell chime. As soon as she saw who it was, she tried to force a smile but she could feel it crumbling at the edges.

"Martha," Robert said at last, "I think we need to talk."

"Oh yes? What is this? The let's-forget-anything-happened moment, now that the war is over? Is that what you think?"

Robert was looking at Martha in that way that used to annoy her so much, almost patronising, as if he had a smirk hidden away somewhere. So she just stood there with her arms crossed and waited.

"I hoped I'd see you last night at the celebrations."

"I was a little busy."

"Yes, that wouldn't–"

"I don't know why you think it's so funny," she said.

"I don't and it isn't. But that's an unusual noise for your house isn't it? Or have I missed something?" Robert asked, raising his eyes towards the upstairs bedroom.

Martha could hear Angela herself now and she swore under her breath, wondering if the door bell had woken her up.

"Yes, it's Connie," Martha said, "that's Angela. Her baby girl! She had it last night."

"In your house!" he laughed.

"She needed some help, didn't she?"

"I guess she's been on her own for some time."

"What's that supposed to mean?"

"I mean Harry has been conspicuous by his absence. It can't have been easy for her."

"No, but Connie's been dealing with it," Martha said.

"So this was all part of her plan."

"No, Robert, it just happened."

"As these things do, remember," Robert added.

Trust Robert to remember that, she thought, always looking for the brighter side.

It had been one of their father's oldest expressions and knowing the response it gave, he would try hard to nurture the moment of affection it gave them, some fleeting chance to draw the family together without the hand of God. It used to be so predictable that they sometimes tried to anticipate these odd moments of light-heartedness. Now, it was enough to at least let her open the door to him.

"Wasn't waiting for him to say it, the most exciting part?" Martha asked.

Robert didn't respond and for one moment Martha wondered what this visit was all about.

"I've got to talk to you, Martha," he said at last.

"Well, that's something," she said looking over her shoulder, "I was beginning to think you had forgotten why you were here. Billy will be back soonish, so you'd better come quick."

She led Robert into the parlour and sat down.

"Yes?" she asked in a tone which she hoped convinced Robert that she wasn't about to put on the kettle, after seeing him settle in one of the armchairs.

"You're not going to believe this?" Robert said.

"Try me."

Robert cleared his throat as if a speech was coming.

"Mother gave me a present, after father died. Don't look like that! I was hardly expecting anything. Certainly not his Bible."

"Father's Bible! He gave you his Bible!"

"That was my reaction too but it got worse when mother said that he had to say he was sorry."

"Perhaps he meant to give it to you for your birthday and forgot. You know how scatty he could be."

"No, no, no" Robert went on, "it was nothing like that. Anyway, I just put it away on my shelves and forgot about it."

Robert hesitated.

"Until?" Martha asked.

"Until yesterday morning when I came across it looking for something else. Seeing it again filled me with the same rage and disgust I'd felt when mother had first given it to me. That's why I just hurled it against the fireplace."

Martha looked at her brother and wondered where this was all going.

"I'm glad I did."

"Made you feel better, did it?"

"No! This fell out of the Bible when it hit the wall."

From his pocket Robert took out the folded parchment paper and gave it to Martha.

As soon as she saw the handwriting, like Robert, she recognised it. Starting to read, her eyes began to blink as if unable to take in the words in front of them. She closed her eyes, opened them slowly and then reread the words as if hoping they might not say what she feared.

"Oh my God, Robert," she said, trying to hold the note back to him with her shaking hand, "it can't be true? How–?"

"How could he do such a thing? Because he had to."

"Had to? What do you mean?" she asked.

"He was so guilty that he wasn't capable of being given a second child himself. That he hadn't used the 'power given to him' properly. Otherwise mother would have been able to have a second herself. You know what Father was like, he must have taken it as a sign that he had opened himself to God and that a way had been found."

"You can't believe it's true?"

"I've been thinking about little else since I found it. Or maybe it found me."

"Oh, Robert," she said moving closer to him with her outstretched hand, "will you be able to –?"

She paused. Robert took the note from Martha's hand and put it back in his pocket, "Forgive him?" he asked.

Before Robert could answer himself, Martha heard the front door close and then Billy's voice,

"How's nurse Martha then?"

As Billy came into the room and saw the two of them, he stopped. His frame seemed to fill it, as if there was now little space for anything else. Martha looked at Billy waiting for him to break the silence, but all he seemed to be doing was staring at Robert. Then he started.

"What's this then," he asked, "more well-wishers for the new mother and baby?"

Robert was shaking his head.

"No, I came to talk to Martha. I had no idea–"

"Well, there's a surprise," Billy cut in. "Keep yourself to yourself now, don't you? Suppose it's safer that way."

"Stop it, Billy!" Martha said turning to Billy and giving him a look that she hoped would tell him it wasn't the time.

"That's right. Trying to protect your bloody brother now. I'm sick of it," he said going through to the kitchen.

"God, why can't you two...?"

"Don't worry, Martha, I'll be going," Robert said.

But even as Martha shouted, "Wait, Robert!" she knew it was already too late.

"God, what is the matter with you two?" she shouted in Billy's direction, as she heard the front door slam, "Why can't you just give it a break for once?"

Martha was trying to catch her breath. On all sides she could feel this pressure as if she couldn't move without straining a part of her. There was Connie upstairs, needing all the rest she could get, worried that she'd already overstayed her welcome and she had her brother telling her he'd been lied to all his life about his parents. And now she had Billy wanting to dig up a rotting patch of resentment that had been festering since the war started.

"You just don't understand, do you?" she screamed. But as soon as the words were out of her mouth, she recognised them for the bait Billy would take them for.

"No, of course I don't, because that's how you feel about me most of the time now."

"Billy, that's not fair." she said, though she regretted her tactless remark, "Because this is different."

"Oh, yeah?"

"Yes, I've only just found out myself."

Billy was silent, staring at her. Then he said, "Well, are you going to tell me what it's all about?"

"It's not for me to do that, Billy. That's Robert's choice."

"Oh, I see. Even though you two are so close, joined at the hip aren't you, you're not allowed to say anything."

"I can't Billy, so please don't ask."

"More family secrets, is it? God, I should have known better."

"He'll tell you when he's ready, Billy. That's all I can say."

"Like I said, I need to change out of these clothes and have a wash."

Martha could hear his heavy steps on the thin stair carpet and she prayed he would be quiet getting another pair of overalls out of the back bedroom.

She slumped onto the sofa and lifted her feet so that she could rest them. If only she could close her eyes and remove these pins that seemed to be digging into every part of her body.

It already seemed an age since it started yesterday morning when she heard Connie's shout as she left the house. If the day had been brighter, Martha would have left earlier and Connie would have missed her. But since then it hadn't stopped. A day and night nursing Connie, watching her body weep with the joy of a new-born next to her, a night so full of dreams she couldn't sleep, a bad-tempered reaction to Connie's needling remarks about Robert, Robert's discovery of their father's deception to him and now a stand-off between the two of them.

Nothing yet was ready for tea. Every day she had a hot lunch at the factory, but come evening, Billy was ravenous and could eat everything she put before him. But today she decided to wait. When he'd been in and out of the bathroom and changed out of his work clothes, he came into the parlour with his usual air of expectation. Martha tried to look as nonchalant as she could, even though her head was fit to bursting.

He looked at the empty table and then at her.

"What's the matter?" he asked with a tone of incredulity.

"I suppose you are at the moment, Billy Hilton, if you really want to know."

He stopped and looked awkward as though he didn't know where to put his big frame.

"What about this for starters?" she said. "First you expect me to tell you about my conversation with Robert even though you have no intention of changing your attitude about him. Then you come downstairs expecting me to have a meal on the table waiting for you though I do work a full shift every day and leave the house earlier than you sometimes."

She paused for a moment, long enough to see the look of puzzlement spread across his face.

"And that's not all," she went on. "On Monday just before I got off the bus I spotted a queue outside Bishops and Sons. Do you know what you do when you see a queue? No? You join it because you're never sure what they might be selling. There were at least thirty people when I joined it so I waited with them. For just one second I thought I might be able to bring something interesting back for tea. After an hour of waiting, I got to the front. *Custard powder*, Billy. That's all that was left "

The tears were swelling in her eyes and before she could stop herself her whole body was heaving and sobbing.

Billy went forward and lowered himself to the floor so that he was sitting with his shoulder against the edge of the sofa. He reached out and took Martha's hand and then he brought it to his face, "Don't cry," he said kissing it.

Of all the attempts which Billy made at reconciliation after they had fallen out, there was nothing that made Martha wither more than his formal and self-conscious attempts to show some affection. With this gentle man kneeling before her, she pulled herself off the back of the sofa and put her other arm around his neck. Sliding her hand away from his mouth, she leant forward so that he could kiss her salty tears. She could feel his hands on her back, squeezing her and smell the tar soap on his face. They found each other's lips. "Ssh," she said taking hold of his hand and pulling herself to her feet, "hold on tight."

Taking care not to tread on the squeaky boards on the stairs which they knew well, Billy followed Martha up the stairs and into the small bedroom at the back of the house. They stood there in the middle of the room, for one moment uncertainly looking at each other.

"Let's close the curtains," Billy said, releasing Martha's hand and turning towards the window.

"No," she said reaching out for his shirt and pulling him back to her, "we've had enough darkness. We've got lights again! I want to see your face."

It seemed so quiet. Standing still, inches away from each other, she began to unbutton the collarless shirt he was wearing, while Billy's fingers fumbled with the small buttons on the cuffs of her blouse.

8

Martha

"Do you hear what they're saying, Billy?"

Billy walked past her and went into the kitchen. She heard the bathroom door shut. At times like this it was Billy that needed holding. After their misfired attempt at love making upstairs, Billy blaming Angela, or Connie or both, he had stormed out of the house. She just felt relieved to see him back home.

"It was on the news," she shouted, "something about concentration camps. They've found thousands dead. Gassed!"

Her head was still full of it when Billy came out of the bathroom, buttoning his shirt before rolling the sleeves up, but as soon as she started talking again, she could see him looking at the floor and trying to avoid eye contact.

"You alright?" she asked.

She could see that his face looked red and sore, as if he had a rash.

Billy nodded.

"Where did you go?" she asked.

"Down the patch," he replied in a voice that was barely audible.

"Oh, Billy Hilton, come here," she said, throwing her arms around his neck, "you look as though you need a proper…"

Before they were even close to him, Billy grabbed them and slowly pulled them back down in front of her so that she was standing like a naughty schoolgirl in front of her teacher.

"I'll be OK," he said, "I want to be outside." She watched him turn around and walk out of the kitchen door into the yard.

It had been small enough to start with. But like others, they'd had to dig a shelter. By the time the hole they'd dug at the far end of the yard had been covered with corrugated iron then concrete and last of all earth, to stop it being visible from the air, the yard had visibly shrunk. After making steps on the banks at the side of the shelter, they planted vegetables there and over the top. There was still a fenced hatch at the bottom end of the corner where they'd had a rabbit. They'd fed it like a proper guest and been looking forward to celebrating the end with a bit of meat. But oh no, somebody had to take it, didn't they? They probably did it for a joke, Billy had said. Martha had been beside herself at the time. It felt like waiting for Christmas and then being told on Christmas Eve that it had been cancelled. She knew she shouldn't have taken it so badly but she couldn't forgive people who could be so cruel and selfish.

From the window, she could now see him digging up a trowel of earth and riddling it gently from left to right, his tanned forearms were bare in the evening sun. The longer she gazed at him the more she wanted to hold him. But given the state he was in, Martha knew him well enough to realise that she couldn't find him at the moment and that she'd learnt that he only went there when he needed somewhere to hide.

Extract from Robert's diary

What a day! After missing Martha the evening before, the desperation I felt to talk to her had grown even stronger. Sleep had come fitfully, broken by the sounds of celebration that seemed to go on through the night. As soon as one died down, another seemed to take its place.

In the end, I waited until I was ready before walking to Hestor Street. On my way there I passed the remains of street parties: broken bottles, half-charred furniture, piles of ashes scattered by the wind and bunting still hung across streets, like leftover washing lines.

As I turned into her street, I remember seeing a can lying on the road. Running up to it, I kicked it as hard as I could, and then watched, while it flipped in the air somersaulting and spinning before hitting the ground with an empty echoing sound. There was something about getting ready.

It had always been like this.

On the few occasions that I visited Martha, I'd felt Billy's derision as soon as I stepped into the house. As soon as Billy found out that I had applied for exemption, he made no secret of his disgust. The penalty I had served for wanting a total exemption only gave Billy another string for his ire.

"You deserve to go down for a year or two, not just one bleeding month," he had said to me, after he had made sure Martha was out of earshot. Since then I'd been wary of being with him, realising that we moved alongside each other as easily as tectonic plates.

But meeting him last night was like seeing Billy for the first time...

Now, standing on the doorstep, I thought how strange the house looked and sounded. I'd been there so infrequently that I might have been seeing it for the first time. It was one in a row of terraces, 2 up 2 down, which though built of red brick, had over time been blackened by the soot and grime blown over from the mills. In fact, had I not remembered the number 23, I might have imagined that I had the wrong house because from somewhere inside I could hear the sound of a baby crying.

That's when Martha opened the door. She was hesitant at first and seemed to be wary of letting me in. I recognised the features: the strident tone of her voice, and the pose – the hip jutting out, her head forward like a boxer, and her arms crossed. Something about it made me smile. I was thinking of Martha and the rages she could get into, but when I asked her about not being at the celebrations, she told me about Connie's baby. Connie! I can only wish her luck. Tough being left on your own but then everyone makes their choices. Maybe at the time she thought her beau would stick around. Then I had one of those flashbacks, hearing something that father used to say and that helped get me inside the door.

As she read the note she was as incredulous as I had been. Before we had time to talk further, Billy came back. I caught his eye before Martha had spoken to him and for a moment he said nothing, just looking at me. It was strange. Martha kept looking from Billy to me and back to Billy, exasperated by what she saw as the gulf between us. He didn't say anything and then the next thing I knew he was trying to kick me out of the house as quickly as I could. I took the hint.

That's why I decided to go to the allotments. Digging and clearing out the weeds and watering the vegetables often clears my head and I needed that. There's no pretence about it.

If only I'd had longer to talk to Martha, I might have felt as though I was able to understand what it all meant. It was always going to be difficult to talk about it. Martha sounded *far too preoccupied with Connie and the baby to be able to listen to his own, still to him, unbelievable tale.*

At the moment, he was still a stranger to this new-found identity. He'd seldom heard father talk about Auntie Agnes. Something in his memory had her living on the other side of Telford. Only now was it clear why his father had been so quiet about this side of his family. Because when Agnes died, she was already on her own. I suppose that's when his family ceased to exist.

The allotment was on a slope. At the top end of the field there was a small metal kissing gate. Tied to an old wooden pole, someone had erected a sign which read Dig for Victory. Anyone who had a garden big enough to grow vegetables would be doing so. If they could, they'd keep chickens for eggs and maybe rabbits for meat. Those who hadn't, like me, would have arranged to get a small plot where they could grow cabbage, peas and beans, -anything that would supplement a meagre diet and make it more a little more varied.

I went through the gate and walked a little distance up the slope until I came to my strip. Ever since I started digging here, I'd looked forward to being on my own, looking after the soil, turning it over with a hoe before planting seeds. Sometimes there were others tending their own strip, often putting horse droppings down as compost after digging out the weeds.

The sun was getting lower. I took off my jacket and draped it over the fence. It was just after cutting back a bramble which was growing against the fence of the field and had started to weave its way into the allotment on that side that I heard a voice behind me, asking me if I'd found any more family secrets.

Looking over my shoulder, I could see Billy walking down the slope carrying a shovel. Why did Billy have to do it? I asked myself. What right had he to start prying? I dug my small fork into the ground and left it there. Oh God, I thought as I sat back on the uneven ground bordering the turned soil, what does he know? Surely Martha wouldn't have told him anything?

Going back to the beans, I couldn't stop thinking about it. If Billy did know anything, then surely he would have made more of it than he had? Anyway, I needed to get some water. Or maybe that was an excuse. Picking up the bucket I always carried, I walked towards the tap at the far end of the field, quite close to the plot Billy was working on. As I passed, I could see Billy digging a new strip two spit deep.

"That'll help to feed more mouths," I said without thinking and walked on to the tap. I'd almost filled up the bucket before I noticed the shadow behind me. My hand darted forward to turn off the tap and put the bucket down. I suppose I must have turned quickly because my shoulder caught Billy's outstretched arm.

"Billy!" was all I could manage.

"Hoped I'd see you here." I was about to make a quip about that making a first, but something about the look on his face stopped me.

"Martha–" he started and as his eyes began to move around as if not sure where he wanted to look.

"Did she tell you I was down here?" I helped.

He nodded but then continued.

"And something else too."

"Billy, you know I can't read your mind. You're going to have to tell me."

"That was the strange thing. She said you'd have to tell me. So that's why I'm here. Waiting. To listen."

I shook my head trying to rid it of the mesh of thoughts and fears that were knitting together into some impenetrable haze. Martha, a different sort of sister which made Billy's connection to me even more strained.

"It's difficult, Billy. You've got to believe me. It's like my whole world has been shaken up. Do you remember those toys we used to play with? We used to shake them up and down and then wait for the flakes to come back and settle."

It was hard to make out the expression on Billy's face. I seemed to be looking directly into the sun, and was screwing my eyes together to shield them from the glare.

"You always did talk in riddles. Did you know that?" Billy said.

I could have talked about the struggling attempts I'd been making recently to write occasional lines of poetry – most of which were closer to riddles than rhymes – but I decided I couldn't miss this chance – to have a conversation with Billy which didn't end with him never wanting to see me again. It was a goal worth aiming for.

"Could you move a little, Billy? The sun's dazzling my eyes and I really can't see your face."

To my utter amazement, he shuffled sideways and stood on the other side of the water trough and waited.

"That's better," I said. It's now or never I thought.

"You see, I found a letter. It was given to me a while ago just before father died. My mother had given me his Bible and there was a letter hidden inside. I think it was their way of saying that I would need a faith to live with the contents of the letter. I only discovered it because I threw the Bible against the wall in a fit of anger. You see Billy, a Quaker upbringing did little for my spiritual journey, or Martha's."

I could see Billy looking at me and today I noticed how soft his eyes were. Gentle undulating crinkles edged their way around them. I didn't want to lose him in this, confession – for that's how it seemed.

"It was written by father but it was a secret they shared. You see Billy, I wasn't their son. Father's sister had died in childbirth shortly after Martha was born and as she was on her own, father was asked if they could look after me. They took it as a sign from God and treated us as twins. Which to them, before God, we were."

As I stopped talking, everything seemed so quiet. The only sound I could hear was someone's wheelbarrow creaking its way up the other side of the slope. At last Billy spoke,

"It's like different lives, isn't it?"

I paused, not quite able to believe what I had just heard, then carried on.

"You're so right, Billy. Ever since I read those words I've been trying to find a path that I can weave through my existence, that can make some sense of it."

Billy was looking at me now in a way I hadn't seen before.

"One minute you think you know someone. I mean you've grown up with them and that should be enough. But then-" He stopped.

"Then?" I wanted to hear his words.

"It all changes. And it's as if you're seeing them for the first time."

"I thought you didn't do poetry, Billy! I'd be happy with that line."

I could see his mouth stretch into the shadow of a smile. "So you do think we can change, Billy?"

"Well if it's not you, it's me, and right now I seem to be the one looking and wondering what the hell's happening."

"Or both of us? Everything's changed now, Billy, hasn't it? Like I said at the celebrations. This looks like the end of something."

Billy was standing no more than two feet away from me and his face now seemed lined with the weight of the new *possible worlds that like birds were circling around him. Doves or hawks? he clearly couldn't tell.*

I stretched out to put my hand onto his wiry shoulder.

But the next thing I knew, Billy's right hand had lashed out and struck my hand away. I stumbled backwards, shouting, "Billy, Billy, there's no-" I never finished. With Billy's large frame in front of me, and with my back to the wooden fence, I was at the edge of the field now. Like any creature who feels they're cornered, I probably panicked. Putting my right foot against one of the bars of the fence, I pushed myself forward as fast as I could and crashed into Billy at the top of his thigh with my shoulder. Billy could not have been expecting it because the jolt took him off balance and he fell over with me trying to pull myself free. But before I could move, I felt a pair of strong hands lifting me and rolling me sideways. With my back on the rough ground, I tried to pull away but Billy was too quick and first held down one leg and then the other with the weight of his lower body. The next thing I knew Billy had straddled me, so that I couldn't move my legs at all. He'd got hold of my arms and was holding them above my head. I tried to open my eyes properly and focus but I must have got some dirt in them.

That's when I knew he would hit me. I was waiting for it. With those strong hands of his, Billy could probably have broken my jaw or punched me in the stomach til my insides felt as though they'd been through the mangle. I suppose I waited. It was only when I felt the sun off my face that I opened my eyes. Billy's huge torso was blocking out the sun and his face was so close to mine that I could see the sweat edging past his eyebrows, before falling onto my face. I could only look into Billy's eyes. They looked so sad. That was the last thing I saw before his fist caught my face.

9

Martha

From outside she could hear the sound of trams in the distance.

Throughout the night images had flashed before her – Billy sweating, anxious, telling her to stop, Connie's weeping breasts, and feathers falling from the sky in a graveyard. It wasn't Billy's fault there was no room, but she couldn't move him when he was settled. Taking a couple of blankets with her she went downstairs and lay down on the sofa. She couldn't remember how long it was before her tears were wiped away by the comfort of sleep.

Early morning sounds and light chinking its way past the curtains were enough to wake her. Outside on the street Martha heard the sound of a door slamming. That's when she heard one of the stairs creaking. She waited, hoping it wasn't Billy coming down with his soft shaken face and muttering about being left alone. But that was the only step she heard. The front door was opening slowly and the next moment she saw Connie standing there. In her hand she was carrying the basket.

"Connie?" she called.

"I didn't realise you were down here," Connie said.

Martha tried to laugh.

"The bed in the backroom is big enough for half of Billy," she said, "I think we're both better off like this."

"Oh Martha," Connie said, putting her things on the table by the door and coming towards her, "I shouldn't be doing this."

"Don't be so daft."

"I've made up my mind Martha. We're going home, Angela and I. It's time we made our start together."

"You know you don't have to, Connie."

"I do. And before you mention it, this has nothing to do with last night. That's over, OK?"

Martha nodded and then started getting up from the sofa.

"But there's something I wanted to give you," she said going through to the kitchen. She reached up and pulled down one of the glass jars. From inside it she pulled out a book.

"Here," she said, tearing some coupons from the book and pushing them into Connie's hand, "take them. If your angel doesn't turn out a beauty like her mother, I'd never forgive myself."

Martha closed Connie's hands around the coupons, lent forward and kissed her on the cheek.

"If the midwife calls, I'll tell her you've gone home."

By the time Martha was back on the sofa, Connie had slipped the latch and was gone.

Connie

Connie wanted to carry the basket, because without it now, she'd have felt empty. She knew she couldn't have stayed longer with Martha. Finding her downstairs this morning, inconsolable but unable to say what the matter was, Connie took it as another sign that she needed to leave.

When she'd walked to Martha's two days ago, she could remember little apart from the noise inside her head. Today the streets were different to her. Looking about her now, she thought it seemed so quiet, as if the day had somehow forgotten to start. There were so few people about, and those that were she thought walked past with a different purpose. Part of her wanted them to stop, notice her with the basket, peer into the basket and see the angelic face, pass generous comments and then leave her to her daydreams.

By the time she reached home, she was thinking about the changes that she'd be making to the small house. The back room she'd be converting into a nursery. When she could she'd find some new drapes for the room. Perhaps she could ask at the hardware shop if there was any paint she could buy or even wallpaper. How she looked forward to seeing it transformed into a beautiful nursery. At the moment it was filled with some of Harry's boxes. She remembered him talking about some music sheets and books. But when he'd been away for all that time, she'd started to clear most of his stuff in her head and some of it in reality. It was the only way to operate. She couldn't think how many times she'd said that to Harry in her dreams, as if trying to find some final justification to him for the state she now found herself in.

All she could do when she reached home was collapse in the softest chair she could find. But not before taking a cushion from the two-seater sofa so she could sit on it.

It was when she was coming back with the cushion that the front door bell rang. Her first thought was that someone had seen her carrying the basket into the house and wanted to see the baby. Opening the door, the postman must have seen the look on her face.

"Are you Mrs Connie Morris" he asked, pulling a letter out of the large satchel he wore around his neck.

"Yes," Connie whispered, suddenly aware of the frighteningly limited number of possible reasons for getting a letter. She'd heard of too many other mothers, wives, grandmothers and girlfriends finding out about the fate of their loved ones in this way. Staring at the letter in his hand, for one moment she froze, unable to bring herself to take it.

"Well, are you gonna take it, then?" he asked and with a boyish grin added, "they're not all bad you know. He might be alright, after all."

Connie snatched it from the postman's hand and was sorry for him when she slammed the door in his face. She had to be alone. All over she felt herself twitching, frightened at what the letter would say and horrified at what it might not say.

Easing herself onto the cushion, she reached for the polished black lacquer box from the table. From it she took out the silver letter-knife – one of the few relics of her parents that held any sentimental value for her. Though her hand was shaking, she slit the telegram, paused and then slowly opened it.

"Dearest Connie,
It's over! The Russians…..

She could hardly read it. It was as if she had waited for this moment, one that would wipe out the sense and reason that had been channelling her life for the last nine months. She stared at the words. They were like a tunnel opening in front of her that she was running down along, afraid that she would never reach the end, but too frightened to stop for fear of what might be following her. She hardly heard the knock at the door.

Billy

Perhaps this is what a journey to hell is like, thought Billy. The steelworks were surrounded by a thick black smoke. As the bus approached the factory, he could see nothing. Because the smell was foul, they'd keep the windows shut. But the smell still stayed with them afterwards. As soon as he got home he'd scrub himself to try and get the stink off him. Sometimes when he travelled to work he might catch a glimpse of them, the soldiers from the Pioneer Corps, by the huts in the fields.

But he was proud to be working here, helping to produce equipment that was so badly needed. They'd forge anything from bayonets to tank armour. Coke wagons littered the floor to keep the furnaces fisting at the right temperature. Inside the noise and heat seemed even more intense than usual.

This morning he wished he felt more like his usual self. He could barely keep his eyes open and wearing the goggles made him squint at the dials in front of him. He didn't remember sleeping.

Billy was up in the crane box when it happened.

His hands were on the controls and he was trying to move a long rod from the bay to the furnace. His right hand was bandaged with a piece of cloth which he'd tied in a hurry around his fingers before he left. He knew he'd done something to his knuckle. It had ached all evening and this morning it had been swollen and purple. Martha hadn't noticed it. Getting off for the six o'clock shift meant that she was as clockwork about getting out of the house as he had to be. This time he must have caught the lateral control with the edge of the bandage because instead of moving the rod vertically from the pile the lever started rotating the rod. The rod caught the edge of some metal sheets and sprayed them across the floor like spreading cards. As they fell the high-pitched clatter reverberated throughout the floor. Even wearing earplugs he could hear the screeching sound. He knew they were sharp enough to slice through bone.

Billy saw the supervisor waving at him to get down out of the crane.

"Christ," he said to Billy, "what the hell were you doing with that pin? I thought you knew how to operate it properly?"

"I do," Billy murmured, "I'm sorry. It won't happen again."

"You're bloody right it won't! You don't know how lucky you are there was no one around when it happened. Do you know how sharp those sheets are?"

Billy nodded.

"They'll go through bone like a knife through butter."

"I don't know what happened," Billy said.

"Too right you don't know. No one gets into these crane boxes unless they're ready for the job," he said eyeing Billy's hand. "Looks to me as though you've been in a fight. Hurt it, did you?"

"Not serious."

"Well, of course it bloody is, if it stops you doing your job properly."

Billy put his hands up to his face.

"There's no shame in it, son. We're all tired. But that makes you dangerous. That's why you're going to be stopping off early. Just make sure you come back fit. D'you hear me?"

Connie

It was Robert. Connie didn't know how long someone had been knocking at the door, but it pulled her out of her reverie. She hadn't expected anyone. It might have been the timing of his visit so soon after learning that Harry was on his way back. The knock was like a taunt from the devil and she was afraid to open the door. Shuffling across the carpet to the window in her slippers, she glanced outside to see who it was. But at the moment she caught sight of him, she found him staring through the window at her. Robert!

When she opened the door to him, her knees seemed to buckle underneath her and she almost fell into his arms. If he hadn't caught her she would have fallen over the front door step. Perhaps it was the strange relief she felt but as soon as she felt held by him she burst into tears.

Robert turned her round and led her back inside.

"Connie," he said, "I think you'd better sit down."

He was about to lower her into the closest chair when she shook her head and pointed to the one with the round cushion. It was only when she had settled herself in the chair and wriggled around on the seat to lessen the discomfort that she found herself staring at the crumpled piece of paper in her hand.

"Can I get you something?" he asked

She couldn't answer. In her mind and heart she seemed to need everything: lines to be curves, daytime to be night-time, today to be yesterday. She needed the impossible.

"I knew you'd been at Martha's," he said, "because I was there yesterday."

Connie looked at him with a puzzled expression and he must have seen it because he continued, "But I couldn't stay long. I think you were sleeping."

"Sorry."

"No need. I didn't know you were there. I went to see Martha, but she told me you'd come over to hers and that the baby had been born there."

He was looking at the baby now. She'd left the basket on the table.

"Congratulations," he said, "Pretty baby, isn't it? He's got your mouth."

"She."

"Sorry. It's not that easy to tell from here. What are you calling her?"

"Angela."

"Angela? Any reason?"

She shook her head.

"It's a beautiful name."

She could have hugged him and she'd have dissolved on him again. He'd always been Martha's brother first and Robert second. Always the type to keep to themselves at school, Connie had had nothing to do with him until he was of interest like all the others who were big enough to smoke and wear trousers. And she remembered his indifference to her and many other friends of Martha's.

"You should be proud of yourself."

"It's not that simple, Robert," she said, holding out the paper for him to read. "It arrived this morning."

He took the telegram from her hand and read it.

"You didn't expect him to return?" he asked, with his slow even tone that made her feel he wasn't judging her.

"Well not back then. How could I? All I heard was that the bomber had gone down. Missing in action –first presumed dead. Suppose that's why I gave in. So there I was already in the pudding club when I get a letter from him after he's already spent months in a camp. I've tried to reply to his letters."

All she could do was close her eyes and shake her head at her stumbling attempts to find words that might have been full of warmth but were always empty of truth.

"And the father? Did you decide this together?"

"Oh Robert, don't! I didn't decide anything. It just happened. You know how hard it was to resist those gorgeous GIs. They had everything, didn't they? Belonged to a different world. That's what we thought."

"Is he coming back?"

"I think life's going to be complicated enough without adding him to my life. He certainly doesn't seem to want to know anything about that little angel," she said pointing at the basket. "Might be enough to keep him over the Atlantic for all I know."

"So Harry survived! Always did have a certain knack about him, didn't he?"

Connie began to sniffle. "For months I thought he was dead, Robert."

He nodded and turned his head towards Connie.

"Of course you did."

"But I didn't wait, did I?" Her head fell forward.

"That's gone, Connie. And you won't be able to change it. You've got to look forward, haven't you?"

"But Harry will never look at me again," she said lifting her head and putting her hands in front of her face.

"'Course he will. It'll be hard at first getting used to the idea. Depends what sort of state he's in."

"What do you mean? They'll be free won't they? After being POWs everything will seem like heaven."

"Maybe on the surface. Underneath they'll all carry scars, Connie."

She watched him get up and take a step back towards the window. On the sill he must have noticed the picture of Harry in his uniform.

"He was so proud," she said.

"Looks it – gritty. Full of determination."

"You know they tried to stop him enlisting because of his breathing. Had it since he was a boy. But he went back and back and the last doctor he saw was prepared to be a bit vague about Harry's condition. That's how he got in."

"Couldn't take no for an answer."

"Oh no, Harry wouldn't be beaten. God! Unlike you by the looks of things. Blimey, I've only just seen it. Someone's landed you a right shiner." He turned so that Connie could get a full view.

"What a beauty! And don't tell me–"

"Yes, you're right Connie, I got hit by a wall!"

"Oh yes. I know that one. Not like you to get into fights, Robert, is it? Thought you were against that sort of thing."

"But anyone can fight to defend themselves, don't forget."

"Is that what you were doing?"

"I'm not sure. I think we were confused."

"We?"

Robert was silent.

"Don't mind me, Robert. It's none of my business."

Connie smiled and looked at Robert. Ever since she'd been friends with Martha, Robert had never been far away. The same age, of course, the same class, the same town. They'd grown up together. His stand over the war had taken many people by surprise.

"Can't have been much fun inside then. Pretty rough there, I suppose?"

She looked up and saw his head turning away. "Sorry you probably don't want to talk about it."

"That's OK." he said, turning back to Connie again. " No, we weren't much liked. *Conchies* we were called. But I was in a first offenders' prison."

"With other conchies?"

"That's right. It had been agreed that we should be considered as first offenders no matter how many sentences we had served."

"What was it like?"

"Not a bad place. Full of Jehovah's Witnesses as well as COs. They spent most of their time trying to convert us. When they offered me a conditional exemption if I did hospital or relief work, I couldn't refuse – I was doing it anyway."

Connie was lying back in her chair. Her blonde hair fell to her shoulders and she noticed Robert looking at her.

"What's the matter?" she asked.

"You're glowing!"

"Like a flare?"

"With the flush of rude health."

"Oh, very poetic," she said, closed her eyes and then asked, "but I don't suppose I should be surprised by that. Didn't Martha tell me you're a bit of a writer?"

Robert gave a low chuckle.

"Robert, why did you come today? Oh, don't get me wrong," Connie went on, "it's lovely to have visitors. I've been waiting to show my angel off to everyone."

Robert was silent.

"I know," she said, "you came to see the baby."

Robert turned his head towards the basket and back again.

"No," he said, "actually I came about – Martha."

"Martha? Whatever for? Your sister has been like a bedrock to me. As loyal as she could possibly be."

"And to me too, given how much Billy hates my guts."

"He's never quite got over it, has he?"

"Well he's never made much of a secret about it. He thinks I'm on *the other side*."

"Surely Martha can–"

"It's not been easy for her defending someone who is on the side of conscience when everyone around her was on the side of the country. In other countries I'd have been shot."

Connie frowned and then continued.

"Is that the problem? You're getting between her and Billy?"

"I don't know, Connie. That's one of the reasons I came. You've shared most things with my sister over the years, and if anyone knows what's happening to Martha, it's you."

Connie let out a short giggle.

"We've had our secrets Robert, I'll tell you that. But what's happening to her now? Can't really help. I'm a bit tied up in other things."

"She just sounded very tense."

"It's not much fun having uninvited guests. Being turfed out of your bedroom, without warning. Give her some due," Connie said.

"I don't know. She sounded different. And she's always spoken her mind."

"And looks pretty good on it too."

"That'll be those lunchtime meals she gets at the factory."

"Could be! Don't fancy being searched every day though. Couldn't risk having any metal on them with all them explosives around. Some of the girls who work in the powder department have to spend every night trying to scrub their nails clean. And they all have to wear protective clothing. Even so it doesn't keep the yellow powder out – even their knickers are yellow! No, she can have it all as far as I'm concerned."

For a moment Connie was silent.

"It's been lovely talking, Robert. It makes a change from talking to Angela – a bit one-sided at the moment – or going round and round in circles worrying what's going to happen when Harry returns."

There was a knock at the front door. Connie looked at Robert and asked him to see if he wouldn't mind seeing who it was.

"Who is it?" she called a moment later.

"It's Martha," he called back.

"Don't just stand out there," Connie shouted from the parlour, "tell her to come in off the pavement."

As Martha walked into the parlour, Connie could see she was still wearing her work clothes and her hair was still tied back ready for the protective netting she had to wear. She could see the two of them passing quick glances at each other, as if each was waiting to see what the other would do.

Connie told them both to stop being so formal and sit down.

As the silence deepened between Robert and Martha, Connie started,

"Would someone mind telling me what's going on around here?"

She looked from Martha to Robert and then back again. "Well?"

"Martha and I are trying to sort out one or two things at the moment," Robert said. "Nothing to worry about."

"I see," Connie said.

"How are you feeling, Connie?" Martha asked.

"Bloody tired, thanks. But she had a good feed earlier so with a bit of luck…" Connie held up both hands with her fingers crossed.

"I felt so awful seeing you go this morning."

"Don't Marth," Connie said, "you were there when I needed you. Like I said this morning, this is my home, sorry this is our home and I've been waiting for this. I mean it's not as if I didn't get any bleeding warning! I've had nine months to get nest building."

"So you think you're going to be alright."

"Fine, so long as I don't start thinking about what's going to happen. Christ, I only got the news this morning, Marth."

"What news?"

"She's talking about this," Robert said, coming forward and giving Martha the telegram that he was still holding.

Connie could see Martha's face as she opened it up. With her eyes widened, her mouth fell open for a moment before she started to smile.

"Harry's alive! And he's coming home, Connie! " Martha said, moving towards her.

"I know that now," Connie said, putting her hands up to her face, "but he was dead when this one started life inside me. I only have to think of him and I'll be in pieces."

As if shocked to hear the news confirmed by someone else, Connie stumbled backwards and just caught the side of the chair before she lowered herself onto the cushion she had put there. Martha went forward, sat down next to her and threw her arms around Connie's neck.

It started as a faint whimper and there was a slight scuffling of the blanket from the basket on the floor.

"Doesn't she sound like an angel?" Connie gasped, trying to get her breath back. "Always starts off like this. Doesn't take her long to build up though. Midwife says she's got a good pair of lungs."

"Did she say anything else helpful?"

"Regular feeding, Connie Morris. That's her rule. They don't need feeding all the time, she says. Don't give in too easily."

"Easy for her to talk."

As the crying got more intense, Connie levered herself to the side of the chair and took the baby out of the basket.

"I'm sorry," Connie said, "maybe I need some time to take all this in. Anyway, sounds as though I'm needed."

Robert

Robert needed no further cue and left asking Connie to let him know if he could help her with anything. Martha followed him outside.

There they stopped and waited. He wondered who would be ready to start talking. Everything around him seemed so still for a moment.

"What do you think?" he asked at last.

"She's tough is our Connie. She'll survive."

Robert looked at Martha and wondered when she had ever been without this hard-nosed streak.

"And Harry?" he asked.

"It's hard to tell what sort of state he'll be in. He'll not have eaten properly since he got caught. There's only so much hardship the body can take."

"I know but he's coming back. Having blocked him out for so long, she's going to have to find some space for him, isn't she?"

"She's frightened?" Martha added.

"Frightened of what?" he asked.

"Of Harry! He's so unpredictable. And you know what he's like when he gets the bit between his teeth. He just won't let go."

"She's scared of telling him," he said.

"Wouldn't you be? Think about it. He leaves his new

wife and returns to find that she's had a child from some passing GI who's buggered off home in the meantime. Scared! No, not scared. She's terrified of what he'll do to her. There's no way of telling what he'll do when he knows."

"Does he have to know?" he asked, without fully considering where the question was leading.

"What! Harry is her husband! They do live together!" she exclaimed.

"I mean until it was safe, couldn't the baby live somewhere else? Connie would just have to visit every day."

"But it's a baby!" Martha said.

"Yes," Robert went on, "that's why it's possible. The mother may be important but not the surroundings."

By the time Robert left Martha to turn back down the road, he almost thought he saw a smile creeping across her face.

10

Connie

It was still quiet.

Angela hadn't yet woken and Connie was luxuriating in the comfort of dreamy sleep and waking, for once, before her angel.

Little by little she was managing to adjust her life to the new demands. The baby was feeding well – that's what the midwife had told her when she came yesterday. She'd done one or two tests on Angela to make sure everything was working as it should be.

"Get her out into the open air. It'll do you both good."

So today Connie had decided to take the midwife's advice. She thought she'd take Angela out this morning. A little while ago she had picked up a pram which had been discarded. It needed some attention but Martha had asked Billy to have a look and see if it could be repaired. He'd given it some oil and straightened out the forks that were bent. It didn't look new yet but it was no longer a disaster. The first time she moved it, a terrible scraping sound came from the wheels as they turned. If Martha hadn't been with her she might have walked past.

"Go on," Martha said, "you know you're going to need one."

"But this one looks as though it's been on air-raid duty every night for the past six years."

"Nothing that a bit of oil and elbow grease can't put right. I'll ask Billy. He likes doing that sort of thing."

"You're lucky with your Billy, aren't you, Marth?"

That time, Martha had just smiled.

So this morning she thought she'd take Angela out in the pram. It was much too big for her, but Connie knew it would make her feel better. A lovely morning met her as she wheeled the pram outside. There were occasional light clouds but the sky was bright and Connie felt it was a good sign for the first trip out. She'd put an extra blanket in the pram just in case.

Connie thought she'd walk with Angela to Jessop Street. That's where they had some stalls on Friday morning. Nothing much ever to buy there. But it was as good a place as any to pick up anything different for the week. In her purse she had her own coupons and the ones which Martha had given her. She remembered the midwife's firm words.

"Protect yourself and you'll protect the baby. Feed yourself and you'll both be fed." It was much easier for Connie to think of spending her coupons that way.

It's funny, thought Connie, how people disappear when you want them. Here she was, pushing the baby out for the first time, proud as anything, just waiting for someone she knew to spot her and come over and start making lovely cooing sounds over the baby. But it was all so quiet. The few people she saw seemed too absorbed in their own business to have time to look at Angela.

Then she saw Mrs Granger.

She was one of those women who'd pick up the gossip, curdle it in their mouth and then spit it out like foul-tasting liquid as fast as possible. The last time Connie had seen Mrs Granger had been on her way to Martha's when she'd felt the bitterness on the edge of her words. Back at the barrage balloon factory she could remember what Mrs Granger had said, "Cheap women think it's fine to go with GIs when the real men are fighting for their country. Worse than the enemy, they are."

Connie had tried to avoid her ever since.

Now that she was walking towards Connie, though marching would be a better word, Connie kept her head down hoping that she had other matters to keep her busy. It wasn't until the pram had almost passed Granger that the pram pulled up as Granger caught the loose tasselling of the hood.

"And who is this newcomer to Olthorp?" she asked spreading her ample frame across the pram, "well it's a sleeping–"

She never finished. As she turned her head and caught sight of Connie's face she let out a guttural grunt. Connie half expected her to spit.

"I don't forget faces and the good people around here won't forget what you have done either. This," she said indicating the baby with a flick of her wrist, "will be your reminder of what you've spawned from your moment's indulgence. It won't leave you." She walked off without another word. There were two other women coming up behind Connie and she was aware of how they sped up as they passed her.

By the time she returned home, she was shaking so much she thought she'd wake the baby sleeping so close to her. If only she had met someone with a familiar face who'd not chastise her and be ready to share in the pride she felt. She looked at the faces when she got to the shops, hoping for some small sign of recognition, smiling at strangers, waiting for their returned sign of goodwill so that she could engage with them. But the longer she stayed the more she felt that like Granger, they despised her and the baby as if they knew all along about her and the GI between the sheets. And she thought they were there with a jauntiness about them which was new, which she longed to share but couldn't. She couldn't bear to look at the stalls or the signs telling her to '*Celebrate the end of the war with a bit of fun – buy your bonds now.*' She wanted to turn away and hide her baby.

That's what she did. Pushing the pram faster away from the market than she did getting there, she was back inside the house in twenty minutes. She pulled the pram over the front door step, inside the house and then slammed the door. Standing there with her back to the door, she stretched her palms out against the peeling paint and said to herself "I don't want to see them anymore."

Billy

Billy couldn't remember having a day off work since he started at the works. He'd always prided himself on his ability to carry on with work when others were down with illnesses. Martha had rude health herself and there had been an unspoken assumption between them that they wouldn't take time off work, unless they were desperate.

He sat by himself on the bus back to town. They were mostly women on the bus, most of whom he recognised but none he was on first name terms with. Putting his coat against the window he nestled his head into it and let his mind drift off. Whatever mood he was now in, he couldn't shift it. His body knew something was wrong – that he shouldn't be sitting down in a bus at this time of day.

Little had changed when he got back to Hestor Street.

There he found the quietness of the street unsettling. Row after row of closed doors with few people about. It was like stumbling into a life that was running parallel to his own but which he never touched. Now moving from one to the other, a crossing over, made him feel like a trespasser into foreign territory. A stranger so close to home. He wished he'd been able to persuade his supervisor to let him stay. Just before Billy left he'd told him how much better he was feeling.

"Look Billy," he said, "there's tons of molten steel smelting around this furnace alone. One tiny error and it's not just you that's going to get incinerated. I'm not taking risks with your pride, got it?" And he walked away from Billy, leaving him to join the group of women who were waiting to get onto the bus.

When he got home, he washed and changed into his other pair of trousers. It was as patched as the pair he had on. A pair of braces hung from the wire rack on the back of the wardrobe door. He took one and fastened it to the front and back of his trousers. Before he put his arms through, he lay down on the bed. Tiredness had its own colour for Billy. Everything turned brown. It was like his eyes couldn't quite take in light of certain wavelengths or had somehow merged them into a murky earth colour which spread right across his field of vision.

He must have been in a light sleep because he remembered dreaming. The sky was a clear blue and the heat of the sun had made him take off his shirt while he banged nails into a roof where he was mending tiles. And then he started falling away from the roof and just as he was about to hit the ground, he woke up sweating.

Looking out of the window now, he was trying to decide if the sky was blue or a darkish grey. But it doesn't matter, he thought. Pulling on his braces and finding his boots in the hall, he walked out of the house. He needed to be outside. It didn't matter where.

At the end of the street he passed a woman dressed in what could only have been a utility frock, bought with the requisite number of coupons, who was pushing a battered-looking pram. Inside it he could see a box of powdered egg substitute. The green box with the blue label had become a familiar sight. She'd bought the bigger 9d box. He thought she looked sad, as though the end of the war was going to mean little change in routine for some time to come. Or perhaps there was a defiance about her as well. She wasn't going to be pulled down by the scarcity which she had been feeling for so long. *'You had to get by'* seemed to be scored into the harsh lines on her face.

Billy carried on up past the cemetery and it wasn't until he got to the allotment that he stopped. He'd walked this way so often to look after their plot that it was probably instinct for him to follow the same route. It hadn't been a conscious decision to follow it, but as soon as he saw the familiar ash-lined field with the gentle slope up towards the houses on the east side of Percy Street, he followed the pavement up the hill before going through the metal gate. There was no one else about.

Without hesitation, Billy followed the path down through the allotments to the bottom end. Until he saw it, he couldn't even remember leaving it there. His spade was lying on the ground next to his patch on the side closest to the fence. The two-spit digging which he'd started yesterday had taken him about a third of the way down. Yesterday he'd been thinking about another row of broccoli. Before picking up the spade, he put his coat over the fence.

Lifting it up, he ran his forefinger along the edge. It wasn't sharp enough to cut his finger. He could see a weal there now. Holding the spade as usual it felt cumbersome. His right hand felt thick and puffy. He swapped them over so that his right hand was the lower.

Digging was difficult with the hand. Most of the work had to be done with his left hand, digging up the earth and piling it ahead of the next cut. The ground was getting summer hard. He brought the spade down onto the ground and almost jumped onto it with one of his boots so that he could dig it into the right depth. And then he'd throw the earth forward and put the blade down a spit below the surface and then again, dig, kick the spade in, and throw the earth away. Move to the side of the first cut, dig, kick and throw.

Faster and faster he went. It little mattered that the one edge wasn't straight. He'd sort that out later. Now he wanted to finish what he started yesterday. He was trying to blank out his mind, to free it of the images that kept coming back to him. Dig, kick and throw. He was doing it in a rhythm of grunts and sounds of the blade cutting through the surface before hacking its way to the hardened lower level. Nothing would stop him and he carried on with the sweat dripping from his head and stinging his eyes.

Taking a red and white spotted kerchief from his pocket he wiped his wet face and head and looked at the allotment again. Clutching the spade he began to walk up the hill staying close to the fence. It wasn't difficult to spot. The runner bean stalks gave it away. Down by the water tap he knew the old bucket was there. Left from yesterday. It didn't take him long to find it. It had been overturned and someone had been using it as a seat. The top of the bucket had been sheared off, but the lower end had no holes. He couldn't remember how many trips it needed because it carried so little water. But when he left the allotments, he carried away with him the rich aroma the ground was giving off. It was the least he could do and if it wasn't noticed he'd have to try another way to say he was sorry.

Extract from Robert's diary

By Friday evening, I couldn't think straight. It had been one of those weeks which felt as though a stream had started trickling through my life which over the course of the week had grown into a gushing river, destroying the usual landmarks that I used to navigate a safe passage downriver. Showing the letter to Martha had done little to restore my faith because of her own failure to understand what it all meant. It was as if I was alone, floating on a raft with little to trust but the brittle planks of my own conviction to keep afloat. Meeting Billy down at the allotment had only built up the current around me, shifting the predictability of the river bank even more. Perhaps this was how it felt to come back now, I wondered, after years away at the front. Nothing could look remotely the same for those returning, with their wives and children often changed out of all usual recognition.

I hadn't decided to walk along the towpath for any reason other than needing the calming influence that water had on me. But as soon as I saw the bridge ahead of me, all I could think of were the allotments which ran down to the canal at that point and of meeting Billy there. Turning through the kissing gate, I followed the path that I usually took to the rows of beans and other vegetables that I'd planted. When I left there, I couldn't remember what sort of state I'd left my patch in. Now approaching the small strip, it looked as though I'd finished hoeing out the worst of the weeds from the beans. But looking down at the gently furrowed earth, there was something about the neat rows that was different.

For one moment I just stood there staring, before it came to me from another sense. That smell! I'd come to recognise it – that pungent release of aroma that always followed the rain. Turning my head over my shoulder, I looked up into the still, clear sky. My eyes scanned across to the bottom of the slope where the old bucket had been left next to the tap. Though riddled with holes, I knew it could still carry water. And it was down there that I'd last seen Billy. I could remember Billy jumping off him before walking away towards the road. Smelling the damp earth now, my face began to flicker into a nervous smile.

11

Martha

Martha couldn't remember the last time they'd been to the coast.

Blackpool was never that far away but somehow there was always some better reason for not going. Last night, she and Billy had sat watching the end of their meal disappear in silence. Billy hadn't spoken when they got back inside and she knew better than to keep trying to dig it out of him. When the plates had been cleared away, she mentioned it again.

"What do you think, Billy?"

"What?"

"You know. What I said out in the yard about getting away."

He was sitting still, gently nodding his head.

"Where to?" he asked.

"Anywhere you want."

For someone who liked to ponder the possibilities sometimes before making up his mind, she thought he was quick to answer and then he smiled, as if savouring the prospect.

"Blackpool."

"Well, you're not one to take the easy option are you, Billy? Blackpool, eh? Can't say I've ever been. Have you?"

"Once," he said.

"Not the biggest travellers, are we?

"And then it was a time ago. It's probably changed."

"We all change, Billy."

Martha told Billy she'd overheard someone at the factory talking of a coach trip there. 'Not a quick journey' they'd told her, 'but worth it when you're there.'

That's why they had decided to leave early. And it didn't matter that they couldn't really afford it, because this was Billy's choice. She wanted to help him as much as she could. He'd been out of sorts this week and she couldn't be doing with much more of it. A trip away like this couldn't do him any harm, she thought, and when there, they could do whatever they wanted.

"I've just been up the Tower once," he said as the coach approached the city. "You should be able to see it soon."

Martha knew for certain that she'd never been up it in her life before.

As they turned a corner, the department store seemed to slip sideways and the next thing she saw was the tower. She reached out for his hand.

"I'm glad we came," she said.

She'd heard how Blackpool always had been a popular holiday resort. Some came for the tower itself, some to walk the pier or see the circus, some to go dancing in the ballrooms or even idle away hours on the beaches.

Billy's shirt was soaked with sweat as they walked along the front towards the pier. He'd been hot on the coach and as soon as they got off a wave of warm air hit him.

"Come on," said Martha, "I'll race you to the seaside. Last one there's a donkey."

She was off.

Usually when she played these sorts of games with Billy, his sense of pride would not let him be beaten easily. She'd always been quick at running and still had a small silver cup, engraved with her name that she had won at school for *Most Improved Athlete.*

"Slow down, Martha. Save your running for the beach."

Without answering him, she slowed to a walk and waited for him to catch up. The disappointment showed in her face: the lines around her mouth were marked rather than hidden by the fullness of her rosy cheeks.

"It looks so exciting, Billy. It's difficult to imagine how big it is until you're here. I can't believe I haven't been here before."

She blamed it on coming from a Quaker family.

"Why don't we do the sort of things other families do?" she'd asked her parents in a petulant tone that was always guaranteed to lift their eyebrows when they heard it.

"We don't need it, that's why," her father had retorted "the true life is a life of simplicity." But the question was never answered as far as she was concerned.

"I don't call this simple living," she'd once said to her father after a row about the time she was supposed to be back, "this is backward living. I thought we'd moved on from the stage where women–"

He didn't let her finish and she was too frightened to try again.

As they walked along the promenade, Martha thought what an odd pair they must look: Billy a good foot taller than she, wearing dark trousers over his work boots, a sky blue shirt – courtesy of a raffle at the factory – which had stud pockets on the front and over his shoulder he carried his jacket; Martha with her white frock with red polka dots and her woollen cardigan, folded and carried over one of her bare arms. Light and dark; small and large. Were they always such a contrast she wondered?

Though she could see he was happy to idle slowly, gazing at the stalls which were trying to do their best to get customers, Martha wanted to explore.

"In you go, in you go. You'll never be disappointed. Fill the lungs, sing and feel happy," the shill said, with his arms outstretched like some drunken signpost so that before they knew it they were ushered inside what looked like a tiny shop. A man dressed in a dark jacket and black bow tie was playing at the piano. Standing next to the piano and accompanying him was a large redheaded woman. She was singing popular songs at request.

"'In My Arms'" someone shouted. Many inside the room nodded in approval. You never could go wrong with Vera Lynn, Martha thought.

They stood there and she could feel Billy's hand hunting for her own and for a joyful moment or two she allowed herself to wallow in the occasion, the relief that she felt and the release that came with it, the sense of anticipation of having a life to look forward to, the gratitude for having survived and the joy of something about to start. She put her head on his shirt and she could feel his hand now pulling away from her own and threading itself around her shoulders uncertainly, like a nervous suitor on a first date.

"Come on then, who wants a sheet? Take the music home with you. Bring the stage into your parlour. Sing it there, as many times as you want. Come on! You'll only regret it if you don't. Now's your chance" the shill said as he saw folk drifting out of the shop. Martha nudged Billy and they moved towards the door.

As they came onto the street, they blinked in the bright sunshine. All they wanted to do was to drift away and soak up the atmosphere of celebration that had now become infused with the air they were breathing. Without hesitation, they went down past the shops in the direction of the Tower.

Walking down the street, Martha noticed that there was little in the shops of any value and the streets and buildings still looked as though they were part of a theatre of war, unable to wake from such a long dormant period of inactivity and lifelessness. Not even the faces of the people she passed looked ready for the next part of their lives. Even if she couldn't see that shadow of threat and insecurity lining the thin faces of people in the streets, she certainly hadn't yet seen them filled with expressions of life, hope and optimism.

By the time they got close enough, she could see that the Tower was closed. If she'd been honest, she might have guessed that. Having been closed for so long, it was unlikely to open for some time to come. Though she didn't want it to lessen their excitement when Billy said,

"No matter." A part of her wished him to get mad, like she did so often. She knew he was trying to soften her disappointment. It made her want to run again.

"We could always go to the dunes," she said, "it won't take that long."

Extract from Robert's diary

Even though it was May, there was still a chill in the air and as I left my room, I couldn't stop thinking about the dream which had woken me up. Giant nasturtiums had been growing everywhere and so long that they'd wrapped their thin branches around my body, with the tubular flowers

smothering me until I was gasping for breath. The more I tried to look after them, watering and feeding them, the more dense they became. Nothing else could be seen but the fluffy violets and cream cones of colour that sprouted from the rich earth. And if I couldn't water them then it began to rain so hard that I was soon trapped in the earth as if it was thick mud, strangled by clusters of flowers.

I wasn't surprised to find myself dreaming because I'd spent the evening thinking about the allotment and my patch but I was still shocked by its viciousness. As soon as I woke up, like a thirst that I couldn't quench, I knew what I had to do. Dressing quickly, I was still kicking my feet into my shoes as I left the house.

How could it only be a few days since the note had fallen out of the Bible, I asked myself. It seemed like a heavy chain which had been draped around me before being thrown into the water. It felt as though I was thrashing around in the water all the time trying to find a way to cut myself free. And the vision was with me all the time. Other ideas came into my head but were quickly taken over by images from the past. At odd times during the day I'd see father working at his desk writing one of the openings for the next meeting. Father showed no sign that he ever heard me when I came into the room. Martha and I called it the study, though I could only recollect a collection of Waverley novels inherited from a distant uncle and a selection of Bibles which had been accrued over the years. On the walls there were a couple of prints of religious images. Mustard curtains on the wall added to the sense of torpor and airlessness in the room. Sometimes we would play games counting how long it would take their father to notice them waiting. Once I remembered counting to three thousand and eleven and having to stifle the urge to scratch an itch on my bare leg for fear of giving the game away.

As I walked up Hestor Street, I was rehearsing possible opening lines over and over until I felt like a ventriloquist's dummy. Even when I had been before the court, I never remembered feeling like this. By the time I knocked on the door, I was reeling with giddiness. Even my face couldn't hide the meeting we'd had earlier in the week. By now the bruising had turned to a faded jaundice colour that only made me look unwell. I was prepared to live with that. Back at work I had been ribbed for my shiner. Colourful tales were quickly invented to explain it – most supposing it had been received saving a woman's honour, with adversaries changing from wicked stepfathers to unscrupulous landlords to merciless pawnbrokers as the day wore on. But each time I saw my face in the mirror, it reminded me of a visit I still had to make.

By the time I reached their house, I started laughing to myself. For how long had Martha and I been living in the same town, unable to make contact with each other? Now for the third time in a week I was knocking on their door, with a renewed sense of apprehension about where this was leading.

I'd been there a couple of minutes waiting when the lady from number 26 came out.

"There's no one there today."

She was shouting down from the upstairs front room of the house.

"She told me they were leaving at the crack of sparrows this morning. Trying to get to Blackpool, she said."

"Blackpool?" Robert repeated in a tone of incomprehension.

"That's what she said. Who am I to doubt it?"

"Both of them?"

"Aye. They wanted to go to the seaside. Celebration, I think it must have been. Good journey though, isn't it? Can't

think when I last went there. Anyway, mustn't keep you."
She shut the window and disappeared from view.

I turned around and kicked at the ground as I left. What did the woman mean when she talked about celebration? The end of the war? I knew Martha well enough to know that she wouldn't go swanning off to Blackpool, with all the cost involved unless she had good reason to. Martha was tighter with money than he'd ever been. I couldn't help feeling that something had happened to make them decide to go off for the day and I wanted to blame myself. That's when I decided to visit Connie. She was as likely as anyone to know what was going on and I'd known her long enough to expect an honest answer – if she could give one.

When I got there, Connie didn't seem surprised to see me. Maybe nothing can shock her at the moment? Angela was sleeping so Connie gave me a cup of tea, courtesy of a neighbour who'd passed over her tea coupons to Connie. For a few seconds there was silence as I looked around the room. There was precious little there: a framed souvenir postcard from Westbury-on-Sea, the radio on the mantelpiece and some old magazines. Nothing showy about the room, but then Connie had never been one to go over the top.

I'd picked up one of the magazines when I heard the sound of sobbing coming from the kitchen. By the time I reached Connie, she was in floods of tears and it was all I could do to get her to come and sit down in the parlour and try and calm herself.

"Now you just sit there while I go and fetch that tea," I said.

There were tea leaves still in the teapot from the last brew. But I poured in the boiling water and hoped that a minute would do something to dredge out some taste.

Poor Connie! I'd been as surprised as anyone when Martha told me about the pregnancy. On one level I think

I was shocked by Connie's decision to keep it, but other options weren't any easier. She could have paid someone in a backstreet to get rid of it or handed it over for adoption. Knowing how much Connie had longed for a family, she wouldn't have considered having an abortion. And giving it up for adoption would have broken her heart. Harry was missing, presumed dead and a new man had just walked into her life. That's what Martha had intimated. But then getting the telegram telling her that Harry was a POW had left her tearing herself apart with the fear and guilt.

Over tea I asked Connie how things were going and she started telling me about the reaction she'd had when out walking with Angela in the pram and how miserable it was making her. She said how condemned she felt and how she was beginning to imagine people muttering behind her back about sleeping around and how she had got it coming to her.

I tried telling her not to let it get to her, because we were all so different and that didn't make one person better than another. It wasn't our place to do the judging, I said. Knowing why I was there, I talked about her staying with Martha and Billy and hoped she didn't feel judged by them.

Connie couldn't have been clearer. She knew how Martha had put herself out for her, even giving up her bedroom. I quipped about Billy grumbling at that and that's when Connie talked about Billy having had an accident down at the works when he dropped a steel pipe from the hawser. I asked if she could remember when it was and she was sure it happened on Thursday. She told me that he had been sent home and told not to come back until next week.

When I suggested he could do with a rest Connie gave me a wink and said she thought it was plain as suet pudding that Martha had been broody as hell with Angela around the house. Probably having the time of his life, she added.

Martha

After they left to walk away from the front towards the dunes, Martha was smiling. There was something in the air: the warmth, the gentle breeze blowing the grass on the edge of the dunes. To her it looked like something out of a film or a book. She could see the heroines she had read about as a teenager walking off with their lovers to deserted meadows, or being cast by the spell of the full moon. Now, it was her turn. All she wanted to do was to walk along the dunes and find a hollow of sand where they could lie together, away from prying eyes.

"How far are we going?" Billy asked.

"Billy Hilton, I don't want anyone to see me with my knickers around my ankles if that's alright with you."

She stopped, turned towards Billy, looked him in the eyes and kissed him.

"So we need to find somewhere we won't be disturbed."

She was acting like a teenager on her first big night out and the element of danger was making that prospect all the more exciting. There was a fresh glow about her, made by the wind and the sun.

She wished the same was true of Billy. In his face she could see uncertainty and his high forehead looked creased with worry-lines.

"Come on," Martha said, pulling Billy away from the sea towards a bank of dunes surrounded by tall marram grass.

She thought it was a perfect spot and Martha threw herself onto the sand and held out her arms for Billy to join her. Taking one of his hands in hers, he lowered himself gently down onto her. She had such fine dark hair, and she loved the way he played and stroked it rhythmically with his fingers. Martha reached and pulled him towards her. There was a taste of salt on each other's lips and he could feel his body on her as she wriggled beneath him until she was ready. In the distance she could hear the sound of an accordion playing a haunting melody. Taking her arms away from around his back she lowered them so that her hands were between their bodies and she could feel him.

The next second Billy rolled over onto his back.

"What's the matter?" she asked.

She could see his eyes were closed. He picked up a pebble and threw it away as if in disgust.

"I can't. Not right now. That's all."

"What d'you mean, you can't?"

"I don't know what it is."

"Do you mean you don't want to?"

"No, it's not that. It's just…"

"Well Billy, I can't start a family on my own, you know?"

Martha knew that Billy could sometimes get himself to places where it was difficult to find him. She'd be able to see something about the look in Billy's eyes – some never-never land that he was visiting. If he was there now it was really poor timing, she thought.

"Open your eyes, Billy. They don't hide anything from me."

She could see his eyes flickering as he struggled to open them.

"That's better! Look at me, Billy," she said resting on her side, "you've not been yourself this week, Billy. Ever since you came back – Wednesday night, that was it – it's not been you there, has it?"

She watched him and waited for the words to form.

"Maybe it was difficult for you with Connie and the babe. You should have told me if it was."

"No, it's nothing to do with Connie," he said.

"Well, that's one thing out of the way. You're sure?"

"Trust me," he said.

"That's a relief, 'cos we haven't seen the last of dear Connie. I told her we'd help her out when Harry comes home. If that's OK with you?"

Billy nodded.

"We'll manage," he added.

"I know we'll manage, Billy, but you frighten me when you're out of reach. We really need to see eye to eye about things at the moment," she said drawing her finger down the side of Billy's face. "And another thing you need is rest."

"I feel tired."

"And you look terrible. Sure as hell don't know why I could fancy you at the moment. Looks like you're carrying the weight of the world."

"Not me," he said getting up and pulling Martha to her feet, "I'm still your Billy."

Martha looked at him.

"Sometimes I do wonder," she said.

12

Robert

Robert knew it should have been a time for celebration. For the first time in too many years, people were able to sit in their rooms without blackouts and were able to go about their business thinking that there was some point in planning for the future. The clock was going back – even street lights were back on. Bunting was still hanging across the streets, but it had the look of yesterday's party which someone still hadn't cleared up. One paper shop had in its window a picture of Monty being saluted by a row of German officers, another still had the slogan '*Make do and mend*' spread across its front.

The people Robert passed in the street looked as though relief was sewn into their smiles. He hoped it wasn't too early for joy of course. The war reports in the newspaper reminded the British public that the war with Japan hadn't finished and the Forgotten Army was still advancing through Burma.

As Robert made his way towards Hestor Street on the mill side of Olthorp, he was wondering how long this period could last. Was it to be another fool's paradise which would blow up in their faces in time? When could they start taking this new-found belief in themselves and the future for real?

This morning it made him think about his father with a certain gratitude. His father, ever the optimist, had always been intolerant of those who preached that there was no point in trying, because the end was always just around the corner. He said you needed to live each day as a building block for the future. Now with the end of the war, it seemed to Robert as though a curtain had been lifted. Everyone had the chance to look ahead and believe that there was everything to live for. That's what he was trying to do.

But he also knew that there were others who would not want to forget what had been done in the name of freedom.

'It's easy for you to say things like that, Robert,' he could hear Billy saying, 'because you haven't been there, have you? Not down in the mud, in the trenches, not living with fear every second of the day and night. Not fighting them baby-bayoneting Nazis.'

Robert had usually heard about these lectures from Billy second-hand. When he visited them, Martha tried to explain why Billy would no more have Robert in his house than let someone take over his allotment. But if ever Billy saw Robert, he always took the chance to remind Robert that he owed his life to the men who were doing a real job.

Of course, Robert knew that in part Billy was right. No, he hadn't been physically down there with the rest of them. His way of helping the lads had been to pray for them. Robert had tried not to let it bother him when Billy made a cheap jibe at his expense – making him out to be a traitor to the cause. Somehow he had grown used to it.

Thinking again about Billy made Robert relive that moment in the allotment when Billy knelt on him with his broad swarthy features looming above him. There had been a moment and it was just that, when he'd caught the frightened, puzzled look in Billy's clear blue eyes, as if he'd been found in someone else's house and couldn't remember who he was visiting or how he had got there. Billy had been staring back at him when that look of pain, almost fear had covered his face. That's the last image he had of Billy.

"This is a surprise," Martha said, opening the door to Robert.

"Hullo, Martha. I called yesterday but you weren't in. Your neighbour," he said pointing to the house on the opposite side of the street, "told me you'd both gone off for the day."

"Aye, that's right. Managed to get to Blackpool. Well," she said, stepping back a little so that Robert could come into the house, "are you coming in or not?"

"You look tired Martha."

"Well, that's not bleeding surprising is it?"

"Sorry!"

"Apologies don't get the meals cooked or the clothes darned when you're working."

"I was only–"

"Yesterday was the first day off I've had in I don't know how long. And working with the room screened by blackouts means there's no ventilation and the noise of the machinery is bleeding deafening. It's not been much of a holiday, I can tell you."

He could almost hear their father telling them to stop bickering.

But looking at Martha now, Robert could see that her eyes were red and realised that she must have been crying. Martha, crying? He couldn't remember when he last saw her tearful. Even at their father's funeral, she had been unable to show any emotion. Robert was so puzzled by the look on her face, that Martha said she had to ask him twice if he wanted a cup of tea.

"I'm worried about you, and no, don't say that makes a change," he said going up to Martha and holding out his hand, "because I can see you've been crying, Martha, and you never cry."

Martha looked at Robert's outstretched hand for a moment and then did something which Robert could never remember her doing before. Lifting one of her crossed arms away from the front of her smock, she edged it forward until it was hovering above Robert's. Then, with her head falling forward, she held onto his hand while pulling herself towards him and collapsed onto his chest with an explosion of sobbing.

Robert put his arms around his sister and held her as firmly as he dared.

"There now," he said, "steady, steady, steady."

As soon as he said it, he recognised it as one of their mother's sayings. He couldn't imagine what had made him remember it at that point but it was one of her foibles which they both remembered with a certain fondness. She'd use it with them when they were upset or angry or tired or out of sorts. Sometimes it seemed the only way to offer comfort to her children.

"Remember how bad it had to be before she said it?" he quipped.

The memory made Robert want to laugh. Beneath his arms, Robert could feel Martha's stifled giggles as she too remembered their mother's reliance on a particular verbal bandage which was thought to be suitable to fit all ailments. Within seconds, Martha was off herself.

"The pudding!" she shrieked.

"Of course," Robert replied, "the one which father had bought from the fair."

"For a farthing!"

"And then insisted we eat it, even though it tasted like muck."

"You were in tears," Martha remembered.

"And mother was doing her best to swallow, even though it was plain that she didn't like it either."

"I didn't cry, but I remember hating him for it, and especially when he told you off for crying."

"And all she could say was," he paused.

"Steady, steady, steady," they both chimed together.

For what seemed like ages, they were seemingly locked together in a laughing embrace. Then rather abruptly, Martha pulled away

"I'll make the tea now, shall I?" Martha asked, as she started to take cups off the dresser and put a pan on the hob to boil.

Robert was still in the back room, looking out at the yard with the shelter at the far end where the vegetables were growing. To Robert that morning, it all seemed to belong to another world.

"I came to see Billy," he said.

"Hang on a minute, Robert, I'm just waiting for this pan to boil. Won't be a minute."

Robert stood there, wondering what had made him say those words. He hadn't thought about what he was going to say at all. Even if Billy had been at home, he didn't know what he could have said to him. Billy might not have registered him at all, making Robert feel that what he had felt or seen at the allotment was part of his imagination. But today, like yesterday, there was a part of him that needed to see Billy, to find his eyes again and see what they were telling him.

"Sorry! It takes a bloody age to boil anything. But it's hot and wet even if it's tasteless," she said passing Robert over a mug, which he nestled between his hands. Martha sat down on the chair closest to the kitchen.

"Come on! No need to stand on ceremony in this house. You should know that!"

Robert gave a low laugh and stayed where he was.

"I said I came to see Billy."

Martha looked up and stared at Robert. She started to tilt her head from side to side as if to check whether she had heard correctly.

"Sorry, Robert, maybe I'm a little slow today, but is there something I've missed? I mean since when has Billy done anything other than insult you about the stand you've taken?"

"I need to talk to him."

"Need? Robert, I don't think you two have spoken civilly to each other in the last five years!"

To Robert, the more he talked about Billy, the less easy he felt about explaining what was going through his mind. It wasn't about words. Words would probably destroy everything that he felt so excited about.

"Yes, I need to see him, Martha."

"Why, for God's sake?"

"That accident at work?"

"What about it?"

"It was probably my fault."

"Robert," Martha started, "you are beginning to make me feel like I've been living somewhere else recently. What's it to do with you?"

"I saw him. Billy."

"So what?"

"On Wednesday evening."

Martha sat back in the chair and folded her arms.

"At the allotment," Robert continued.

"You're right. I do remember him going there that evening."

"It wasn't planned."

"What wasn't?"

"Meeting there. In fact, as soon as he saw me, he was up for it – as usual."

"What?"

"Having a scrap!"

"Why?"

"I don't think he enjoyed finding me here with you earlier that day, locked up with family secrets. It must have looked to him as though I was going through the past – a time which didn't include Billy Hilton. I don't think that made him feel any fonder of me."

"But that wasn't your fault!"

"No, but I needed you to tell him that – when Billy was feeling calmer. Guess that never happened."

Martha shrugged.

"So, I suppose this fading shiner," she said getting out of her chair, standing in front of Robert and running a finger down the side of Robert's face, "was our Billy's handiwork."

"You got it," Robert laughed. "That's what I want to see him about."

"Oh God, Robert, you're not going to have another fight, are you?"

Robert was caught between saying too much and saying nothing at all.

"No. Maybe I want to see if he meant it."

"What! Bloody well looks like it, doesn't it?"

"Like I said, I need to talk to him."

"Well, he ran off cursing me a while ago. Why don't you start at the allotment? That's his usual refuge."

"Did he need one?"

"Robert, let's forget about it now, shall we?"

"If that's what you want."

Robert turned towards the door.

"Why don't you ask Billy, if you see him? We've got no secrets, remember."

Later, when he closed the door behind him and turned down the street towards the allotments, Robert could hear the word *secrets* hammering inside his head. It was less than a week ago since he had come across that secret kept by his father which would haunt Robert as long as he lived. Now here he was doing it himself, covering a piece of himself with his own shame and guilt. He was beginning to wonder if the lessons would ever be learnt?

13

Billy

Billy remembered his dad telling him that the land between the canal and the road, down to the railway arches, had been used as allotments ever since the council bought it. He'd followed his father down here since he was a lad, and when his father died, keeping up 'his patch' as his father had called it, seemed the most natural thing to do. Like others he had received packets of seeds and had been grateful for them. He'd also be looking forward to receiving his 'Digging for Victory' certificate from the mayor.

Billy had always been keen on keeping his patch tidy. He couldn't call it anything else. If there was one part of his life that had been influenced by his father, it would have been his love of gardening. As soon as his father began to leave his own patch untended, Billy knew that he was sick. When Billy thought of his father's decline, he saw the patch, strangled by weeds and nettles, and dandelions growing where once he had grown sprouts and cabbage, runner beans and tomatoes.

Now, Billy's patch was like a best friend to him. Needing some peace and quiet, he'd stroll up the road, go under the arches and then through the bottom gate. Often talking to himself as he was planting or hoeing, cutting or seeding, he'd treat it as his confidant. Sometimes he'd be able to go back with a clear resolution in mind after chewing it over while he cleared the patch. He was hoping that would happen this afternoon.

He couldn't understand why Martha was in such a rush. One minute the idea of starting a family had been in the background for both of them. Then all of a sudden it was like Martha couldn't think of anything else. Billy couldn't blame her, mind. What with Connie and the babe in the house, it was a bit like having your face rubbed into it. That's why he'd hoped it would be a bit easier without Connie there. But it wasn't to be for long because what Martha told him yesterday meant that Connie and Angela would be back with them as soon as Harry was back in the picture.

Yesterday! Could it have been more difficult? Not that he could blame the sand dune fiasco on Connie. She was nowhere near Blackpool beach! Somehow he felt as they walked away from the pier that Martha was building up to it. He also knew that his wires were crossed at the moment and he didn't know when they would get untangled. Nothing seemed to be simple at the moment.

Martha certainly didn't take kindly to his excuses on the beach. But she was even more wound up when the same thing happened this morning when all Billy could think of was getting a bit more sleep. Usually she hardly needed to touch him and he was excited but at the moment there was little Martha could do to make her feel that the effort would make any difference.

"You're no use to me in that state, Billy Hilton," she said.

He knew that but he also realised he couldn't tell her why because he hardly dared guess himself. It had started on Wednesday evening, right here in the allotments. That much he knew. He could still see Robert's face as he lay on the ground, looking up at him, with his silver blue eyes. He could still see the sweat running down from Robert's head and earth stuck in his curly hair. Some part of him had wanted to untie the kerchief from around his neck. Folding it once and then again, with one hand he'd wipe the sweat from Robert's face and with the other, brush the soil from his hair. But the closer he came to his neck the harder it became and the urge within him got louder and louder until he thought he would scream. That's when he lashed out – to stop the noise.

Since then, he'd nearly killed someone at work and had been made to look by Martha as though he wasn't even up for it. Who was this? Not the Billy Hilton he knew or anyone else for that matter.

That's when the allotment seemed a better place for him to be. He'd left home as soon as he could, slamming the door behind him.

He was digging up some rhubarb when he heard his voice. At first he thought he was dreaming.

"Hullo, Billy."

Looking up, he saw Robert turning in from the lane that ran alongside the canal. Getting to his feet, still holding the rhubarb, he just nodded.

"I've been to your house," Robert said.

"What's the matter? Wanted to have another soul-searching time with Martha, was that it?"

"No, I went to see you."

"Me?"

"Like I did yesterday. But you were out."

"Aye."

"Blackpool, wasn't it?"

"So?"

They were only a matter of feet apart, but to Billy at that moment they might have been in different valleys.

"I came to talk about Wednesday," Robert said.

As soon as Robert said it, Billy could see Robert's face again as he lay on the ground, helpless, with the sweat dripping from his face onto the earth around him.

"Yes," he said, "I thought you might."

In the silence between them that followed, the train passing so close to them, the noise of the rattle seemed to deafen each of them with its layers of familiar sound.

Pushing the fork down hard into the earth, Billy willed his body to move towards the low wall, where Robert was standing. He'd covered only a few paces, when Robert jumped over the wall and landed neatly on the edge of the allotment.

"Where'd you learn that?" Billy asked, edging further forward.

He came as close as he dared to Robert, before pointing to the bruising on Robert's face.

"I didn't mean to do that," he said.

As if to confirm what Billy was talking about, Robert began to touch that still discoloured side of his face.

"You had every right to be angry with me."

"But if I wanted to scrap with you for being a conchie, I'd have done it properly."

Billy saw Robert nod his head and start to smile.

"It wasn't a bad effort! I can still feel it. Even the bruises are only just going," Robert said.

For a few moments Billy stood quite still, feeling Robert's eyes all over him.

"I didn't know what to say. Frightened, I was," Billy said.

"You weren't the only one. I thought you were going to pummel me. That's probably why I couldn't speak."

Billy saw the smile at the edge of Robert's mouth.

At the top end of the allotment, in a patch closer to the road, a man wearing a cloth cap was turning over the soil and talking to a small boy who was holding the wheelbarrow. Billy had seen them earlier and now caught the sound of their voices drifting over the allotment.

"Lucky there was no one about to see me then! I'd have been–"

"There wasn't," Robert cut in.

"I'm sorry," Billy said, rubbing his dirty hands down the side of his trousers before holding out his hand. "Robert?"

Billy couldn't remember when he had last called him by his name. Maybe he never had done before. The word and all its associations were still ringing in his head when he felt Robert's hand in his own. His eyes seemed locked onto their hands as they held onto each other. Without knowing what to think, they shifted and the next moment he found himself staring at Robert's face. For the next few seconds, with the two of them standing there so close to each other, surrounded by canes stuck into the ground at odd angles with shoots growing along them wild and untrained, Billy couldn't speak and the silence seemed so intense between them that neither was able to hear the words of the old man until he was almost upon them.

"Sorry to bother you," the man said after clearing his voice, "but I was wondering if you youngsters could lend us a hand."

As soon as he heard the voice, Billy's hand loosened and he pulled away, turning towards the speaker.

"It's just that me and me lad were digging and we need some help," the man explained.

Without hesitation, Billy went over to pick up his fork.

As the man muttered his thanks and moved away

walking back up the allotment, Billy looked at Robert just standing there. He seemed unable to move in any direction.

"Guess, it's not the best time now," Robert said.

"No," he agreed.

"I'm glad I came," Robert said, "because I needed to see you."

"And I meant it," he said, "about being sorry."

"I know."

"Do you? I'm glad. Been thinking about nothing else."

"Me too," Robert added.

"I've been a zombie, since it happened. Christ, I nearly killed someone at the works."

Robert shook his head.

"I'd better go," Billy said, turning around and walking over to the old boy and his lad, taking a fork with him, "but I won't be long," he shouted back.

14

Martha

Martha couldn't wait for the election to take place.
Like everyone else she'd felt so optimistic at VE day.
Since then it had been more of the same in many ways.
Like rations, which people had been hoping would be lifted
come the end of the war. But what happens, she asked
herself. Rations get cut! As if we haven't been living with
rations long enough and tight enough already. Going past
the empty shops made her feel that she was still waiting for
life to be returned to her.

On the side of a house she saw GOD BLESS OUR LADS
FOR THIS VICTORY painted in huge red and blue letters.
Elsewhere names had been written on walls: Roosevelt,
Churchill, Stalin and Monty. Martha had heard Churchill
on the radio a few days ago and thought he sounded tired,
as if he belonged to another era. He may have done his bit,
she thought, but there is still no reason why he should stay
in charge until the war with Japan was over. There would be
an election in June, they'd been told. It couldn't come soon
enough for Martha.

Many of the lads were coming back. She'd seen some
already, walking downtown in their smart demob suits,
as if they thought that would be enough to win over the
hearts of women. But they were coming back to a different

country too. How many of their wives would have been working in their lives before? How many would have ever experienced the conditions in some of those factories? Martha knew it was a different country now after six years of wartime. That's why it needed a different government. She knew they must be ready for change.

By the time she turned into Hestor Street, Martha was tired and she could feel herself about to break out into a cold clammy sweat.

As soon as she saw him, sitting there with his head in his hands, she could feel her stomach tighten as if she'd heard someone call "Gas!" He got to his feet.

"Should I feel honoured? Is this more–," she started.

"Martha," he said, cutting her short, "it's Billy. There's been an accident."

All Martha could do was stare at Robert as if unable to believe what she was hearing.

"What do you mean an accident?" she asked.

"He was helping out a young lad at the allotments. The boy had Billy's fork. He must have hit a bomb with it."

"Oh my God, Robert, no. Not Billy, no not Billy."

"The boy was blown to bits in front of his grandfather. I think Billy must have been a little way behind the boy but he's suffering from concussion."

"You mean he's –" Martha could hardly bring herself to finish the sentence.

"Alive, yes, but unconscious."

"Oh Robert," Martha said, coming towards her brother and holding him by his arm, "I've got to see him now. Will you take me to him?"

"That's why I've got the ambulance."

By the time they arrived at the hospital, Martha couldn't hold herself back. She jumped out of the ambulance as soon as it stopped and ran inside the hospital. Robert caught up with her as she was outside the intensive care unit (ICU), but no sooner had she been taken inside than she came rushing out, saying,

"Oh my God, Billy, what have you done?"

Robert tried to hold her to calm her down but she had been so frightened by all the machines and dials that she felt she had been dropped into some nightmare vision of hell.

It was only after she had been persuaded by Robert to go in and sit with Billy lying there in the ICU, with the heart monitor beating out its regular pattern that she felt her wild heart beat beginning to calm down. Reaching out with one hand, she clutched Billy's hand and started to stroke it with her other. But it was the banks of machines, blinking their coloured lights at her that seemed to mesmerise her. All she could do was stare at them.

"Talk to him," she heard Robert say, "he needs to hear your voice."

For one moment, her mind blanked.

"Billy, it's me, Martha," she began, aware that her eyes were beginning to fill. She looked towards Robert and saw him nodding at her and putting his thumb in the air as if telling her to carry on. She took a deep breath.

"Robert told me what happened down at the patch. About the boy and his grandad needing some help. Trust you, Billy Hilton. Always wanted to be the glory boy, didn't you? Never could miss the chance to be the hero. Well, you know Billy, that's just one of the things you do that I fell for. Everyone else comes first. I suppose that includes me and nothing's changed since… we've been together. Nearly two years now and it's not stopping…"

Martha couldn't manage any more without bursting into tears and she knew that was the last thing that Billy wanted to hear. She squeezed his hand again before getting to her feet and running for the door.

On their way back from the hospital, she tried to tell Robert how hard she found it and the next thing she knew she found herself apologising for her clumsiness.

"There's no need," he answered. "Most weeks I have to deal with people traumatised in one way or another. Each person's reaction is different and it's always unpredictable."

Martha felt relieved to hear it and put her head back against the hard seat. She let the rumble of the ambulance along the uneven surfaces calm her as much as she could. Then she sat up sharply, as if pulled out of her reverie.

"How did you know?" she asked.

"Know what?"

"About Billy? That he was at the allotments. That he had been injured? Well?" she probed after waiting for an answer that never came.

"I was there," he answered.

"At the allotments? At the same time as Billy?"

"Yes," he said, "until about a minute before the explosion."

"I don't believe it. Did Billy know you were there?"

Martha looked across at him. It was at times like these that she wondered whether she really knew her brother at all. The longer he was silent, the more amazed she became.

"Yes, we were talking," he said at last, "when the old man came over with his boy to ask for someone to help him with some digging, the boy pointed at me before the old man walked towards Billy."

Martha started shaking her head,

"Wonders... and then you saw Billy walking up the slope of the allotment towards the far end."

"I guess so. I was back on the towpath walking away from the allotment when I heard the explosion. It was so close I knew it must have come from there."

Martha put her head back and closed her eyes.

"Not a good time for you, Marth," she heard Robert say, "let me know if there's anything I can do."

"You're right. I hate being on my own. Still that won't be for long because of Connie."

"You're helping her out again."

"Somebody has to. Harry'll be home in a few days. Some homecoming he's going to get to find his wife with a baby that doesn't belong to him. Connie's scared through and through and I don't blame her. I only wish I could give them something decent to eat. I'm fed up with eating dried egg and milk!"

"Maybe I can help out. I'm getting more than enough from my patch to keep me fed. Why don't I drop you off some carrots or a swede or some kale?"

"Are you sure? Oh, that would make such a change"

"I wouldn't offer if I didn't want to and then you can cook one of those special pies that we used to drool over. Not that they came often. You remember the ones that mother used to spice up with anything that she could find and then--"

"Hey, hold on Robert. What's got into you rambling on like that? This is my street actually and you've just driven past the front door. What a state – the two of us! Too busy reminiscing. Not like you really. Let me off here then and Robert, thanks for your help today. I couldn't have managed."

"Tomorrow? Will you be going to see him?" Robert asked.

"'Course I will! But it's OK. I'll get there myself from now on. Don't you worry."

That's when she got out of the ambulance and started walking back to her front door.

She was so caught up worrying and thinking about Billy, that it wasn't until she was almost at her front door that she noticed him. A young man, with ginger hair, was getting to his feet where he'd been sitting on the pavement, right outside her front door.

There was something about his manner that made Martha wary even before she had spoken to him. Tallish, he kept his head down as he approached Martha and if she hadn't spoken he would probably have walked straight past her.

"You looking for something?" she asked as she passed him.

The man looked up at Martha. She noticed how pale he was and what shifting eyes he had. He couldn't keep them still for a second and they didn't stop moving as he spoke to her.

"Maybe," he answered in a way that she couldn't recognise where he was from.

"You were standing outside my door, that's all. And there's not many that do that unless they want to see me or Billy."

He was wearing grey trousers held up with braces and she noticed the turn-ups were dirty and torn. On his head he wore a hat which had a striped bandana around it. To Martha, there was something quite comical about him.

"Well," she repeated, "did you or did you not want to see either of us?"

"No," the man answered.

"Fine," Martha said, turning her back on him and moving towards her front door, "because I've got things to do."

"I was looking for Robert. Robert Chalmers."

Martha stopped and turned around to look at the visitor, who claimed to know Robert and to be looking for him. She couldn't for the life of her find anything familiar about him and she didn't know whether to be worried or intrigued.

"Why would that be?" she asked, trying to sound as ordinary as she could.

She could see the man hesitating and starting to kick the ground with one of his feet, like a horse stamping the ground.

"He's a friend," he answered at last looking at Martha.

"A friend? If he's a friend then why don't you know where he lives?"

"Must have lost his address. Knew he lived in Olthorp, though."

"Lost his address? Bit careless for a friend."

He didn't answer so Martha continued.

"Why did you come to this house then?"

"I asked someone down the post office. They reckoned that a Chalmers lived here."

"Is that right?"

"Yeah. That's you, isn't it?"

"Kind of. Why?"

"Like I said, I'm looking for Robert."

"I'm getting that too."

"Well," the man said turning away, "if you won't tell me where he is, you'd better tell Robert that Stewart's looking for him. He knows I'll find him."

Extract from Robert's diary

The day hell returned!

As I left Billy and walked away from the allotment along the towpath, I felt a glow all around my face. Part of me wanted to stop, turn around and run back where I had come from. I'd keep on running up the slope until I'd see him again. He'd be there, standing, or bent over as he tried to help with the digging.

But I looked into the water and knew that if I found my gaze it would be a beaming reflection. At last! I'd seen him. Billy! Billy, after all these years! Nothing made sense, but then why should it? Looking around me as I walked along the path and under the bridge, I thought it all looked so beautiful with the barges moored alongside and the overhanging trees with their sweeping branches full of leaves. How could this make sense after the horrors they'd all lived through. But here it was – new life and hope!

And now Billy! As soon as Billy called my name, I felt as though I'd been touched with a very soft hand, gently stroking my face. When we clasped each other's hands and held them there, I could feel the rough calluses on his palms and see his blue grey eyes fixed on mine. My hands were still tingling and again and again all I could see was Billy's outstretched arm and hand waiting for my own. But I didn't need to decide because it was like returning a touch already given. And as our hands met and each gave their own clench of strength and pressure from different fingers at different moments, I knew things could never be the same between us again.

Even as I had walked away from the allotments, all I could think about was that look on his face. Confusion and edginess had given away to an honesty and simplicity. For once his steel blue eyes were smiling. I noticed a scar just above his right eye. My hand could still feel his lingering touch.

That's when I heard it.

It sounded like a dull reverberating thud, like one that had come from somewhere deep underground behind me. Looking over my shoulder towards the allotment, I saw smoke lifting from the ground, between the arches and the canal. For a moment, I tried to stop it making sense, wanting to find something surreal about such sounds set amongst the innocence of the toiled-over allotments. But the part of me that was tuned into the daily ravages of war took over, the wires joined up and shocked me out of my reverie and I knew that the blast had come from somewhere too close to the allotments. Without waiting, I ran along the towpath as far as the allotments. That's when I saw the smoke rising up from the top of the slope I screamed,

"No!" and then again, "No!" before I turned on myself and ran back along the towpath towards the gate at the bottom of the allotments.

As I turned in at the gate, there was some part of me that was beginning to feel that I was making the tragedy more real with every step I took. But nothing could stop me and I started shouting, "Billy! Billy!" and running towards the smoke. By the time I reached the top of the slope, I couldn't see anything clearly. Where the top end of the allotment had been, there was now only a crater.

"Billy!" I screamed again, forcing myself to walk into the hole left by the explosion. Even as a trained emergency worker, I could never prepare myself for the gruesome gore of war – the scattering of limbs, heads detached from torsos, feet shorn off from legs and parts so unrecognisably human that I couldn't touch them without recoiling and gagging.

Lying on the ground, its tines sticking out of the ground like some monstrous claw, with the handle burnt off, I recognised the fork that I had seen Billy give to the young lad. Next to it there was a piece of fabric, which I thought I recognised as the boy's shirt, now stained with blood. I turned away from it and bent over, retching.

That's when I heard someone moaning – a noise which came from further down the slope in the direction of a row of blasted, twisted canes, where tomatoes were growing. Running away from the crater, I jumped over rows of vegetables, through the swirling smoke, following the groans and all the time shouting, "Billy!"

I could never have seen the old man's feet. The next thing I knew I was falling headfirst towards the ground, my arms coming out instinctively to protect myself from the fall. But rather than the sudden jarring of hard ground, they fell on something soft. The next moment I found my head buried in someone's chest. One glance at the jacket and I knew that I had found Billy. But lying there against Billy's inert body, with my head against his chest, I knew there was no need to do what I had done for the FAU in every other emergency situation. Through the jacket I could hear the slow beat of his heart and I lay there, with my wet face buried and my shaking hand following the contours of his face.

It was only as I pulled away from Billy, that I realised that I could still hear the groaning and it was coming from the old man whose prone body lay a few feet from Billy's. Turning, I could see blood coming from the old man's shoulder. I pulled off my shirt and tore a strip from it which I used as a bandage, all the time talking to the man, explaining what I was trying to do. As I bent over and tried to move him into a sitting position, the old man's hoarse voice was trying to tell me something.

"Save your breath," I told him.

"No, no," the old man wheezed, trying to find the strength to speak, "Adam." That was all he said.

I knew that there would be a time for the man to learn that Adam's young body was now spread in pieces, around the allotments. Just as easily I feared that he would never understand it. Already I had seen too many such accidents which went beyond the reason of words. Now, all I could think of doing was to try and save the man's life while he still had that desire left in him. Going back to the road, I ran along the pavement, waving and shouting to some people who were waiting at the bus stop.

"You've got to help. Three people have been hurt in an explosion in the allotments. Look," I said pointing behind me, "you can still see the smoke!"

Perhaps it was the word allotments that did it. Three of them followed me back to the slope. There was a woman amongst them.

"Are you sure?" I asked turning to the woman and appealing to her with upturned hands, "it's not pretty."

"I've seen enough," she said before adding, "who am I looking for?"

"A young boy, Adam," I said.

While the men and I were busy carrying Billy and the old man back down to the ambulance, I could hear them tutting about the bloody war being over. The woman said nothing but went about scavenging amongst the earth and debris for parts that belonged to Adam. She never complained and quietly gathered as many as she could find and placed them together in a small crater made by the explosion.

"There," she said at last, "at least you can tell the family where the boy's buried." As I went back to the ambulance, I saw them making their way back to the bus stop.

I took them both to the hospital where I stayed with Billy as long as they'd let me. Within minutes he was put on a trolley and wheeled through to the ICU. They told me to leave and as I left the old man, he clutched my sleeve,

"Don't leave him there," he croaked.

A row of plane trees runs along the edge of the allotments. Now there's a small mound which is marked by a cross made out of a couple of small branches. Every hour I pray it's the only one that will be needed.

And Stewart! What the hell was Stewart doing in Olthorp? As if I needed any more surprises today. I saw him as we came round the corner coming back from the hospital. Couldn't bloody miss him with that striped bandana of his. I don't know what I was talking about to Martha but it must have been nonsense because my head was somewhere else. Shocked is one way of putting it. What on earth was he doing here? And how the hell had he tracked me down. I couldn't remember what I'd told him when we were inside. Maybe I had opened my big mouth and talked about Olthorp. Then I suppose I had no idea that Stewart would hang onto the information and use it. It's almost as if he planned the whole thing.

After dropping Martha, I drove away as quickly as I could because I needed to be back in my room, to try and make sense of the day. I couldn't remember making a conscious decision to do so, but a few minutes later I found myself driving past the allotments. As I turned to stare at the terrible killing ground, my mind couldn't tear itself away from the memories that sparkled and froze at the same time.

15

Robert

Last night was one of those nights when Robert knew he wouldn't be able to sleep and the hours would stretch endlessly into the early morning. Even when he did sleep, his mind was filled with such foreboding images that it came as some relief when at last he pulled back the curtains to reveal a day that was itself only half-formed. Sunlight was struggling to filter its way through the banks of low clouds. For Robert it was as if the day was not yet ready for life.

By the time he reached the hospital, he'd rehearsed what he was going to say to Martha, were he to meet her there. For how long he could keep up this pretence he didn't know. There she was, digging away for answers about why he should have been there at the allotments at the same time as Billy. He couldn't blame her! After the protracted friction between them over his CO stance, how likely was it for them to be sharing time together when digging spits?

"You can go and sit with him if you like," the nurse said when Robert had found his way back to the ICU and asked how Billy was. "No, you won't find much change in him."

"Any idea how long it might take for him to regain consciousness?" Robert asked.

"Now there's a question," the nurse replied, "that none of us can honestly answer. All head injuries are different.

Some who do recover may still be prone to fits for some time to come. You can't rush nature sometimes."

The more she talked, the more Robert was filled with a deepening leaden gloom. How could such a thing happen now? After surviving raids as often as they had? But there was no reason for it. Did all death seen so senseless, he wondered? After re-reading First World War poems, Robert had tried to find his own words for the horror that the next generation of combatants had faced. He knew so little of what they had suffered and yet part of him felt that were he to have had all the facts before him, he would have been even less likely to have his mind changed about the stance he had taken.

As he went into the room the first thing that struck him was the noise made by the various machines to which Billy was attached. It sounded like someone was sucking water through a toothless mouth. Sitting in a chair by the bedside, Robert tried not to turn his gaze to the monitors which gave out a shadowy picture of Billy's hold on life. Instead he looked at Billy's face. He could see the face that hung above him as he lay prone in the allotments: a ruddy complexion under a mop of dark hair, with the edged lines made by toiling at the mills and living with the perpetual uncertainty of war snatching some of his boyish innocence.

How long he waited there he couldn't remember, but when the nurse came in, she talked about the never-knowing being the hardest part about head cases.

"You can never tell when they'll come round," she added, "sometimes it needs a trigger. Like a piece of music perhaps. Maybe his wife would know. Suppose she'll be coming back today."

It was like getting an electric shock.

"I'll ask her when I see her," Robert muttered, realising perhaps for the first time since the explosion that Martha would never be expecting to see him at Billy's bedside. He turned, as if half expecting to see her there coming into the room with a look of utter disbelief on her face.

He didn't need to. As soon as Robert got home, he managed to persuade the others in the house to lend the radio that usually sat in the kitchen on top of a dresser base. It was an old tube radio in a wooden case with dials at the top and adjusting knobs at the side – ironically, German made. But then he knew how many of them were. He didn't wait. Took the radio back to the hospital and prayed for it to do its magic.

By the time he came back home, his head was still so full of the music he might want to be brought round to, that he hardly heard someone calling his name as he went into the kitchen.

"Rob. Some guy came calling for you, just after you left. Told him that you had taken the radio to help out at the hospital. Seemed it was the least we could do. Hope that's OK."

He shook his head. This was what was what he feared. Stewart had found him. Olthorp was not a big place and Stewart had already tracked down Martha. It was only ever a matter of time before he was found. Whatever music playing in his head earlier had now given way to a monstrous dull thumping – an ever-present reminder of the explosive limpet that would be clamped to his back as long as Stewart was around.

Since Robert had started visiting Billy, he had managed to avoid a meeting with Martha in the hospital. A quiet word to the nurse was usually enough to find out when Martha was next expected and she'd kept Robert informed about how pleased Martha had been by the idea of the wireless.

Immediately after transferring a young woman with severe abdominal pains to the hospital, Robert had taken the chance to come up and see Billy.

"You're a bit late today, aren't you?" a nurse asked.

He recognised her from an earlier visit.

"Yes," he replied as if rehearsing his lines, "I thought I'd make sure the radio was still working, because it's seen better days."

"Well, it was when I walked past there not so long ago."

"But it hasn't done anything for Billy then," he asked.

"You can't hurry it."

Robert started shaking his head. He didn't need to have the same negative message given to him like a medicine that he had forgotten to take earlier. There was nothing about what she said that lifted the sense of being like a trapped animal waiting for the trapper to finish it off.

Turning into the ward, Robert prayed for some change. How he wanted to see Billy's tanned face restored to replace the ashen mask that now covered it. Even as he heard the music, which sounded to Robert like a brass band, he felt as though it was leading him into a tunnel which got darker the further he went into it. The closer he came to it, the more the sound of clashing cymbals and the howls of the bugle began to mock him. Without hesitation he went up to the radio and turned the tuning knob until he found some piano music which he didn't recognise but which seemed to him to have a sadness and beauty that he had never heard before. The notes seemed to build up to a crescendo of finger-light suspense and then drift down the keys with notes shadowing each other with magical ease and delight. The more he listened to it, the more the music sounded to him like a string of chords that was familiar but which had been lost. Hearing it now, it took him back to images from the past that he seemed to have buried: training with the FAU at Manor Farm, where he remembered the sense of camaraderie amongst the COs, though few of them came from Quaker backgrounds, learning how to march there and being asked to put up blackout entrances; working as a medical orderly in an ambulance in London before being allowed back to Olthorp as a driver himself. It seemed such a strange route that he had taken and for once Robert allowed himself to be overtaken by the memories.

As he came out of his reverie, he was aware of two things: the music had stopped and Billy's head was turned towards the side of the bed where the radio was placed and where Robert was sitting. Lifting himself from the chair, Robert leant forward and clasped one of Billy's hands with both of his and started whispering,

"Billy, Billy, are you there? It's me Robert."

As Robert watched, he could see tiny flickers of movement on Billy's face and thought of the blood forcing its way along arteries trying to establish connections that had been wiped out by the explosion.

"Nurse," Robert called out, and again "Nurse!"

By the time she appeared at Billy's bed, his eyes had gradually opened.

"Right," she said, putting her hand on Robert's shoulder and asking him with her eyes to make space for her, "That's wonderful, isn't it? Nature won't be rushed will it? Let's see what the doctor has to say about the patient, shall we?"

Robert left the side of the bed to make way for the doctor to make his own examination. But getting to his feet he suddenly felt very weak, as if the blood had drained from his head. Had the nurse not turned round at that point and seen the look on his face, Robert might have been the next casualty. As it was, she pushed Robert back into a chair and told him to put his head between his legs.

It wasn't long before the doctor arrived. Without saying anything, he began to shine a small light into Billy's eyes.

That's when Robert decided he needed to get some fresh air.

Still walking with a slight sway and shaking his head to re-orientate himself, it wasn't until they were just yards apart that he realised he was walking towards Martha. Whether the sight of him there at that time was so surprising that she hadn't taken it in, he couldn't say. But the look of surprise was mirrored on both faces.

"Martha!" he exclaimed, "Billy... I've just seen him. He's coming round."

He could see her looking at him now and for once the lines on her face seemed to switch between happiness, concern and puzzlement the closer he moved towards her.

She came up to Robert and clutched his arm.

"Tell me he's alright. That I've got Billy back again."

Robert was about to smile and tell Martha that the nurse was with Billy when he suddenly felt nausea rising in him. Afraid that he would be sick on the shiny waxed linoleum floor, he rushed away from Martha in the direction of the toilets, waving his hand and hoping he could keep his stomach inside him until he got there.

16

Robert

The comings and goings in Robert's house were so irregular that the lodgers rarely ate together let alone passed the time of day with each other. Every person seemed content to fill their own space and maintain a certain distance. That's why when Robert returned from the hospital that afternoon, his head still full of seeing Billy and talking to him again, someone in the front room had to shout twice until it registered.

"That you, Robert?"

Robert put his head around the door.

"Thought it was," the man said, "it's that light uneven tread that gives you away."

"What is it?" Robert asked.

"Thought you'd want to know that you've got a visitor."

Robert looked at him to see if he was about to break into laughter and tell him it was only a joke. But the expression on his face, which Robert hardly recognised, didn't change.

"Honest! Came about two hours ago."

"Who is it?"

"Some bloke. Said you'd done time together."

Robert slowly shook his head. No, it couldn't be. Not now!

"That's right, is it?" his house mate asked.

Robert had always tried to keep quiet about his past. This time he just nodded.

"Well! Who would have thought it? Where? Halstead?"

"Yeah."

"You had it easy! Anyways, he's in yer room."

As Robert made his way up to the third floor, each step felt as though he had to will himself forward with every ounce of willpower. It was some time since he had seen Stewart, but one part of him had lived another life in that time – a life that he was wanting to savour as long as possible.

He could see the door was closed as his feet dragged to the top of the stairs. Thinking of this uninvited visitor sitting inside his room surrounded by his books, letters and incidental attempts at poetry scattered over the walls, made him feel utterly exposed, his clothes stripped off him.

Taking hold of the rough handle, he pushed the door wide enough to see Stewart lying on the bed. Surprisingly, Stewart had had the courtesy to take off his boots which Robert could see were tossed towards the corner of the room on the covering that was so threadbare you could see the floorboards.

"You've no right to be here," Robert said, walking into the room and opening the half sheet that doubled as a curtain.

"That's no way to greet an old friend. I've come a long way to see you, Robbie. You've not been easy to find."

The sound of that name transposed from the dark confines of prison life made Robert shudder. He felt it like a clinging creeper that was trying to smother him.

"It's no good," Robert started, before Stewart cut him off.

"You see, Robbie, that's where you're wrong. You see it was very good for us wasn't it?"

"That was then."

"Exactly. When there was no freedom and if the screws knew what we were doing they would have taken us apart. Not so?"

"What's your point?"

"Look at us now! We're not inside. No one can touch us. And there's everything in front of us."

Robert saw the words like flares shot up into the sky, illuminating the intent behind the words and the reason for his arrival. But Stewart was lying there quite still, with his hands underneath his head and his elbows folded back as if embracing the comfort around him.

"How did you get my address?"

As soon as Robert asked the question, he knew the answer with a sickening stab of inevitability. When you were inside, you kept most things to yourself, but he realised that he must have mentioned Olthorp without thinking of its possible consequences.

"We were sharing things then, Robbie. I thought it meant something."

"Oh, for Christ sakes, it did."

"Didn't we talk of times after the nick?"

"Yeah, we did. But that was different."

"Why?"

Robert swallowed hard. He couldn't deny that meeting Stewart hadn't been exciting. The constant need for absolute trust and secrecy had given their contact its edge. And a way of flicking two fingers at a system that had put them there to start with. But one touch in the allotment had changed all that.

"You seem to find the words difficult. Maybe I can help."

Robert looked at Stewart's face. There was the beginning of a smile, not with amusement but with sneering contempt.

"There's someone else, isn't there? No, don't look so surprised. I'm beginning to know Olthorp. You're not that hard to follow. And when I got to the hospital, I just asked the nurse if the radio was still useful. She told me that his friend was busy testing it out, pointing towards the ward. But from the door, the only busyness I saw was your gentle caressing of the patient's face. I guess I had seen enough."

"It looks like you have."

"Christ, it didn't take you long to forget about me. One moment it's all Stewart this and Stewart that. The next moment? Gone!"

"Did I ever say I would be waiting for you?"

"That's not the point is it? I risked having the shit beaten out of me inside."

"You weren't the only one."

"I thought there might be a reason for it."

"Don't get all tacky now, Stewart."

"So it didn't mean anything, did it?"

"I'm not saying that, Stewart. I was glad it happened."

"That's something I suppose."

"But that was then and I can't change what's happened in the meantime."

"So?"

"What?"

"Well, are you going to tell me anything about him?" Stewart asked.

Robert shook his head.

"I mean what's he got that I haven't? Or don't we discuss those details anymore?"

"For Christ sake you've got a nerve, haven't you?"

"Robbie, I'm pleased for you. You deserve it."

"Perhaps you'll be pleased to learn that the whole situation is about as complicated as it could be."

"How so? You always were one for keeping things simple, eh Robbie?"

Looking at Stewart now, Robert thought he could pass him on the street without recognising him. His ginger hair had grown and the face full of stubble made him look like a person that Robert had never met before. Today there was something about him – the dark greasy fringe of hair that he flicks away from his forehead, the unkempt look, the clothes stained and dirty – which made Robert feel nauseous.

"Get out of my room and get out now," Robert said.

The tone of Robert's voice must have taken Stewart by surprise. His hands came up in a mock surrender.

"Take it easy. I've just spent the last day or two hitching my way up the country to surprise you."

"Next time, you can wait for the invitation."

"Oh, it's like that is it?"

"Yes," Robert said, standing over Stewart's prone body.

He waited for Stewart to roll himself slowly off the bed, with the least urgency he could muster.

"Bye, Stewart," he said, going over to the door and waiting while Stewart put on his shoes, picked up his bag and coat and lolled towards the doorway.

"You can say sweet bye-byes, Robbie, but don't think that your Stewie is just going to walk away from this. Oh no, seems like I ought to be introducing myself to your family. I mean, I've met your sister haven't I? I wonder what she'd say if she knew how her darling brother was one of those 'sad young men'. Guess she'd be in for a shock, don't you?"

Robert heard Stewart's footsteps recede along the corridor before he slammed the door.

17

Connie

Connie knew she couldn't wait any longer. She had to get Angela settled into her new home before Harry returned. The telegram had said he'd be back the day after tomorrow! If she delayed she could risk everything. She'd been thinking of nothing else for so long that she couldn't make a mistake now.

But that didn't make the prospect any easier. Without Angela, she knew that a part of her would be aching from night til morning. With Angela she might be the laughing stock of people like Mrs Granger but at least she had something that was a part of her, which she loved more than anything that she could have ever imagined.

What she hadn't bargained for was the visitor she received that morning.

She was throwing away some tea leaves into the compost bucket when the front doorbell rang.

As she opened the door, the look on her face must have turned from one of surprise to one of shock.

"Robert, is that you?" she asked, recognising the familiar brown long coat with the cord belt around the middle. "Bringing me good news of Billy, I hope?"

Robert turned around slowly.

"Yes, he should be out today with any luck."

She had to bite her tongue because for once she thought he looked awful. Grey bags under his eyes made him look as though he hadn't slept in a while.

"God, what have you been up to? Come on, you'd better come in."

It wasn't until Robert had come into the house and sat down in the chair offered to him by Connie that his tongue began to loosen.

"Sorry, Connie," he started at last, "but I didn't know where else to go."

"You don't have to say anything. Don't forget, your Martha is like family to me."

"She doesn't know I'm here. I couldn't stay in my room because…"

Robert put his head back and closed his eyes.

Connie knew that visiting her was a sign of Robert's desperation. Here she was trying to keep Angela away from the public gaze, quite out of touch with anything and anyone about her. What help could she possibly be to Robert? But then she wondered whether Robert would have really come here to talk to his sister. Ever since Billy's accident, Martha had seemed more and more cagey when talking about Robert. Knowing the history of antagonism between Robert and Billy, Connie didn't find it surprising that Martha had tried to get between them but somehow Connie felt everything was different now. So why was he here?

"Look Robert. Whatever the matter is, I think you'd better spit it out. Not much good trying to help you if I don't know why you need help, is there?"

Robert put his hands behind his head and started to explain.

"Someone's looking for me, Connie," he said at last, "let's just say it would be better if I stay out of the way at the moment."

There was something in the look that Robert gave her. His eyes were wary, twitching, unable to settle. She'd never seen Robert like this before – taken over by a mixture of fear and confusion. He must have seen the concern spreading over her own face.

"It's alright, Connie," Robert went on, "there's no danger of him finding me here. I covered my tracks."

"Well, that might be the case, but I wouldn't know it from the way you look. Never seen you like this before, Robert."

"I don't know what to feel or think at the moment, Connie. It feels like having a boil that I need to burst but can't because if I do, it'll get infected."

She waited for him to speak but she could see, she'd have to wring it out of him.

"Who is he?" she asked and then as quickly, "and why is he after you?"

He started to shake his head.

"It's a long story, Connie, I'm not sure I know where to begin."

"Well, you can start it where you want. I'm not going anywhere out with Angela today. Not in this bloomin' weather."

Robert told her that he'd been desperate to talk about it to someone since Stewart had appeared in his room, from nowhere by all accounts. After taking off his boots and settling into one of Connie's arm chairs upholstered in a gaudy floral pattern, he told her how it had started on "B' wing at the prison where Stewart and he both spent time as COs.

He told her how days had passed painfully slowly and he described each day mentally crossing off one of the small panes of leaded glass that were at the top of his cell. There were only twenty of them, so he had to treat each piece of glass as five days. That would be enough to get him out. When he came to the end of a row, he had to stop himself from celebrating as though it was a month. There'd be another two panes before the end of the month.

Connie asked Robert if they'd shared a cell. When he said they hadn't he started to elaborate on how they met.

Stewart had apparently 'spotted' him in the dinner queue and been amazed at the way Robert reacted at the 'incident'.

"Bloody starving, I am," a con had said muscling his way forward in the queue that day, with mutters following him all the way to the serving hatch.

As he passed Robert, he elbowed him in the ribs.

"You don't need to hurry Jonny Boy. I can see your mom fed you with the best side going. I'll just squeeze my little self past."

It didn't take much to do it. Robert stuck out his foot as the man passed and down he went, throwing his plate up into the air as he did so. The sound of the metal plate hitting the floor was enough. The whole canteen erupted like schoolboys after a prank. The con knew it was Robert. He came back to the queue scowling, muttering "Funny! Funny! You think that was funny! I'll soon show you what funny is. It's Jonnymeboy scraping the shit from his face in the bog."

Before he could do anything to stop it, the man had hit Robert in the face. He must have been wearing a ring because a gash opened up on his cheek. As soon as it happened a crowd of men gathered around to pull the other guy away from Robert. It was clear that wasn't the most popular con on the wing if their comments were anything to go by. That's when the screws moved in and took Robert away.

"I'd have been so frightened," Connie said, "I'd have hidden somewhere."

"That's the thing with gaol. There's no place to hide. Anyway, I never saw the man again. He lost his ring, had a fight with someone else that night and then got moved."

When they took his food away, Robert continued, he felt as if everyone was looking at him. Robert had never intended to make a spectacle of himself. In fact as he sat down, he couldn't remember deciding to stick out his foot. On any normal day he wouldn't usually have gone in for that sort of retaliation. But it was bad timing.

He thought it had all started after he'd received that letter from his mother. It had turned him upside-down. She'd written so few letters to him that he knew, as soon as he saw the familiar writing, so light and feathery they looked as if they'd blow away.

She was writing to tell him that his father had passed away. She didn't go into details but mentioned his sudden illness. The funeral was to be in a week's time at the church, she wrote, and hoped Robert could be there in spirit.

"It was so typical of her," Robert said to Connie, "to be stoic like that. And to block out that terrible sense of fear and isolation that she must have been feeling. Without father, I didn't know what she'd do with herself."

Robert shook his head as if in lament for a situation out of his control.

"Don't you worry," Connie remarked, "women have a much better way of rebounding than men sometimes. You see."

"It made me feel so angry that I couldn't be with her when it mattered."

Robert carried on with his story.

He told Connie that Stewart had come over to him

while he was eating after the incident and told him that he advised Robert to get the cut cleaned up properly.

"No knowing where that ring's been," the man said.

"'Course," Robert answered.

"I'm Stewart by the way."

"What you in for Stewart?"

"CO."

"Christ, you'd think they'd put us to better use than stick us in this garbage can."

Whether Stewart was thinking about anything else at that stage, Robert didn't know. He told Connie how he seemed to see a lot of Stewart in the days afterwards and then they managed to eat together and spend a fair amount of time in each other's company. COs were given a much more lenient time than some at the prison. Otherwise they could never have got as close to each other as they did.

Connie had listened to Robert without interruption and could now feel her jaw drop and lock in an expression of bewilderment as Robert came to an end. For a moment she didn't know what to say.

"Sorry, Connie, " said Robert, filling the silence, "it's really not fair to burden you with this right now."

Connie looked at Robert and started shaking her head.

"Robert. You! I'd never have known. Couldn't have guessed. Are you going to talk to someone about it? I mean, get help?"

Robert kept quiet. Connie thought she saw a slight shake of his head.

"So, where are you going to go?" she asked.

"Go? I can't go anywhere. I'm not hiding."

"So what are you doing here, then?"

She saw Robert close his eyes for a moment.

"So he's come looking for you, Robert?"

"Yeah, that's what he says."

"What did you expect?"

"But I told him at the time that it was the excitement of doing something to put two fingers up at the system. It didn't mean anything to me then?"

"It don't work like that Robert, does it? If someone presses all the buttons for you," she paused "even if.....then you'll do anything to make sure you do the same for them. That's why he's here."

"That was then, Connie. But now everything is different."

"Why's that? Time and place aren't going to change the way you feel about someone."

"Not sure I believe that anymore."

"Stop talking in riddles, Robert."

Robert laughed. Billy had used the same expression that afternoon they met at the allotment.

"How long have I lived here, Connie?"

"All your life."

"Like you. And like all the others around here. I've known them all my life."

"So?"

"One minute you see someone you've known all your life like a distant mirage. Next day there's something about them that's changed so much it's like seeing them for the first time."

Connie looked at Robert. She saw the short-cropped fair hair and his freckled face and wondered what it would be like to live with the excitement of falling for such a person. He looked back at her and she held his gaze as she examined his clear blue eyes like a curiosity. They were honest. She thought they were asking her to look further so that she could understand and know who it was that had so changed Robert. Only when she saw the edge of a tear crawling down his ruddy face did the images start falling into place. Robert coming to tell her about Billy's accident at the mill and his feeling responsible for it in some way, hearing of the tension between Martha and Billy and of his friend in the nick. It made her realise that he wasn't going to have to give anything else away.

"Oh God, Robert, no. Don't tell me you're…"

She didn't dare find the words. Robert, whom she'd known for all those years and whose life had been weaved with her own through Martha.

"How could you?" she shouted, "You, me, Martha, Billy. We've been together for so long. And now? Can you see what you're doing, Robert? You're trying to tear us apart. And I'm not going to help you do that."

Connie

Connie had waited for as long as she dared.

Putting on her coat, and carrying the torn pieces of sheet that she had been using as a nappy, she picked up Angela, wrapped in the blanket, and opened the front door. For once everything outside the house looked unfamiliar and unexpected. She looked up the street where she'd be walking to see if there was anybody about, watching. There were few shops on the street and even if the butcher's was open, she knew there was little chance that anyone would be there because there was nothing yet to buy.

With her free hand she held onto the knocker and pulled the door to.

There! For weeks now she had been thinking about nothing else. Even Martha had tried to prepare her for it by talking about what she wanted her to do if this or that happened when she was on her own. Connie had been amazed at this change in Martha. Ever since she married Billy, with Connie egging her on and wanting to hear about their plans for children, Martha had expressed no interest in the matter whatsoever. There were days when Martha had nearly bitten her head off for asking.

"There's a time and a place, Connie, isn't there," she'd say, looking at Connie as if trying to fathom where her friend found the time to think about such matters. As soon as Connie found out she was pregnant, she'd told Martha. But even then Martha's concern had been about how she was going to manage. She seemed to want to distance herself from the joys and agonies of what it was to be a mother. As if she wasn't ready for it. That was then.

But now it was very different. Martha was all over Angela whenever they visited and for the first time she had been asking Connie the ins and outs of it all. What did breastfeeding feel like? How did Connie know which breast to use? How often did Angela get the bottle? Was she sore still? Was labour as bad as she thought it would be?

"You'll be a Readers bloody Digest of pregnancy soon, you will," Connie had told her, "time you started putting some of this theory into practice yourself."

Martha hadn't replied and Connie reckoned that if she and Billy were trying to start a family, she wasn't giving anything away. Connie had been aware of the mixed messages that she received from Martha at times about her staying with the two of them but had said nothing. Martha said that Billy didn't mind and that he could usually sleep through anything. But Connie knew he had been fed up with having to move his collection from the box-room to make way for she and Angela. And Martha had been unusually secretive about where the need for extra money had come from.

"You'd tell me if you wanted the space for anything, wouldn't you, Martha?"

"Don't be so touchy!" was all Martha had said.

But Connie knew that it would be easier to get into a routine at Martha's before Harry returned. The last thing she wanted, apart from trying to convince Harry that everything was normal, was to hurry off to Martha's to find a baby that wouldn't settle. As soon as she saw the telegram she knew it would be Harry. He said he should be back in a couple of days. Two days! The recent letter and then the telegram made her feel that there was a juggernaut picking up speed and coming down the road straight towards her.

She couldn't yet imagine Harry coming home, nor visualise what he would look like, or how his body was scarred. She didn't want to think how he might be affected by the experiences he had been through. If only she could find a way of getting him used to the idea of Angela before revealing the extent of her deception.

She was pleased there were so few people about the streets of Olthorp that morning. It meant she could let herself into Martha's house without attracting attention. The baby had started crying when they crossed the street and she'd been trying her best to rock her as she walked to get her off to sleep again. Wrapping her inside her baggy coat seemed to have helped a little. She wondered if Angela was cold. 'Course she was only skin and bones. The last thing Connie wanted was for Angela to catch a chill.

As she let herself into the house, the first thing she saw was Billy gathering up some things from the scullery. Even when the weather was bad Billy seldom hung about the house. He'd be down the allotment or in the shed at the back.

"Billy!" she shrieked.

"Yes, it's me, Connie. You've not just seen a ghost."

"Billy......I just didn't expect to see you here. Thought you were still in–"

"Hospital?" he answered for her.

"That's right. Martha told me you were lucky to be alive, that the– "

"–other young lad wasn't so lucky? No, can't say he was. Took me fork and went running up to the top of the allotment. Next thing I know there's an almighty blast and pieces of the boy start flying all around me."

"Billy, I'm so sorry."

"It's not me you should be sorry for but the lad's granddad. He was waiting at the bottom of the slope when it happened."

Connie closed her eyes and shook her head, with Robert's words clamouring in her head.

"And you?" she managed to ask.

"Lucky not to be closer to them. It was all over so quick."

"How are you feeling now, then?"

"I only just got home and I'm already sick of hanging around. Don't know when I'm going to get back to work."

"You've had a serious injury, Billy. You need to take it easy."

"I don't need anyone else preaching to me, Connie. Anyway, I can see you've got your hands full at the moment," he said nodding towards the pram.

"Martha, she did speak to you about this, didn't she, Billy? That I needed somewhere for the baby."

"Ay, she did that. You've heard from him then?"

"Sent a telegram. Billy, he'll be here the day after tomorrow."

"Didn't take him long then?"

"Age and length of a service would normally get out first. But he's been sick and a POW. That helped him in a funny sort of way."

"Two days then? I've cleared away my things. There's not much room but it'll give you a bit more space."

As Billy came forward, Connie could see that he looked miserable.

"Billy, we won't stay here a minute longer than we need to. I promise. If there was another way round this, we'd take it."

"I know. Let's hope you don't have to."

"And Billy," she started without having any idea what to say, "there's another thing." She paused. "I'm not wanting to interfere and you can tell me it's none of my business."

She could feel Billy's eyes on her now. Staring at her.

"It's just that……Robert came round and we started talking. Oh no, he didn't want to tell me anything. But you know me, I started putting the pieces around him together. And somehow, wherever I put them, Billy, I found you."

Billy pulled back as though someone had pushed him. Connie had clearly said enough and she could now see Billy's face starting to crumble into a look of desperation.

"If Martha wasn't my oldest friend I wouldn't have said anything. But from where I'm standing, Billy, you seem to be playing a very dangerous game."

Connie could hear the tick of the carriage clock on the shelf above the fireplace.

"That's where you're wrong, Connie. It's no game — games have rules. You know where you stand and what you have to do. That would be easy. But where I am. I've never been there before, wherever that is."

She could see Billy shuffling as if trying to find somewhere to hide.

"All I'm saying, Billy," she said and paused, "is that you need to be very, very careful. Everything has a price, doesn't it? Just think about what there is to lose – not just you. All of us."

18

Harry

Maybe this was the last stage, thought Harry.

When the Fortress had picked them up at the airfield, a few miles from the camp, he was in the second plane to go. He didn't know where they'd be landing, and he didn't really care. All the way home he was struggling to get his breath and by the time they were over England, he was dropping in and out of consciousness. When he came round, he had pain that was spread throughout his whole chest. Eventually he was spoken to by one of the doctors.

"You're lucky to be alive. Pneumonia is not a kind bedfellow and until you got here, your body wasn't in much of a position to fight it at all. How do you feel?"

"Bloody awful at the moment."

"You'll improve over time."

"Thanks."

"We won't be able to keep you here for long though. One war may be over but there's another one in the far-east that still has to be won. Casualties from there will be keeping us busy, I'm afraid."

Harry nodded.

"As they say, for you the war's over though. It'll be off to a disembarkation camp from here. Not sure how long the lads are there at the moment. Not more than a couple of days probably. But at least you'll have the chance to get in touch with your family. Then off to a Dispersal Unit and then to a Dispersal Centre. How does that sound?"

Harry couldn't quite believe that he was out of hospital. But here he was at the centre with many other Air Force servicemen, being sorted into various squadrons. All of them looked older than him and from what he overheard they'd had a longer service record.

The first thing they did was to give them each a Release Book which had a number of pages, each perforated and ready to be torn out. Harry noticed that a couple of pages were already missing which he later found out had been taken while he was at the camp and forwarded to the Regimental Paymaster.

"It'll make sure you get the right pay and anything else owing," he was informed by the NCO who was busy calling out names and reminding men to "take your books next door. You'll be a civilian soon enough."

"Can't wait, sir" said Harry, before adding. "Any chance of sending a telegram? Missus probably doesn't even know I'm alive."

"Had a few crossed wires, did we?"

"That's one way of putting it," was all he could bear to answer.

"Next door. They'll tell you where to go for your telegram. It'll cost you, mind."

They asked Harry for his name and number. When he had confirmed both, a clerk stamped his book and tore the relevant page out. Half an hour later, four more pages were stamped and torn out before a final stamped page which another NCO informed him would be needed at the civilian clothing depot.

Armed with a temporary ration card and a stamped page to obtain a ration book and a certificate for free medical treatment, Harry followed the directions he was given to the postal service.

Out of hospital. Nearly there now. Back day after tomorrow. Harry ooxx

His next stop was the quartermaster's stores.

It was never going to be a comfortable journey.

Because VE day had taken the pressure off the railways to be used to convey troops, food, shells, fuel and other necessities, Harry thought it would make the possibility of travelling easier. But the coaches were still crammed with people relishing the chance to travel again.

"Have you got a cigarette?" the woman asked Harry. She was leaning against the window opposite a compartment that was full of officers.

She looked dressed to the nines. Even at this time of day, he could see that she had taken the trouble to put on some makeup – probably gravy, he thought. Who cares? She's obviously meeting someone, somewhere.

"Here," he said, taking out a packet from the pocket of his suit, "keep these."

The woman looked at him and smiled.

"Are you sure?"

"Take it," he said, holding out the packet to her, "I don't smoke anyway. Can't! Doc said they'd kill me. I was given one by someone down at the demob centre. Dunno where he got them from. Nicked 'em probably."

Harry couldn't remember when he last struck up a conversation with a girl on a train. Mind you, he couldn't call her a girl, not if you looked the way she was dressed. This woman had a style about her. He could see her looking at him out of the corner of her eye.

"Where's the suit then?" she asked, pointing at his ill-fitting coat.

"What?" he asked.

"I thought you said something about demob. Didn't they give you a suit?"

He laughed to himself wondering if she'd understand what made him do it.

"Yeah and a raincoat and a trilby and a pair of shoes," he said, patting the suitcase that was next to him "The suit's under my coat. I'm keeping it warm."

"Didn't feel like wearing it, you know, showing it off a bit? I thought all you lot did?"

"No, you're right. Just couldn't be fagged to carry me old coat, that's all. Reckon it's time I showed it off to the world."

Taking the heavy worsted blue overcoat off made Harry feel for one terrible moment, exposed and guilty. He'd been thinking of that fiver in his back pocket since he hurried away from the centre. Putting his hat on as he left made him one of hundreds of identical men. He knew they'd never find him.

Down at the centre, the place had been chaotic. Men everywhere being given their demob box. But there were others – it wasn't difficult to spot them – men with slicked back hair, jackets with KKK pads in who were roaming the table offering £5 for the box. Harry had seen this and reckoned that it was about time he picked up an easy fiver. With him he carried a battered suitcase which had his other few possessions. After he had been given his box he found somewhere to change. Over the suit he put his overcoat that had been given to him and inside the demob box he put the rest of his army gear.

Waiting until he saw the spiv – he could recognise one anywhere – looking harassed and agitated, he went up to the man and asked him how much he would give him for the demob box.

"A fiver!" he heard.

Harry simply put out his hand and said,

"A fiver it is then."

No sooner had the man pulled out a wad of notes from his back pocket and counted five into Harry's hand than Harry put his case down in the middle of the pile of other demob boxes that had been party to the same exchange and walked off trying to wait until he was outside the depot before bursting into laughter.

Much as he coveted the way he did it, he couldn't break the news to this stranger on a train, whom he'd only set eyes on ten minutes ago and who would walk out of his life in another couple of hours. Right now it was a lark to be in her company. If they got off together at the same station, he might even buy her a drink. As she looked out the window he glanced down at the case she had put between her feet.. More like a vanity box than a case for clothes. You'd get gloves inside but not much else, he thought. But that's when he caught sight of a label hanging from the box. Wonder where she's come from? His chest might be buggered but his eyes were still good. Now if you play this one right Harry Morris, he said to himself, you might get a bottle out of this corker. He leant over and made as if he was tying up a lace. It brought the label even closer. Nothing took long.

He moved away to look at some of the other passengers in the carriage. After a little while, he turned around and moved towards her.

"What's yer name then?" he asked, before saying "no, don't tell me. I've a way with names. Every picture tells a face. Yours has definitely got the look of Dorothy Lamour. Or maybe a Betty?"

"Get away with you!"

"I'm serious. If you want, I'll put my money where my mouth is."

"What money have you got?" she asked.

"Say you'll match it and I'll show you."

"I don't believe you've got anything."

"Try me."

"Alright then," she said

From his back pocket he pulled out the tight wad of creased notes and taking them between his thumb and forefinger, began to stroke it before her eyes.

"Crikey, where'd you get that then," she said in a tone which Harry hadn't yet heard from her.

Harry played it down as he was getting used to doing. Don't make them think you're excited by it. Make it a joke. That was always his motto.

"You mean to say you're ready to lose a fiver if you can't get my name right."

"Only if you are if I get it right."

He paused to let it sink in. There was never any point shocking people. They had to be ready to part with their money or you'd get a reaction. More than once he'd needed to be quick on his feet to avoid getting into serious trouble. Harry thought generosity was one thing but that didn't mean he had to lie down for any sucker, so he stuck out his hand.

"Is that a deal?"

By now he could see a flash of uncertainty cross the pretty woman's face. Make up? Perhaps he had overplayed his confidence. Never show them too much too soon, because they need to think they're in with a fair chance. Harry put his head down as if reflecting on the possibility of losing his new-found wealth to the first person he met on a train.

"Deal!" she said, taking his hand and shaking it.

The train was slowing down. He knew the journey

would never be quick. Stopped at every station it could. Still he'd find a way to lose himself when the time came.

"Made your choice then?" she asked.

Harry looked at her. It wouldn't do to be cocky about winning. He thought she might get loud and hysterical.

"No," he said, "I'm going to have to think about this one. Your face has depths that others don't have."

Flattery always helps he thought.

"Is that yer choice then?"

Harry tilted his head from side to side as if viewing her face from as many angles as he needed to.

"Give me time. There's not many who do this as quickly as Harry Morris."

"Well?" she asked, "found it have you."

There was uncertainty in her voice now, as if the possibility of losing her money had glued up her voice box. He could have left it there, but the demob business had given him a thirst.

Harry screwed up his eyes and started to shake his head. Then he put his hands together and rubbed them, like Fagin, and slowly a smile spread across his face.

"It's not been easy this time," he said, "but I'm as close as I'm ever going to be."

"Spit it out then."

"Thelma," Harry said and then again, "Thelma. That's all I'm seeing."

It was the look that did it for him. One minute so in charge of their lives and the next made to feel as though someone had picked them up and stuck them onto a nail which despite their wriggling, they couldn't ever get off. It wasn't the time to laugh.

"I don't believe it."

"That's what they all say, the first time."

"How did you do it, then?"

Harry tapped the side of his head.

"It's all in here luv'. A complete mystery which most will never be able to comprehend."

The woman scowled at him.

"Now don't take offence, but I think that concludes our business, doesn't it?" he said, raising his eyebrows and looking at her expectantly.

The train was coming to a station and from the window Harry could see the lines of passengers waiting to get on. Another beautiful timing, Harry son, he said to himself.

He could see that it grieved her. He watched her manicured hand fluttering above her bag as she opened her wallet and then extracted a note. He couldn't see the size of the purse, but he'd be surprised if that was the only one in it.

Though she had it in her hand, even at this stage she was hoping that something would intercede on her behalf. There was a hesitation.

"Fair dues," he reminded her.

"Here," she said, thrusting the note towards him.

As if on cue, the train stopped and a few passengers carrying their meagre holdalls or muslin bags or duffels moved past them towards the door. Harry waited until they had gone and new travellers had climbed on board. As these scurried down the compartment, desperate to find a seat, Harry merged with them and did his disappearing act.

He never did see the woman again.

What a journey! He began to think that he would never get there. The train seemed to stop everywhere and each time it slowed down passengers would put their faces up to the window, rubbing off the condensation to see if they could recognise the station they were coming to. 'Course the signs had all been taken down at the beginning of the war, hadn't they! Nice of them to think of putting the bleeders back though. But as he cleared the moisture from his own steamed up window, he could see the familiar spire and he knew that he was getting closer to home.

'Home!'

How many times had he thought about this moment. He was glad he'd managed to send a telegram to Connie. Let her know he was on his way. They'd been told that relatives had been informed of their return, but he knew that they could never know for certain when it was going to be. And one point he thought maybe he'd surprise her and just arrive back in Olthorp. But the thought soon passed.

What was he expecting? A red carpet? He didn't know but there was still something inside of him that rumbled when he tried to think of life back home. It was as if he couldn't put the picture back together as it was. Every time he tried to something else changed. One day the shops were gone. The next he couldn't find his way back from the pub because too many landmarks had been flattened by Jerry. Another time, he couldn't find his old mates from the works. Someone would tell him that they were in the graveyard and he'd wake up in a sweat.

It was so late by the time he got off the train that there were few people about. That's alright. Nothing could touch him at the moment. First the demob suit and then fleecing a fiver off Thelma. Mind you he didn't feel bad about it. Loaded, she was, decked out in her finery.

He'd be needing a train to Olthorp, but that wouldn't take long. He should be home in an hour and a half. Midnight at the latest. That was before he found someone to ask about the next train.

"You're too late. Last one left ten minutes ago."

Harry's face fell.

"You're having me on, aren't you?"

"Wish I was, sir. No, you'll have to wait for the 6.25. But don't hold your breath. There's nothing like a war for scrapping the timetables!"

As Harry walked away he heard the man laughing at his own joke. That's all he needed – a nine hour wait at the station! No, he wasn't up for that. He'd carry on and find some way of getting there. Putting his bag over his shoulder, Harry left the building and walked outside.

It might have been the start of summer but the skies were clear and there was a sharp chill in the air. Harry pulled his coat tighter around him and began to walk away from the station when he saw a bus pull in at the side of the road. He hurried over to it and spoke to the driver.

"I'm heading for Olthorp," he said.

"Well you'll no' get a bus there now."

The driver mentioned another town in the right direction where the bus would stop. He told Harry it might not get him to Olthorp but at least it was a mite closer. Moving, thought Harry, was usually better than standing still, so he got onto the bus.

It was good to be out of the wind. To be honest, he didn't feel too bad. Hungry for sure, but he reckoned he'd be in for a big one when he got home. He hadn't had any news recently, but like his doctor used to be fond of saying, *'no news is good news'*. If things had turned turtle at home, he'd have heard.

The bus was a boneshaker and it seemed to groan if there was any sort of incline to climb. Harry let the noise and the vibration settle him deeper into his seat and within seconds he was asleep. You couldn't learn it quick enough when you were in service. If they gave you any time off, you had to use it. For once Harry needed no reminder. The next thing he knew was the driver waking him up and telling him to get off his bleedin' bus.

"Where are we?" Harry asked.

The driver told him.

"You were after Olthorp, weren't you?" he asked Harry.

Harry nodded as he took hold of his bag and unsteadily started walking towards the door at the front.

"Find the Carlton Road first and you won't go far wrong. Shouldn't take you more than an hour."

Harry shook his head as he came out into the cool air. Well, he certainly wasn't going to get there by public transport at this time of night but he was damned if he was going to stop now. There was nothing for it – he'd try his luck with his thumb out.

On his way to the Carlton Road, the place he used to know well enough, but years on, he couldn't remember without asking someone how to get to the road. But on the corner of Marston Street, Harry came upon a pub, The Pig 'n' Whistle. It was standing all on its own. The area around it had been bombed and it stood alone, defying the Luftwaffe to strike it down.

Harry was in no mood to pass up a chance to drink a bottle of stout or two. He wasn't going to get to Olthorp early anyway. Who could stop him? In the back pocket of his trousers the five-pound note was burning a hole in his trousers.

Buggered if he was going to miss out on a chance to get perked. Anyway, he'd won himself two of them today. What was the point of winning if you couldn't celebrate? Provided he went home with one of 'em in his back pocket, who was going to start complaining?

As soon as he went into the pub, Harry could feel drifting eyes on him. There were half a dozen in there and most were twice his age.

Undeterred he went up to the bar, put his small case onto the ground next to the stool he was proposing to sit on, pulled the fiver from his back pocket and banged it theatrically on the counter.

"Next round's mine, folks. It's a lucky day for Harry. Just fill up their glasses for me will you," he said nodding to the barman, "and for your good self too."

"Hear that," the barman announced to the assembled drinkers, "this gentleman wants to buy you a drink. His money's on the counter and it looks clean to me."

"Bloody great," one man shouted, "first you win us the war and now you're buying us a drink. Your next one's on me."

That quickly brought a chorus from the other tipplers who wanted to do the same thing. Harry couldn't stop a smile spreading across his face. You've done it again Harry Morris – found yourself amongst friends when you needed them. And you're not even home yet.

By the time the barman walked Harry to the door, thanked him for his custom and gently levered his unsteady body out onto the street, it was late.

"This is no time to be struggling 'gainst everything," he muttered to himself, "a little bit of shuteye. That should do the trick."

It didn't take Harry long to find someone's front garden to lie down in. Using his bag as a pillow, he put his head down. That night his luck held out with the weather because before he passed out he remembered a sky full of stars.

It was the cold that brought him round. He couldn't have been asleep for more than an hour before the discomfort and the cold nagged him back to consciousness.

Shaking his head as he got to his feet, he put the bag under his arm and walked towards the edge of town.

'Course, there'd be fewer cars about with the rationing of petrol, he knew that, but given his outrageous luck earlier in the day, he felt sure that his guardian angel wasn't going to desert him now. Not when he was so close. So he walked. The longer he put one foot ahead of the other, passing out of the street lights into the darkness of country roads, the more determined he became to finish the journey. There were few cars and he couldn't believe it when the first one sped past him.

"Probably couldn't see my outstretched arm," he said to himself. His mood gradually lowered and after the fifth car had passed him, he shouted. "Where's yer' bloody wartime spirit gone," gesticulating at the fading lights and preparing himself for a longer walk than his body and head had bargained for.

Arriving at a deserted Carlton station at five in the morning, Harry was exhausted and very cold. Nearby he noticed a couple of cars parked and without hesitation had a careful look at each of them. To his amazement, the third one he tried was unlocked. A short time later he was stretched out as best he could on the back seat.

Luck's in again, Harry. Anyway, I'm not doing any real harm, he decided, just having a rest. Surely if the owner returns to find him there, he'll have some sympathy?

Waking up stiff, sore and hungry a couple of hours later was something of a relief to Harry. The last thing he wanted to do was to have to placate the car's irate owner. Without delay he let himself out and went over to the station to buy himself a ticket to Olthorp.

19

Connie

Connie couldn't remember the number of nights she had left Angela. She needed her to be settled there before Harry came back. Without knowing when the charade would stop and feeling such emptiness inside her throughout the evening and night after she left Hestor Street, she had almost decided to come clean and take the baby home and accept the consequences. But now she thought of nothing other than closing up her house as quickly as she could and hurrying along her way until she came to the familiar front door. She'd checked to make sure the back door was locked, and had pulled the thin front curtains back. She thought they smelt musty and she made a mental note to wash them one of these fine days. Wouldn't take a morning to dry them. She pulled her coat off the peg next to the door, put it over her arm, started tying the scarf around her head before heading for the door.

She was trying so hard to get out of the house and up the street, that at first she didn't notice or even recognise him. Connie looked again to make sure. It wasn't the suit which he was wearing – she'd seen enough demob suits in town already not to be taken surprise by that – nor was it the slow saunter which he was making down the street. No, what she couldn't place was the manner in which he was doing it. Each house he passed he was scrutinising, as if trying to find it in his memory. He'd look first at the front door and then cast his eyes to the roof, before making his way down the street.

Then he looked up and saw her.

Unable to say anything and feeling a weight pressing down on her, making her gasping for breath, she felt like running to him and fleeing from him at the same time. In the end her feet wouldn't move and she stayed where she was outside her house, shivering in the morning chill.

"Harry," she said at last, "it's me, Connie. Don't you recognise your wife? I got your telegram," she said, trying to laugh but the nerves made her sound oddly high-pitched.

"That's grand. And I know you had my letters too after hearing from you. But I got worried early on when there was nothing."

"Well it took a while for your letters to get through to me. I heard nothing for months. Not until it was too…." She bit her tongue. She knew it wouldn't be the last time.

He came forward and stopped when he was a few feet away from her. She could see that he was now swaying slightly but trying to stay on his feet.

"Oh Harry, but you're alive! You made it back. I can hardly believe it," she said and as she threw her arms around him, she broke into a shaking fit of tears that had been swelling up every time she thought of the baby.

It was the first thing she noticed. She didn't mean to, but she couldn't help herself. The smell. It was on his clothes – from his new demob suit.

"You've not changed," he said, pulling back a little so that he was able to see her face to face.

Even his saying that made Connie feel guilty. Until a few weeks ago she had been as big as a bloody whale. She still carried some extra pounds that would be shelved as rationing continued.

"What did you think, you fool? That I'd change my hair."

As she said that a smile crossed his face.

"That's my Connie," he said, "just like I said."

"Oh, Harry," she said, "trust you to come just as I'm off to work."

"Take it off then. Christ, haven't I come far enough? They'll understand."

"Bloody right they will! I'll be left with no job at the end of the week, I'll tell you."

"Harry, we'll have to celebrate later. Here," she said, taking him by the arm and leading back towards the house. "Let's get you settled in. You look like you could do with some sleep."

She was shocked by how easily the pretence came to her. How many hours had she spent wondering how she would be able to string a sentence together? Now it was upon her, some part of the threat had been lifted. She had to react out of instinct. It was as if she could do nothing else.

She still didn't know whether to laugh or cry. How many women did she know who'd lost husbands and brothers in the war! And here she was almost resenting the fact that he was still alive. It couldn't be all bad, she thought. I'll have to find a way of making it good for all of us. But she knew she couldn't begin to think about anything else until Harry knew about Angela. The very thought terrified her.

By the time Connie extricated herself from the house, Harry was slumped on the sofa eating the remains of the pie that Connie had been keeping for dinner tonight. Well, she'd just have to find some scraps to make into a soup. Harry would eat anything now.

All the way to Martha's she kept wondering about that smell on Harry. She couldn't place it. But as she had a little matter of a baby to worry about, she thought it could just take second place for the moment.

Martha was still at home when Connie arrived.

"Oh, Martha. Guess what?"

"I know. News travels fast in Olthorp."

"You haven't seen him then?"

"'Course I haven't. But others have."

"Where?"

"It sounds as though your Harry's throwing himself out a bit. Celebrating as he goes."

"Can't blame him can you?"

"S'pose not. Mind you, you'd think he'd be wanting to get back to his missus before he did anything else."

It seemed to Connie that despite the time, Martha had still not forgiven Harry. There had always been something about their friendship which remained edgy. Part of Martha had wanted to support Harry's late decision to get called up. But for her it had been a case of too little too late. That's why she had never really been interested in news of Harry. Of course, when Connie had had no news of Harry for some time and Connie was told that he was 'presumed missing', Martha was the first to offer condolences. Now she thought about it, Martha was one of the first to think nothing of affairs during war time. 'What do you think **he** would do if he were in your place?' she remembered Martha saying. No, maybe now wasn't the best time to start talking about Connie's suspicions about the smell on Harry's breath.

"Anyhow, I'm off to bed. Not feeling too good today."

"It's not Angela, is it? She hasn't been—"

"Christ, Connie, sometimes you act as if we haven't seen a baby before. Billy says she's been fine. Took a bottle from him. Getting quite the daddy, isn't he, bless him?"

Without answering Connie went upstairs to the box room. It wasn't much of a cot, Connie knew that but it was all that she could put her hands on. Picking up the basket as gently as she could, she took it downstairs and put it on the sideboard.

"There, you go and have a bit of shuteye, Martha. I don't want this one waking you up when she gets a hunger inside. She's sure got a pair of lungs."

She wasn't to know how quickly she'd be proved right.

20

Billy

"What's got into you then?" Billy asked, picking up Angela who was still crying. Remembering what Connie had done, he started to rock her in his arms and rubbing her back at the same time. She'd told Billy that it was good for winding a baby, as was putting the baby over your shoulder and patting their back.

When it was clear to him that no amount of rocking was having the desired effect, he wondered if her nappy needed changing. He knew he wasn't an expert at this, but he'd been shown how to do it by Connie. He'd be needing some water and some cotton to clear any mess. But after taking off the khaki nappy, he could see that her bottom looked red.

"No wonder you're screaming. That won't do, will it, Angela? Let's see if we can't find something a bit softer for you and find you some cream. Oh, and here's auntie Martha who's come home just in time for the evening show."

Martha threw her coat over the back of a chair and slumped down into it.

"Bloody hell! That's all I need now! At least I can argue with management. This one's a different game altogether."

"You've been missing the party. This one's been all over the place. Wouldn't settle. Gave her some more milk. Don't say it, yes I did test the temperature. It was perfect. Didn't change anything. That's why I decided to see if she needed a change. Her bottom's raw, poor thing. Them bleeding nappies Connie's been using need throwing out. Horrid khaki stuff."

"She doesn't have much to throw around at the moment, Billy."

"I know that. If she's needing coupons then I'll give her some. Thought that was all you could buy at the moment. Nappies and Utility suits."

"Connie left one earlier. It's one she made up herself and it's in the bathroom. These nappies are bloody everywhere – in this house."

"They have to be washed."

"I know that, Billy."

"You try doing them without any soap. I've seen her doing them. It's no fun."

Martha was silent.

"Looks like I'd better get it then," Billy said.

"Seeing as you work a shorter day than I do at the moment! And put lots of cream on her when you change her."

Though his hands were shaking, Billy picked up Angela with as much care as he could and took her to the bathroom. Over the bath they'd put the cork mat that usually sat on the floor next to the bath. With an old towel over it, it was as good a place as any for changing nappies. Sometimes Billy even thought he was less squeamish than Martha. He knew she'd throw a fit if he let it be known at her work that their hard rank and file socialist shop steward couldn't stomach the mess of really dirty nappies.

By the time Angela was asleep they were both famished.

"What have we got then?" Martha asked.

"As much as we had at nine o'clock this morning, I'd bet."

Almost simultaneously they chimed,

"Cabbage and peas," and then found they couldn't stop the laughter.

"We need that," Martha said, holding out her hand and waiting for Billy to take it, "laughing makes the world go round sometimes."

"Right, as usual."

"Don't you make it sound like a disease. I'm only acting for the best. Like you are with Angela, eh? Who would have thought it?"

"She's only a babe. Anyone can do it."

"Don't you believe it! Oh Billy," Martha said holding out her hand, "you'd make such a lovely father. I think it's time to try and make that happen. Don't you?"

Billy looked down at his feet for a moment and then said,

"I don't want to go waking that baby though."

"You'll just have to be strong and silent then, won't you," Martha said, "like you usually are," grabbing Billy's hand and pulling him to his feet.

They were climbing the stairs when they heard it for the first time – a short strained rasping cough. They stopped and waited. Then it came again, this time for longer.

"What are we going to do?" asked Billy when they got to the bedroom.

"She'll probably settle. Connie's not mentioned anything's the matter with her. Come on, Billy, let's go to bed while we're in the mood, eh?"

As if on cue, Angela then gave out another loud, dry sounding cough. This time it continued as if she had trouble breathing.

"You wait here, Martha. I'll just see if I can do anything."

Billy put on some trousers and went next door to the box room where Angela was in her cot.

"Now what's the matter with you now, eh?" he said picking her up and wrapping a blanket around her as he held her to his chest. He began to rub his hand down her back, much as Connie had suggested and rock her at the same time. When she started her wheezing cough again, Billy thought it worth a try.

"I'm going to get Angela some more milk," he said loud enough for Martha to hear. "I'll put her back for the moment – so don't be surprised if she bawls for a bit. I'll be as quick as I can."

When he came back upstairs carrying the bottle which he'd tried to warm up in his hands, Martha was in the box room, sitting in the old tatty chair, holding Angela.

"What a noise," she said, "it sounds as though she's gasping for air! Do you think she's OK? Billy, she sounds terrible. Feel her forehead. Billy, I think she's got the fever."

"You're right. Here, I'll go and get something you can cool her down with."

"Is that it?"

"Well there's not much else we can do about it. Let's try her with a bit of milk and see if that does the trick."

Settling herself into the chair, and holding Angela in the crook of her arm, Martha placed the teat into Angela's tiny mouth.

For a few moments Angela sucked on it and the short period of quiet made Martha look up at Billy and smile. As quickly, Angela's head rocked sideways for air and the next moment, as she breathed in, the noise of her wail made her sound as though she was suffocating.

"Billy! What's the matter with her? What are we going to do? She sounds as though she can't breathe."

"Robert!"

"What about him?"

"He should know something. He's done some medical training, hasn't he?"

"Babies are different, Billy!"

"Look if he's been trained he'll have learnt a thing or two about most things. Stands to reason."

As Angela started her brassy cough again, Martha turned to Billy,

"Don't suppose we have much choice, do we?"

"I'll go for him," Billy said.

"Hurry, please Billy."

The air outside was fresh and Billy did up the buttons on his coat as he began to run. He had no idea if Robert was going to be able to help but he knew that they would never be able to forgive themselves if something happened to Angela. There was little or no traffic about. But all the way there, he couldn't lose Connie's warnings that stayed as a constant echo inside him.

By the time he reached the house and rang the bell he was shaking and gasping for breath. There were no lights on anywhere in the house, but Robert had told Billy that some in the house kept odd hours. He couldn't hear any noise inside either, so he rang again.

By the time the door was opened, Billy had almost given up hope of raising someone.

"What the hell do you want at this time of night? Don't you sleep?" the man asked Billy.

"Robert. I'm looking for Robert. It's an emergency. A baby needs help. Quick."

"Oh right," the man said, opening the door to Billy, "guess you'd better go and stir him. If he's in."

Billy started to go up the stairs.

"You know where you're going, then?"

"Yes," Billy called back.

He didn't stop until he was on the third floor, standing outside Robert's room. Without hesitating he knocked on the door, saying,

"Robert, it's me," he paused, "Billy."

How long he waited, he couldn't tell. All he could imagine was the look Robert had left him with when they last spoke. There was something desperate about it, as if Robert couldn't ever imagine them not hiding their feelings for each other. It had made him feel worried that Robert was having second thoughts.

The door opened and Robert stood there in his nightshirt.

"When I heard your voice, I thought I was dreaming," he said, with a sleepy smile.

"No, this is no dream, Robert."

As Billy came into the room, Robert threw his arms around him.

"No," Billy said, pulling them away from Robert, "I've come for your help. It's Angela."

Martha

"What did he say it was called?" Martha asked.

"Croup. He said lots of kids under five years have it "

"Doesn't make it any easier for us, does it?" Martha said.

"He said it was normal for babies to make the most terrible sound, like they're desperate for air and can't suck any in. What she needs is moisture, he said."

"Moisture?"

"That's what he said. Try taking her to the bathroom, get a pan of boiling water and sit with her for a few minutes.

Then taking her outside for a short time, maybe ten minutes is supposed to help."

"Boiling water!"

"It's worth a try, Martha. We're not going to get any sleep otherwise."

By the time Billy came back carrying a bowl of boiling water, Martha was feeling desperate about the cries that Angela was making. What was she going to tell Connie tomorrow?

"Put it on that table in the corner, Billy. We want it to be as close to Angela as possible. That's right, isn't it, Angela," she said putting her back down in her cot. "Come on," Billy said, "there's nothing we can do for her at the moment. Let's see if this steam helps."

For the next few minutes, they went next door to their bedroom and tried to talk above the baby's croaking cries from reaching them. Martha was just about to get up again and go upstairs when Billy said,

"Wait! Robert said you've got to give it time."

Martha closed her eyes and started praying that the noise would go away.

"Listen!" Billy said, "I think it's slowing."

Wishing with every part of her for it to be true, Martha crept back into the bed and began to pull the covers over her head. Slowly the gasping calmed down, became slower, less frantic and then went over into the usual pattern of breathing that Martha had heard when she put her head into the room to check on Angela. For some time she couldn't move and when she eventually stretched out her hand to reach Billy, it was met by the sound of his own gentle snoring.

Martha was aware of Billy getting up once again during the night to boil a pan of water which he left in the tiny room with Angela. Usually he would be the first to get up and get Angela's bottle of milk ready, but the next morning it was Billy who woke with a start wondering what had happened.

By the time he got downstairs, Martha was already sitting with Angela in her lap, much as she had tried to do without success during the night. This time however Angela was feeding with a thirst that brought a smile to Martha's face.

Billy grinned at Martha, went up to her and kissed the top of her head.

"What a night," she said.

"She went down at the end, didn't she?"

"Sure she did, but not without ruining our sex life."

"Oh, there's other times."

"Sometimes, I wonder."

"Don't be like that Marth."

"Well, it's not bloody easy for anyone at the moment, is it? How did this one manage to sleep through?" she asked, nodding her head at Angela.

"I gave her another bowl of steaming water."

"I know. Billy, you really can be a mouse sometimes."

"What woke you then? You're not the one to get up early on days off."

"I was so pleased her croaking stopped that when she woke and started her usual gentle whimpers, I almost fell in love with her."

Billy whistled.

"Well, that's a change of heart. The scowl's vanished, I see."

Martha tilted her head towards him and whispered,

"When she's quiet, she's adorable."

While Billy was in the bathroom, Martha finished feeding Angela and put her back in the cot.

The doorbell went and Martha went to the door, expecting to see Connie in her usual frantic state.

There she was, dressed in her 'work' clothes, but this time she was not alone. Standing just behind her was Stewart.

When Martha saw who it was, she just stood there, wondering how they could possibly know each other. He must have noticed the look on her face.

"Sorry," he said, moving a little to one side so that Connie could see him and in a voice that tried to ooze charm, "I don't think we've met. I'm Stewart."

"Who?" asked Connie, staring at the man at her side, trying to take in as much as she could of this stranger to the house.

"Stewart," he answered before turning back to Martha. "I thought I'd come and see you."

"Come in, Connie. Sorry about this," she said moving aside to allow Connie to step up into the hallway.

"Why are you here?" Martha asked him when Connie was inside.

"It's your brother really."

"What about him?"

"I'm worried about him. I think he's making a terrible mistake."

"Oh yes? What kind of mistake?"

"Well, you see we were friends. From the past. We've shared times together and he talked about Olthorp as a way of staying in touch, close, if you know what I mean."

"No, I bloody well don't know what you mean."

"Who is it, Marth?" Billy called as he came into the hallway with a towel draped around his middle.

Martha turned her head towards Billy.

"Someone who says he knows Robert. Wants to talk

about him. Says something about Robert having made a terrible mistake. Dunno what the hell he's talking about."

As Martha stood there she was aware that Billy had come up behind her.

"Look," Billy said, "stop making accusations, d'you hear, and clear off."

"Hold yer horses, will you? Like I said, I'm only trying to help."

"Well you'd help us all by getting the hell out of here. Do you understand me or do you want me to show you what it means," Billy said, taking a step forward.

As Martha put out a restraining hand, Stewart pulled back.

"That's better," said Billy, "and you can keep moving."

Billy pushed the door to and stood there resting his head against the door.

"What got into you then?" Martha asked.

"Bloody drifters. They make me sick. I've no time for them."

"I can see that, Billy. Never seen you get wound up so quickly before."

Billy grunted.

"I'll ask Robert if he knows about this man, Stewart, the next time I see him. What could he have been talking about?" Martha asked, walking back into the parlour.

"Forget it," she heard Billy shout back.

"Sorry about that, Connie," Martha said.

Connie shrugged her shoulders and said as calmly as she could,

"Sounded a bit confused to me."

"Well, I think we're all a bit mangled this morning," Martha said looking at Connie.

"Don't say it! She didn't keep you up, did she?"

Martha tried to explain what had happened, as calmly as she could. Twelve hours later it all seemed an age away.

"Oh Martha," Connie continued, "I just knew something like this might happen. It's so unfair on the two of you."

"That's what friends are for!"

"I feel so awful. Not only do I leave you to look after my baby but expect you to nurse her when she's sick. I shan't do it, Martha."

While Connie went up to see how Angela was, Martha waited for Billy to return and then asked him again whether he had any idea what the man could have been referring to.

"What did he say he was called?"

"Stewart," Martha answered. "He was here before, you know?"

"You never told me," said Billy.

"Didn't I? Probably thought it was not worth the effort. I mean what Robert does with his time is his business, isn't it?"

"Not when it comes into our lives, it isn't?"

"Billy, I don't know why you're getting yourself so het up about it. Since when did my brother's affairs hold any interest for you?"

She was still puzzling over it when Connie came back downstairs.

"What do you think?"

Connie seemed to be so deep in thought that it took a few seconds for her to realise that Martha was talking to her.

"Sorry Martha, I'm so worried about Angela at the moment. I don't know what to think about this man. I'm sure you'll do the right thing."

Martha didn't know if Connie was right but she did know that she couldn't live with the uncertainty any longer.

21

Connie

It hadn't been long since Harry had returned. But every day made Connie feel that the masquerade was adding agony upon agony. She felt a prisoner of her own making and wondered how and when it could possibly be broken. She knew that Harry would be suspicious if she didn't look as though she had been paid. She'd fed Angela and had just put her down. For her, it was one of the worst moments of the day. Each time it happened, she felt that it was the last time she could leave Angela behind as she went home on her own. That day was no different.

"Billy?"

She knew that he was in the bedroom and she didn't want to disturb him. Every day down at the works was hard and ever since the incident she knew that Billy had been supervised more than usual. Billy hated it and talked to her once of feeling out of control.

He opened the door. A towel was draped around his shoulders.

"Thought you had gone already," he said.

"Billy, I don't know how to ask for this. You're doing so much for me already. You and Martha."

"If you don't ask yer never going to get, are you? So best get it over with."

"He thinks I'm working, doesn't he?"

"I hope so."

"Well, I've got nothing to show for it, have I? I know he's been talking about going to the pub every night this week. Oh Billy, I've made excuses so far. But they're wearing thin."

"What do you want?"

"Five bob would do."

Billy raised his eyebrows.

"Thinking of a long night, are you?" he asked.

"I can get it back to you next week."

"You should have said."

"God, how much more do I have to ask you to do for me?"

"And next week?"

"Billy," she said, "I can't go on like this. I call this the dagger moment. Because that's how I feel every time I leave her. Like someone is sticking daggers into me."

"You've got to tell him. Before he finds out, Connie."

"I know Billy."

"Here," he said, taking a note from his back pocket and putting it into Connie's hand, "that's a present."

"Like I said, I'll pay you back next week."

"I don't want it back Connie."

"Don't you need it?"

"I don't know what I need right now."

Connie looked at Billy and tried to find something in his eyes to tell her where he was at the moment. Then she reached up, kissed him on the cheek and went off down the stairs wondering what she could ever do for him.

The light was fading fast as Connie and Harry left the house to go to the pub. By the time Connie got back with Billy's note tucked away in her purse, Harry told her he'd had a wash and was up and ready to go.

"What time were you up then, Mister Brighteyes?"

"When the body told me it was time to get up, if you must know," he said.

"Oh, I am sorry."

She knew that this was one of the hardest parts of her day and without being able to tell Harry why, it became like a permanent sore which little would relieve.

"Midday, was it?"

"Might have been. What's the worry? It's pub time now. That's the main thing, isn't it?"

"You'll have to give me a few minutes then. Can't go out looking like this, can I?"

By the time she came back, Harry was sitting down with his legs stretched out, the paper discarded on the floor beside him, and his arms behind his head.

"Wakey, wakey, I'm ready," Connie said giving Harry's feet a nudge as she stood in front of him.

She knew that Harry always liked it when she dressed up. Not that the choice was much to write home about. Like others, she had to make do with beetroot juice on her lips and thin lines of polish down her legs, 'cheapest stockings you'll get around here' the shoemaker had quipped.

"Well, what do you think then?" she asked, doing a small pirouette in front of him. She knew she was still carrying some extra on her after the birth, but she had done her best to hide it by borrowing one of Martha's dresses. It was dark blue, short sleeved and she wore it with a brooch at the neck. She prayed that Harry couldn't notice the difference.

"I think you'd make any GI's heart melt," he said as he got to his feet.

For a second Connie stopped. Her mind seemed to be slowly emptying itself of all the plans and good intentions until it felt as though it had been drained. To hear him say those words as if he was trying to challenge her made her shrink away from him. He must have noticed.

"Now come here," he said, "I was beginning to think I hadn't waited long enough for you."

As Harry put his arms around her, he must have felt her shivers of anticipation.

"There, now. Like I always said, I think we were always going to be together. We deserve each other."

On the way to the pub Connie was still thinking about what Harry had said when she saw a figure approaching them. At first she paid it no attention. But as the person came closer Connie's heart started pounding. It couldn't be! Not now, she thought. But the closer she came, the more Connie was convinced that it was her, that viper, Mrs Granger.

Connie realised that she couldn't risk Harry hearing her comments. She started to pull him across the road to avoid meeting Granger face to face, when he stopped her.

"What yer doing?"

"I wanted to show you something," she said.

"Can't it wait? We're only a couple of minutes from the pub."

Pulling her scarf forward, Connie tried to melt away from the gaze of Mrs Granger. As she walked along the pavement towards them, Mrs Granger had already seen enough.

"So how did he like yer surprise, then?" she called, stopping to see the two of them hurry their way past her on the opposite side of the street.

Connie didn't know whether Harry had heard Mrs Granger or what he would make of it, but as soon as he asked,

"What was all that about then?" she tugged on his coat and told him that she would tell him in the pub.

All the way she was racking her brains, trying to make up a story that would cover the comment Granger had made. She knew Harry wouldn't let it go. Why couldn't Granger keep her bloody mouth shut? Even while Harry was at the bar getting the drinks, she sat there with her face going whiter and feeling like she had an orange stuffed down her gullet every time she swallowed.

But as he turned to bring the drinks back, the door of the pub opened and a group came in wearing paper hats made out of newspaper.

"Jerry's not getting us tonight, not with these on," one of them said with a roar of laughter from some of the others with him.

They had said enough. Like a warm blast of heat from the fire on one of those long nights when Connie felt as though nothing would ever be able to warm her up again, it came into her head and started to soothe her almost instantly.

Sitting on her hands to stop Harry seeing how shaky they were, she waited until he had taken off his coat, folded it on the seat and was sitting down and looking at her.

"Well?" he asked again as they settled into a corner table at the Lamb, "what's the surprise then? You've got me all excited now."

"Oh Harry, I would've told you earlier but I wanted to wait until I was sure everyone could come. Don't know who I've told about it. Uncle Tom Cobley and the rest – I suppose that's why that Granger woman knew. Mind you. What doesn't that gossip know?"

"Blimey, are you going to tell me, or aren't you?"

Connie leant forward and whispered in his ear,

"I'm gonna have a celebration for you."

"For me?" he asked, pulling away from her.

"Yes, Harry, for you! A homecoming celebration."

"Why, for a while I was beginning to think I wasn't worth it."

"Well, you've got time to think about it now."

"Here's to that then," Harry said and he raised his pint glass, poured the alc down his throat, before banging the glass on the table. "It seems like I've been waiting most of my life for that one and I'm buggered if I'm waiting as long for the next one."

Connie didn't know what to say. Harry had always liked his beer, but he'd never been a hard drinker. In fact in his early days at the mill, Billy had told Martha that they had played one or two tricks on Harry to see what he could take. To start with Harry used to make excuses, but that only geared them up further.

Harry got to his feet and walked over to the bar. He looked over his shoulder.

"What d'you want, Connie?"

"I'm fine at the moment, Harry," she said.

What she meant was that she had only taken a few sips from this drink and for the past five years they had found a way to lengthen the evening by drinking ever so slowly. Yes, it might be alright to be glad that some part of that awful period was coming to an end, but then shouldn't you remember just how bad it had been for so long. Wasn't it a bit like celebrating all those young 'uns who lost their lives. Could have been Harry himself. After all, for some time she thought it was Harry.

The very memory of the change that she had been forced to get accustomed to made her shiver and put her arms around her body.

"Not cold are you?" Harry asked, returning to his seat. "D'you want to know something, I'd forgotten what real beer tasted like. There's nothing like it."

"I'm fine, really I am."

"Now, tell me about this party," he said taking his glass and holding it in his hand, with his arm on the table.

"Well," she started, "it was just an idea about saying welcome home to you."

"Sounds good!"

She still couldn't stop thinking about it and was frightened by all the possible implications of her desperate idea.

"Not too many people, eh?"

"Why not," he asked, "how many am I worth?"

"Now don't be like that. You know it's not meant that way."

"So how is it meant?"

"For family and a few friends."

"Just how I like it."

"Sure you do?"

"Wouldn't say so if I didn't now would I? Something I learnt in the army. Maybe it was the only thing that I learnt."

"What?"

"All you need is friends."

"That's right, Harry."

"No. What I mean is one friend."

"Doesn't sound much to me."

"It's all about quality, isn't it? I mean this mate of mine. Taught me how to survive."

"I thought you were all taught that. Part of yer training, wasn't it?"

"This was different. Surviving and winning."

"What do you mean?"

She could see that look in Harry's eye. He was staring at her now as if trying to get her full attention. Then with a sudden movement of his arm, he took something out of his pocket. It was a blue pocket handkerchief which he opened and fluttered in front of her.

"What's this all about then?" she asked.

"You're just full of surprises, Connie, aren't you?"

"What do you mean?"

"Why don't you look under your hand and see what you're hiding there."

As he said it, she moved her hand that was lying on the table enough to feel something metallic against her skin.

"Lift it up then."

Before she picked her hand off the table, she felt a deep throb somewhere inside. Lifting it up some part of her felt frightened, unable to sense what it all meant about Harry, about the two of them.

Connie gasped as she saw the small shiny shilling on the wooden surface. Taking her hand away, all she could do was just look at it.

"What do you think?"

The trouble was Connie didn't know what to think. So caught up in her own deception, she couldn't imagine trying to move things from the safety of reality.

"You tricked me!"

"'Course I bloody tricked you. Bet you don't know how I did it!"

Connie shook her head.

"And if it wasn't for some lad from Donegal, neither would I! Taught me everything I know, he did. He was a real one, he was. Quick hands, that's what he used to say, takes time and time again. He was a pro."

"What happened to him?"

"Probably making money sitting down still. He was good at that. Not seen him since I left the camp."

Just then the door of the pub swung open and a man dressed in overalls, over which he wore a black jacket buttoned at the waist, walked in.

The barman greeted him warmly and told the man that he'd get his pint in his own jug just as soon as he could change the barrel.

"That'll do me nicely," the man said.

Though inside, he sat at the table with his hat still perched on his head. He looked around him and saw Connie and Harry sitting at a table nearby. Cocking his head first one way and the next, he kept on looking at Harry as if trying to convince himself of something.

Harry went up to the bar and asked the barman to get another one for himself too. As he turned back to Connie, he could see that the last arrival at the pub couldn't take his eyes away from him.

"What you see," Harry asked, "a ghost?"

"Now don't mind, Raymond," said the barman as he came up from the stairs leading down to the cellar, "he doesn't mean no harm. He's just…" and the barman started making circular motions with his hand at his temple.

"Sure he doesn't," said Harry, "but he sure as hell can stare at you."

"Like I said, there's nothing behind it."

"It's pay day today," Raymond said.

"Is it now?" the barman queried.

"'Tis that. Found it. I'll buy y'all a drink."

"That's OK, Raymond," the publican said, "think we're alright for the moment. You hang on to your money. Never know when you might need it."

"Here," said Harry, picking up his new pint and returning to the table, "come over here, Raymond and see some magic."

Connie didn't recognise Raymond. But all the time he was in the pub he never did take his hat off. Holding onto the glass he was carrying, he came and sat down opposite them.

"Pleased to meet you," Harry said, holding out his hand.

Raymond took his hand for the briefest of moments, nodded, looked at Harry and asked,

"Do you want a drink?"

"Why that's just the ticket, Raymond," Harry replied.

As Harry got to his feet, she pulled at his arm,

"What's the matter with you, Harry? You've got a drink in front of you!"

"But there's no knowing where the next one will come from. Bird in the hand and all that. Speaking of which, why doesn't he get you another? What is it? Gin and lime?"

Without waiting for Connie to answer, he put up his hand and said loud enough for anyone in the saloon bar to hear,

"Make that a gin and lime as well will you, Raymond. Connie's got a thirst too."

Raymond turned towards them and smiled.

"Tch," she said, "I'm quite happy with the drink in front of me at the moment, thank you. I don't know why you said that, Harry," and she turned her face away from him to look at the grease stained calendar that was hung onto the wall of the bar.

"It'll be finished soon enough, if I know my Connie."

By the time Raymond returned with the drinks for all three of them, she caught sight of the landlord, whom she didn't recognise, peering over the counter in their direction.

"Now Raymond, tell me something. Do you believe in magic?" Harry asked.

"Magic? Can't say I know much about it."

"Neither did my Connie here when she came into the Flag this evening. But that's changed, hasn't it, Connie," and he turned to her as if expecting her to corroborate his new-found powers. She didn't respond but took another sip from her glass.

"Maybe she's not giving anything away. Doesn't want to spoil it for you, Raymond."

She could see Harry smiling at Raymond as if he was a very small child about to receive a treat.

"Now," Harry said, holding out his hands which were clenched tight, "I've got a coin in each of my two hands here." And he turned them over to show that he was telling the truth. "And you've seen them now, haven't you Raymond?"

Raymond nodded.

"Good," Harry continued "because one of these coins is so slippery that I have to hold onto it as tight as I can. Go on Raymond, feel that fist. Tight, isn't it? Not much could get out of that one, could they?"

Raymond nodded again.

The more Harry talked, the more Connie found herself wondering if she had ever heard Harry like this before. For once he had something of a captive audience and there was something almost ruthless about the way he was hanging onto it. After the first coin disappeared – and she herself couldn't tell how Harry had done it – Raymond clapped and cheered and patted Harry on the back.

"Magic," Harry shouted back over his shoulder to the landlord.

That's when Harry pulled out his pack of cards from his coat pocket with a flourish.

"Harry," she said, with a tone to her voice that she hoped he would hear, "if you're going to spend the evening playing cards, I'll leave you to it."

"What's the matter? Didn't Raymond buy you a drink? It's Raymond's pay day today, remember."

Connie looked at the cards which Harry was fanning across the dark table top and the frozen look on Raymond's face as he nodded at Harry. Picking up her glass, she poured the contents down her throat as quickly as she could before taking her bag and getting to her feet. But even as she left the pub, she realised that there were some parts of her plan which were now getting quite out of her control.

22

Connie

"Christ, you look as though you've been through the mangle today, Connie."

"Working days. They're all hard." she said.

Connie had just sat down in a chair in the parlour after taking off her coat and putting it on one of the pegs in the hallway. She knew that Harry was right, but for quite the wrong reasons.

It was like she'd been on a rollercoaster ever since the meeting with Stewart on the doorstep of Martha's house. It had given her such a shock to see him in front of her that she knew she must have looked very tongue-tied when Martha started asking her what they ought to do. It was clear to her that Robert had not yet told Billy about their conversation. As far as Billy was concerned, Stewart was still an outsider. But she knew that it wouldn't take long.

Oh Connie, she thought, caught between two dear people and she was liable to risk the love and affection of one if not both. She had seen it in Robert's face and heard it in his voice when he had spoken of someone *'you'd known all your life …and suddenly seen for the first time'*. There was Martha for whom the change was likely to become an open sore all too soon and then it had been Billy's turn when he found out that Stewart was looking for Robert. How did we ever get here, she wondered?

She was just imagining what Robert's reaction might have been to find Billy on his doorstep at that time of night, when she became aware of Harry's voice.

"Wakey-wakey! I said I know but you'll be paid soon, won't you? I hope they're paying you double rate on Sunday. That'd brighten you up."

Connie's heart sank. She had little savings and the little that was left she was determined to keep back in case of emergencies. But she also knew that Harry would be aware of what she was likely to be paid and so she couldn't keep up the pretence of working without having some money.

"Why don't we go to the pub tonight?" he asked.

"Again? We only went last night! Anyone would think–"

"What? Spit it out then? Don't you think we deserve this break after what we've been through."

"Course I do, Harry. It's only –"

"Only what?"

"Times have been so lean for so long I'm just not used to it."

"That's why we should be celebrating. Harry's your little earner," he said putting his hand into his back pocket and pulling out a wad of notes.

He spread them like cards on the table and she could see a mixture of 10/- and £1 notes.

"Crikey, Harry, wherever did that come from?"

"Like I said, a good evening down the pub and you can leave feeling quite flush."

"You didn't?"

"What? Take him to the cleaners? He was asking for it. Had so much he didn't know what to do with it. You heard him!"

"But that was Raymond! Everyone round here knows the accident Raymond had when his wife died and how he's not been the same since."

"He'll be alright. Anyway, I didn't clean him out. That's what I learnt. Always leave 'em with something so they want to come back for more."

Connie shook her head and went through to the kitchen.

"I dunno what we'll eat tonight," she shouted back at Harry.

"You're a magician in the kitchen, Connie. Always were."

Connie felt exhausted. But the more tired she felt, the more likely she was to say something which she was likely to regret. Connie had always been the cook in the house. It was one of the few things she still felt grateful for when she thought about her mother. From the hours spent standing by her side in the kitchen, putting dishes together for her father, she had learnt tricks to make meals go further. *"If you knew what to ask for at the butchers, you can make a meal for one day stretch into two or more."* Even now she could hear her mother's words.

If Connie had been able to think about one thing alone, she could have managed. But from the moment she left Angela at Martha's, she couldn't stop worrying how she was. She was praying that Martha and Billy would be able to manage tonight if Angela had another attack of croup. Though Billy was only back part-time still – which he hated – Martha was working full-time and Connie knew that it wasn't fair to expect them to carry on indefinitely. She knew how committed Martha was to staying at work. She just didn't know how much longer she was going to be able to live this double-life, with only half of it shared with Angela.

There was only one other person in the pub when they arrived.

"And what can I get you?" the publican asked.

Harry looked at Connie.

"Well?"

"It's a treat, isn't it?"

"Everyday's a treat, these days."

"I shouldn't. But I will. Gin and orange, please Harry."

"And what about you, Harry? Same again?" the landlord asked.

Connie waited until they were sitting down before she turned to Harry.

"What did he mean? Same again? You've not been here today already have you, Harry?"

Harry didn't respond.

"So, you've been down here on your own, have you?"

"Sorry, I didn't know there was some law against it."

"Well, first you never told me. Second, I thought you might be trying to save any money you 'earned' to help us in the future. Maybe that was too much to ask for?"

Harry's shoulders hunched and the fists of both hands started clenching and then letting go, clenching and letting go.

"Don't you start telling me what to do with my life! I've spent much of the last year being starved at some bloody POW camp. It wasn't a bloody holiday, you know?"

"You didn't have to go! You always said your chest would stop you being called up. Then one fine day you decide that it wouldn't and the next thing I know my fiancée is receiving his call-up papers. I don't understand."

"No, I don't expect you to."

"Why don't you try me?"

"I will after I get in another one."

Harry got off the chair and went over to the bar.

Before he had sat down, Connie had pulled herself up straight and asked him,

"Why do you have to drink so fast?"

"Because all these life and death discussions make me very tired. Beer's the reviver."

"Don't be silly!"

She waited for him to pull the mug away from his lips and put it onto the beermat on the table.

"Are you going to answer me then?" she asked.

Harry's eyebrows met in a quizzical arch.

"Opting in. Why did you?" she asked.

"It's a long story. And even when I've told you it probably wouldn't make any sense."

"Why don't you let me decide?"

Harry took a deep breath, put both his hands around his mug and started.

He told Connie about some lad they had been at school with. He reckoned that Billy could remember him as being about five foot six. But he was skinny as a bean. They all knew that. Harry could only remember the merciless teasing the lad got at school for being such a wimp. The lad was forever getting picked on by the older, bigger boys. Thumping him about the place became a regular past time for many of them.

"Don't get me wrong, mind," Harry said, "we wasn't proud of it."

Harry explained that, like the others, he'd lost contact with that lad after he got called up. Harry thought someone had told him he'd been in North Africa. It wasn't until he heard the news that the lad had been blown to kingdom come after stepping on a mine that he began to ask himself questions. Here was this tiny boy who'd had school made into a nightmare, going out to fight for his country without any hesitation. Where did he get his willpower from? How did he manage carrying a sixty-pound sack on his shoulders in the heat of the African sky? Shamed! That's how he felt. Pure and simple. Shamed!

"You weren't running away from me, then?"

"You don't mean that?"

"See it from where I'm sitting. You marry a man whom you've known all your life who's doing a useful job away from the front line."

"A safe and clean job, you mean! All I wanted to do was to get me hands dirty!"

"And a month after you marry him, he decides to try and swing his medical so he gets his call-up papers."

"So?"

"Like you couldn't get away fast enough. That's how it seemed."

"You're right. Soon as I'd made the decision, I couldn't wait."

"Did you decide after the wedding, then?"

"'Course I bloody did. What do you take me for?"

"I don't know, Harry. Sometimes I just don't know."

"Drink up then and I'll get us another."

"I'm fine."

"So who's coming to the party, then," he asked when he came back to the table carrying the drinks.

"I thought I said I didn't want one."

"I haven't got you one. That's me chaser."

"Well, I suppose the one won't do you much harm."

"Christ, until you've been called up, you haven't seen drinking. Some of them boys could put it back like water."

"And you were one of them, were you?"

"I learnt to hold me own, with me own methods."

Connie had heard enough.

"Harry, I don't know what you're planning tonight. But I've had it. Like you said when I came in through the door. Mangled, that's how I feel."

"Go on then, Connie. Get your beauty sleep. I'll follow

you in a while," he said getting out of his seat to walk through to the public bar.

As they had been talking, the pub had gradually filled with men coming back from work and she saw Harry now finding himself sharing a table with a man who had been sitting on a window seat.

"Mind if I join you?" she heard him ask.

"Help yourself," the man replied. "Don't recognise you," the other said.

"Not surprised. I'm back on Civvy street now."

"Bet it feels good?"

"Sure, but sometimes it feels like one long bloody queue!"

"What were you?"

"In bombers."

"The glory boys?"

"Not when we got hit by one of their Messerschmitts!"

"You bailed out then?"

"Two of us did."

"The lucky ones eh?"

"He was until we dropped into a pack of werewolves who gunned him down when he was about to offer them a cigarette."

"Poor sod. And you? Off to a POW camp was it?"

Harry nodded.

"Tough was it?"

"Bad enough. They all are."

"No attempts at escaping then?"

"That belonged to the 'tally-ho boys'. That's what we called them."

"While the rest of you sat around waiting for the food parcels to arrive."

"Couldn't wait! It was like Christmas every time."

"I bet it was," the man said. "Here let me buy you a drink. Bet you missed this as much as anything!"

"How can I refuse? And then, maybe you'll let me show you one or two of my tricks."

"Card man, are you? Just let me get these drinks. I love a trick or two."

Connie had heard enough.

She swore later that when she left the pub she was going home. She'd got so used to the patterns of her thinking, the flashes, the loops. It was like a layer of her brain that she could never let go of. Everything she did, everything she saw, everything she heard brought her back to Angela. She'd tried to be so hard on herself, knowing that she had to push herself away. Maybe it was the day itself, or the worry about Angela's croup that did it. Within two minutes of leaving the pub, she'd changed her mind and made off in the direction of Hestor Terrace.

Martha

"If that bloody baby doesn't sleep tonight, I don't know what I'll do," Martha said coming downstairs to Billy. "I've got to work tomorrow and I'm buggered if I'm going to let them see me not pulling my weight. Any excuses and they'll give the job back to a man."

"You won't let them," Billy said.

"You want to see the looks I've had already. And the comments. 'Is this really the place for women?' and 'Aren't you worried about your nails, love?'"

"She's going to sleep tonight and anyway we now know what to do if she starts getting wheezy."

"Wheezy! When she has one of those fits? She sounds as though she's suffocating."

"It's not that bad, Martha. Anyway you've always said that you need to stick by your friends when things get rough. Women united? Wasn't that the slogan?"

"Don't Billy! It's not that simple, is it? Oh, come on," she continued when Billy didn't respond, "look what's been happening to us over the past few weeks, almost months. Or should I say what's not been happening to us?"

"You said so yourself that you can't rush these things."

"Rushing! At this rate the human race would die out!"

Martha looked at Billy, sitting there, his long legs stretched out, his hands behind his head. There was a part of her that wanted to shake him when he was in one of these moods. A sponge! That's what he reminded her of. Sucking in everything she threw at him without giving anything back.

"Billy," she said, changing the tone, "I thought we had agreed what we would do."

"That's right."

"Well?"

"We would wait for the end to come and then…"

"Try and start a family."

"Yeah, that's what we've been doing, isn't it?"

"Christ, yes if we had any time to ourselves or if we're not knackered from getting up in the night to give her a bottle or change her nappy, or we've got her hollering from croup until we get so much steam in the room, its running down the window and dripping onto the floor."

"We promised."

"No, we didn't. I did," Martha said.

"So?"

"I should have asked you."

"And if you had I would have done exactly the same."

"Oh, Billy! Stop being such a martyr! All I'm saying is–"

"Yes, what is it you're saying?"

"It can't go on like this! All she's doing is putting off the inevitable. Harry's bound to find out at some point, isn't he?"

"Wasn't she giving him time to readjust? It doesn't seem too much to ask."

"Readjust? Is that what you call it? I heard he's got such a good scam going for him down at The Lamb, the landlord's threatening to ban him! He's been taking money off every single regular and they're fed up to the back teeth with him. So don't let's talk about adjusting!"

"It's not easy for her."

"But look what it's doing to us, Billy! We've been at each other since the baby arrived. Can't seem to find any space for each other at the moment."

Martha remembered that intense pleasure of anticipation, waiting for Angela to arrive. The more she saw of Connie and the baby together, the more she wanted to be there with her own child and feeling that intense closeness while suckling it. Every time she saw Connie's full breasts dribbling milk, she felt this amazing craving. She had never expected to find it so arousing and that's why she could remember jumping on top of Billy that first evening as soon as Connie had gone to bed. They'd managed it, but she could remember how distracted he'd been. It had been much the same since. The pleasure of it, which they used to revel in, now seemed an uncomfortable memory.

He must have read her thoughts.

"So babies aren't what they're all cracked up to be?" he asked.

"No, you're right, it's making me feel I never want to have one. Oh Billy," she said moving over to Billy and putting her arms around his neck, "when I first saw her, I would have done anything to have one. Now I just want her to go and leave us in peace. It's you and me I'm worried by, Billy."

"What shall we do?" he asked.

"We could try going upstairs and lying down together, Billy."

They were at the top of the stairs when there was a knock at the front door.

Connie

Connie couldn't think how many times she had promised herself she wouldn't do this. You've got to protect her – was all she had been repeating to herself – which was all very well she thought, provided that the price was worth paying. Now perhaps for the first time earlier this evening, she had looked at Harry and been shocked by the change, as if she found it difficult to recognise the person she married what seemed just a short time ago. She knew he had been drinking, because she could smell it on his breath. But she was damned if she was going to see him drink away the precious little money she had. That's why she had been so tight with it. But as he had been hard at work finding people to impress with his sleights of hand, he wasn't going to be short of money. Well, not when it still had some novelty value.

Before, Harry always had a mischievous twinkle in his eye – she'd fallen in love with it. Now all she could see was this roguish look on his face, almost cocky, that made her feel he wasn't really with her at all. For the first time since Harry returned, she began to feel that she wasn't prepared to live without some of the joys of being a mother.

Billy opened the door.

"What you doing here, now? Didn't think we could manage? Was that it?"

"'Course not," Connie said, taken aback by the edgy tone in his voice.

"Who is it, Billy?" Martha asked.

"Connie," he shouted back, stepping aside to let her in.

As soon as she came in, she saw Martha coming out of the kitchen. She looked as though she'd been crying and for one moment Connie felt unable to move, desperate to see Angela but embarrassed almost for intruding on a scene that had nothing to do with her. She knew it was unfair to change the routine and come around unexpected.

"I thought Harry was with you?" Martha asked eventually.

"He is Martha," Connie started, "or he was. Oh God, I don't know what's happening anymore. He's not the same."

She could see Martha and Billy exchange glances.

"Look," she continued, "if I've come at a bad time, just let me see Angela and I'll go. I just wanted to see her sleeping. It's been so long…."

The words were barely out of her mouth before she regretted it because she had to run up the stairs choking back the tears. She realised she hadn't even asked how Angela was. Even with the silence around her, she was still praying as she opened the box room door. There was enough light from the landing and from the street lights for Connie to see it. Such a face, framed by a head of dark hair, looked as transparently beautiful to her as anything she had ever seen. Though it had been but days since Connie had seen her sleeping, it was as if Angela's world had changed so much in that time that she couldn't bear to let her away from her for a minute longer. She was frightened that Angela would forget her.

When she went downstairs, they were there sitting at either end of the parlour. She could see Martha still wiping the tears from her eyes.

"Thanks," she said, "and thanks for everything. Looks like she's over the worst, anyway."

She saw them exchange a glance with each other before Martha said,

"Connie, we've tried to help."

"I couldn't have managed so far without you. I mean if Harry had –"

"We can't go on like this, Connie. It's madness, isn't it? It was never a long-term plan, was it? Just long enough to let you break the news to Harry. That's what you said."

Connie felt silent. Now it was clear why the mood had been so touchy when she arrived. But she also knew that seeing Angela had been enough to make her realise that she couldn't live without her daughter either.

"You're right," she said, "she needs to come home."

"Well, there's no rush," Billy said, "is there Marth? She's not poorly anymore."

"'Course not," Martha agreed.

"Will you give me until the party? The homecoming party?"

"That's Saturday, isn't it?" Billy asked.

Connie nodded.

"Are you sure?" Billy asked.

Connie looked at Billy.

"Never been more sure, Billy. I can't bear it anymore. I'll bring Angela home Sunday?"

Neither said anything and Connie was ashamed at her relief that this whole deception and fabrication was at last coming to an end.

"I shouldn't really have come," she added, "it's just that I miss her more than anything. But I have to go. I can't risk Harry getting home and finding me out."

But even as she left Connie knew with growing certainty that she would be the first home.

23

Robert

Robert had been called to the quarries to give some assistance to a man whose foot was a right mess. While setting up a machine on unsteady terrain, a gust of wind had turned it over and the heavy metal had crashed onto the lower part of the man's leg. His ankle bone was clearly visible protruding above his boots. With the help of another worker they had lifted the injured man onto a stretcher and put him into the back of the ambulance.

He was driving the injured quarryman to the hospital when he stopped at the lights. One moment he was watching the trickle of people trying to go about their ordinary lives, chatting together as they walked up the street. The next thing he knew, there was a loud banging noise and he saw Stewart's face clearly visible above the bonnet of the van. He was laughing, jumping up and down and shouting,

"You'd better let me in, Robert. Don't want another injury, do we? I won't go until you've talked to me."

The lights had turned to green and he could hear the horn of the car behind him. Leaning across, he pulled up the passenger side catch.

Stewart had seen him do so and quickly came round, opened the door and jumped inside the ambulance.

"That's better," Stewart said, jumping in as Robert drove away from the lights.

"What the hell do you think you're doing? I've got a patient here who needs to get to hospital," Robert asked.

"Trying to tidy up some unfinished business, if you must know. You've hardly said hello to me and you certainly haven't said goodbye, have you, Robbie? Thought that was the least I could expect from someone who'd shared time with me."

"Well, you're wrong. I've told you then was then and now is now. It's over!"

"Very stirring, I must say. But it's not quite over, is it? 'Course I know where your sister lives... Martha isn't it? Sweet name. My first girlfriend was a Martha. Beautiful brown hair she had. Not that I touched it. Heaven forbid! I never got anywhere near her. Not sure I could have managed even if I did."

"Cut it out will you, Stewart. What do you want?"

"Fifty pounds would be a good start."

Robert looked at him.

"You're joking, aren't you?"

Robert couldn't see Stewart's face but he could still picture that switch from confidante to stranger that he could do at will.

"Not if your new boyfriend's worth it, I'm not. Your sister won't be happy about any of this, will she? No, I wouldn't push me away quite so quickly if I were you. You could at least do me the courtesy of spending some time with me, over a drink perhaps? I'm sure you know somewhere we could go?"

"Or?"

"Or I simply won't go away as you want me to."

"Simple as that?"

"Just as simple as that."

By the time they reached the hospital, Robert couldn't see a way out of this. He knew that the sooner Stewart left the better, but he'd also seen what a stubborn, ill-tempered man he could be if pushed. It wasn't worth the risk.

"You can give us a hand with him," Robert said pointing to the back of the ambulance.

"I'll meet you outside your place at one o'clock then," Stewart said, after putting the stretcher down on a bed in the A & E department and then disappearing as quickly as he had arrived.

Robert turned, looking for a nurse. The next thing he knew Billy was standing in front of him.

"Billy! What are you doing here?"

"Don't ask," Billy said, putting his hands up to his eyes.

"I think you'd better tell me."

"I've bloody done it again, haven't I?" he said, shaking his head.

"What are you talking about Billy?"

"Down at works. We work in pairs like. Must have lost concentration or something. He ended up getting a piece of steel through his sodding hand, didn't he. Went right through him. What's the matter with me?"

"Could've happened to anyone."

"Well, I've never had an accident in my life until… and now I've had two! I had to bring him up here in the emergency van. Christ Robert, I can't go on like this."

"How is he?"

"Doctor's looking at it now."

"And then I see you with that bloke. What's he called?"

"Stewart."

"That's it. The one who came round ours the other day. Wanted to talk to Martha about knowing you or something. Said you'd spent time together. I told him he needed to mind his own business or I'd do it for him."

Robert took hold of Billy's arm and led him further away from the nurse who was sitting at the counter.

"He's right Billy. I met him inside. He's another CO. We became friends, but that was that."

"What's he doing here then? Planned all this when you were inside, did you?"

"'Course we didn't. Never thought I'd see him again. Christ, when I found him at my place the other day, I couldn't believe my eyes."

"You mean that?"

"Sure I do. I ran into him when I was coming here from the Quarries with a patient in the back. He forced me to let him in. Gave me no choice."

As Billy stared at him, Robert could see Billy's forehead wrinkling in an attempt to make sense of what he had heard.

"You've got to believe me."

"And you've gotta believe me too, Robert, that I've got enough to think of at the moment without bringing anyone else into the equation."

"I hope what you're thinking about brings you some happiness too, Billy. Otherwise it's not worth it, is it?"

Robert stretched out for Billy's hand but he had already turned away.

"Just keep him away from me, Robert," he said walking away towards the entrance.

Harry

There was too much empty time as a POW and for Harry he'd think about Olthorp to fill it. The hills overlooking the town would come to mind and the times he and Connie had been up there, in the flush of romance. From there they could see the spire of the church and they'd even made plans for a white wedding. The street names had come back to him, Pencaster, Dewhurst, Trump, and Coles, the newsagent on the corner where they had forced some lad to buy tobacco for them. He smiled. Didn't do Harry any good! One drag of a cigarette and he was spluttering all the way to the front gates of the school.

Walking towards Hestor Street now, with the grey, grimy pebbledash fronts of the two-up, two-down terraces, the masonry chipped, and peeling paint on the windows, he tried to think what it had really been like before. A couple of boys passed him, flicking an old bike wheel along the road with a bit of wire. One of them collided with Harry as he ran past.

"Here. Watch where yer goin', will you?" he shouted after them.

He stopped, turned and watched them running away down the street.

"Kids being kids," he said to himself. That reminded him about a conversation he'd had with Connie. God, what an earful he'd got when he mentioned kids to her. He was only talking vaguely, asking her whether she'd been thinking about it.

"Now? A family?" she asked, "Why do you want to start one now? Don't you think we've got enough to worry about without thinking about kids?"

He couldn't say he'd been surprised at her reaction. Ever since his return he'd been hoping to carry on from where they left off. She couldn't get enough of it then. They'd spent hours in bed. Nothing like how it had been since he'd got back this time when the whole sex thing had been a one-sided affair. He couldn't remember her making up so many reasons for avoiding it. He wouldn't have spent so much bloody time in the pub if he felt that it was worth his while going home. But it wasn't Connie as he knew her. She'd always been the easy one at home, chatting away ten to the dozen. Right now she seemed quiet and apologetic half the time. He couldn't for the life of him understand what was going on. That's why he thought he'd visit her old friend Martha to see if she had any better idea if something was up. Connie had told him that Martha wasn't working Saturdays at the moment.

It was Martha who opened the door.

"Is there anything the matter," Harry asked, "you look a bit surprised."

"No, well, yes there is really," she said, turning round to take her coat off the peg in the hallway and closing the door behind her, "I've got to go to the works. Works' committee meeting."

"Fine welcome that is! On a bloody Saturday?"

"Sorry, Harry. Emergency meeting."

"Christ, don't they work you hard enough during the week?"

"It's not my choice. But that's the way it is," she said, walking away from the house.

Harry stepped alongside her.

"I wanted to talk to you about Connie."

"What's up?"

"She's not herself at the moment."

"How's that?"

"Don't know," he started, "everything really. When I'm with her, it's as if she's not there half the time. Do you know what I mean?"

"Give her a chance, Harry. Don't forget – she'd given you up for dead. Just when she's got used to you not being there, you turn up again like a ghost. Can't be easy can it?"

"And the work!"

"What about it?"

"Well, she's working hard enough but I don't see much money around."

"Perhaps she's saving. Yes, that's what she's doing. Probably saving to put some money down on a house."

Harry looked at Martha.

"And she acts as though she's not interested in me anymore. You know what I mean?"

"You mean sex?"

"That's right! Doesn't seem to have missed it at all. If I didn't know her better, I'd think she was having an affair or something!"

"Get away with you! Not Connie. It'll come back, Harry. I wouldn't worry."

"Well I'll try–"

"That's me bus, Harry. Sorry, I need to run for it."

He watched as she ran along the pavement towards the bus stop, then turned back, wondering why he had bothered to come here at all.

Connie

She knew she'd sounded half-hearted when she spoke to Harry about working today but like a flash he was talking about the benefits of her getting time and a half on Saturdays. With a sigh, her head fell forward. She'd have to blame it on another accounts balls-up when she came home empty-handed again. She put her arms around her body and started moaning, "Oh Connie, oh Connie, what have you done?"

Connie knew something like this would happen. Oh God, how much closer could he come and still not realise what was happening?

The moment she heard the knock on the door, she feared it might be Harry. He always knocked on doors with the same beat as *'one man went to mow'*. He thought it was a humorous calling-card and his few friends hadn't yet convinced him otherwise. Thank God she'd been feeding Angela when he arrived. At least she couldn't cry! But Connie couldn't move either and the first thing she thought of was the coat that she had left downstairs, chucked over the sofa in the parlour. She'd been in such a hurry to see Angela. All he had to do was look in there and he would have seen it. She prayed he wouldn't come in. Martha, bless her, must have known there would be any number of clues strewn around the house, because as far as Connie could hear, she hardly gave him a chance to look inside the house, let alone step inside.

Now that the coast was clear she decided to go downstairs and put on the kettle. At least she'd make herself a cup of tea. There wasn't much else to have. Like everyone else she had assumed that as soon as some peace was declared, they'd lift rationing. Did they just! What she wouldn't do for a banana! She couldn't remember when she last had a peach! Before she left, she went to the window in the parlour and slowly peered round the curtains. There they were, almost at the end of the street. Harry must have been following Martha to the bus stop. Connie put her back to the wall and stood there, without moving, listening to the thumping of her heart. She'd escaped this time, thanks to Martha's quick thinking. But she couldn't count on that forever.

But it didn't take her long to see the baby trail around the house. If Martha hadn't forced him out, he'd have needed only a minute to see them looking so out of place in a house belonging to a couple without children.

It was while she was looking for some tea that she found the tin. There were two £1 notes in the pot. She picked one up and shoved it into the pocket of her flannelette shirt. As she hunted for a piece of paper she could feel her hands trembling. She knew she'd sounded half-hearted when she spoke to Harry about working today, but he was as quick as Jack Robinson to talk about the benefits (for him) of her getting time and a half on Saturday. With a sigh, her head fell forward. How she hated this lying! She couldn't remember when she had ever lied so deliberately or incessantly during her life. But now she also needed to borrow some more money. When would it end? She decided to write her a note.

Sorry Martha, had to borrow money from you – £1. Harry thinks I've been paid! God – I can't take much more of this. Connie xx

She folded the piece of paper and put it between the pot and another glass jar containing coupons.

"Don't even think about it, Connie Morris," she said to herself and turned away from the kitchen.

When she heard the front door opening for one glorious moment she thought it was Martha. It was Billy, carrying some curly kale. As he went into the kitchen to put it into the sink, she prayed that she had left nothing disturbed on the shelf.

"I've got to go," Connie said, picking up her raincoat, "Harry's expecting me back."

"Alright then," Billy said, "I won't keep you. I'll just give the kale a wash. Sure you don't want to stay?"

"I'd love to Billy, but I can't. It's Harry. Sure you guessed that. But if I'm not there, he'll use it as an excuse to look for drinking companions. And that won't be difficult. Then anything might happen."

24

Robert

"Damn him," Robert muttered, walking back down the hill to find a bus to get back home.

It had all happened again: Stewart appearing suddenly from nowhere and confronting him with accusations and demands that made him feel as though he was trapped in a dream over which he had no control. How could this happen now, he asked himself, when he and Billy were wrestling with a history between them of suspicion on the one hand and contempt on the other. The trouble with Stewart was that he couldn't take no for an answer. It had brought him his own share of trouble when he was inside. More than once he had been put in the cooler when he'd had a burst of anger at one of the screws who was trying to persuade him otherwise. He couldn't be faulted for his stubbornness, anyway.

But now it was different. Robert had asked him to go, so apparently had Billy. How many reminders was it going to take to persuade him that Olthorp was just not big enough for the three of them? Meeting Billy at the hospital had been just another piece of bad timing. Robert was not going to get into an argument with him there in front of Billy, and he knew how quick Billy would be to get involved if he thought that Stewart was interfering. That's why Robert had agreed to meet him. Not a perfect venue but then he didn't have much time to give him anywhere else. He had time to get home and have a change of clothes before meeting outside his flat. He certainly didn't want Stewart coming in again because he'd never get him out of there.

From his window on the second floor, Robert saw Stewart's gangling frame coming down the street towards the house. There was something almost jaunty about his stride, even cocksure, and by the time Robert had vaulted his way down the stairs three at a time and closed the door behind him, he could feel the ire rising inside him.

"Glad to see you're being sensible, Robbie" Stewart said closing the gap between them as he continued his approach to the house, "it wouldn't have been sensible to stand me up."

Robert flinched.

Martha was the only person who occasionally shortened his name. His parents had been adamant that it should never be abbreviated. Given what he had recently found out, perhaps that was less surprising. If they had taken on the care of a child christened Robert, they, or certainly his father, would have felt it disloyal to call it otherwise.

The more Robert was with Stewart, the more convinced he became that this meeting threatened to become as difficult as he feared.

"Let's go to the Lamb," Robert said, hoping that the company of strangers might temper Stewart's outrageous demands.

"I'm in your hands," Stewart said, before adding, "but not for the first time."

Robert closed his eyes as he shook his head and took the opportunity of Stewart's lack of familiarity with the route, to cross roads when possible, without warning, leaving Stewart to follow him in silence.

The Lamb wasn't his closest pub, but he remembered taking the landlord's wife to the hospital with a burst appendicitis. The man had been so grateful he told Robert he put a couple of bottles behind the bar for him if he was ever coming his way.

"Yes, I remember now," the landlord said after Robert had pricked his memory, "what'll you be having then? That's two is it?"

"That's grand then," Stewart said, catching up with him at the bar, "a bottle of stout would do me a treat."

Robert could feel his hands clenching and his jaw locking as the words echoed in his head, mockingly.

They found a table next to the window with a couple of chairs. As he sat down Robert decided he wasn't prepared to extend the pretext any longer.

"Even if I could put my hands on the money – which I can't – I would never give it to you."

Stewart gave a smirk.

"You're not that stupid, that's what I think," Stewart said, "because you know how bloody hard it is to find someone. And that's got to be worth more than fifty measly quid, hasn't it? And another thing. Don't I remember your sorry tale about your ol' man who'd pegged it? Well, don't tell me he didn't leave you anything! Or what about your old dear. Or has she copped it too?"

Robert looked at Stewart. It was hard to believe now that he had felt the closeness that he had done towards this man. Perhaps it was the result of being inside, when you fed off scraps of kindness and consolation. He knew how hard hit he'd been by the news of his father. If he'd known then what he knew now, things might look different. But then, he was shattered, miserable and lonely and desperate for the comfort of someone else's touch. All his life he'd been brought up living with a creed of non-violence. For once he felt like being free from that constraint.

"Yes, they're both dead."

The more he heard Stewart's voice the cloudier his thinking became. That part of him brought up on such a strong denial of fighting and violence was being tested as never before. Every word he heard was like a further twist around his faith. But he knew that to give in to his loathing and distaste of what he was hearing would only make him feel that he was the loser in this battle.

"The answer's no," Robert repeated as calmly as he could.

"Oh, I'll give you another chance, Robbie, because I know your sister. Martha, isn't it? Nice lass, she is. Now, she's not going to like what I'm going to tell her, is she? Fine pint!" he said, putting his empty glass on the table. "Now am I going to stay for another? Because if not then I'd better be on my way. You see I've some urgent business to attend to."

"The answer's no."

Though Robert could see Stewart leaving the pub, the images that faced him belonged to a different time and place. How often he had dreaded such a revelation? There had once been a magic that had weaved its way between the two of them, helping them survive in a world that to them looked strange and vicious. If he allowed Stewart to talk to Martha, not only would that piece of magic be destroyed forever but the new elements in his life would be strangled at birth. By the time he put his glass down, it had become clear to Robert that he wasn't prepared to give Stewart that chance.

Billy

Walking alongside the canal had always been a way for Billy to relax and unwind, like going to the allotment. Here the stillness of water calmed him, and the lock with its large turning wheel had an order and simplicity about it that was usually comforting. Today he couldn't find it. Kicking his feet along the gravel towpath as he walked, he knew this was the quickest route to the pub. The sooner he could block out the shouting in his head the better.

Sometimes Billy wondered whether Martha had guessed or whether he'd been acting so oddly that he had given her any number of reasons to question his behaviour. Even so he never thought she'd stoop so low as to accuse him of stealing money! Christ, they'd been living on the edge for so long through the war, he would have thought she'd know him better than that. Why did she think he'd do that anyway?

He needed to talk to Robert. They were linked together on something which was beginning to get out of their control. The first few times they had seen each other, the excitement of the anticipation had wound them together into a state when they felt almost invincible. No one could touch them. What they had was still emerging and yet so perfect that it made him feel as though it belonged to another world which others couldn't enter. Now it felt as though somebody was trying to pull them apart.

"You're in a hurry," he said to himself, noticing someone running along the path towards him. It wasn't until the man was nearly upon him that he recognised the ginger hair.

"Hey, hey, slow down," Billy said standing in front of Stewart, "this is a bit of a surprise. I didn't expect to see you. I thought I said you're not wanted round here."

"Get out of my way."

Billy looked at him. Since he'd first seen Stewart on the doorstep of his house and heard since from Robert about their friendship when inside, he now found himself clenching a fist and feeling a knot hardening in the pit of his stomach.

"The station's that way," Billy said, spreading his chest and pointing behind Stewart.

"I don't need a train," Stewart said, moving a little to one side.

"So where are you going then, and in such a hurry?"

It wasn't much but it was enough for Billy to notice Stewart's mouth turning into the flicker of a sneer.

"None of your business."

"Well this is," Billy said lashing out with his fist, catching Stewart's chin and shoulder and knocking him backwards.

As Stewart regained his balance, Billy was pleased to see the look of shock and anger on his face.

"Don't tell me you're coming back for more," Billy said.

"Look, just let me pass will you? I'm not doing you no harm."

"But I can see what's in your eye. I saw it when you came to the house. Didn't like it then and I don't like it now."

The moment he said it and saw Stewart turn his head away, it all became very clear to Billy.

"That's it, isn't it? You were bloody going there again. To my house, looking for Martha, weren't you?" he said coming forward along the path with his head tilted forward.

"You can't stop me," Stewart said.

"That's what you think!"

"Billy!"

He stopped. It was Robert's voice.

Billy had been so caught up with Stewart that it wasn't until Robert came running under the bridge and past the bushes that Billy recognised him. As Robert came closer towards Stewart, he slowed down.

"You can't do this, Stewart," Robert said, breathing hard.

"I think that's what your lover boy's trying to tell me. He just hasn't got your gift of the gab, has he Robbie?"

If Robert hadn't stood between them, Billy would have thumped him again. Robert had his back to Billy and was facing Stewart. They couldn't have been more than a foot apart.

"I know all about you, don't I, Robbie? Those were tough times we shared together inside and we made the best of them, didn't we? So close, we didn't need many words."

As soon as he said that, he came forward, threw his arms around Robert and kissed him.

Billy had seen too much. Grabbing Stewart's arms he pulled them apart and wrestled him away from Robert. As soon as he did so, Stewart lashed out with his foot, trying to kick Billy as hard as he could in the groin.

"Stop it," Robert shouted.

He was too late.

The shock of the hard edge of Stewart's boot on his thigh was all it needed for Billy. Defending himself was second nature and his reaction was an ingrained instinct.

Catching hold of Stewart's leg he pushed Stewart backwards towards the canal. Losing his balance, Stewart tottered on one leg and then fell over, putting out his arms to break his fall. But he wasn't quick enough. There was no more than a dull thump as his head hit the low row of boulders bordering the canal. It was the deepening silence from the body on the ground that held Billy back. All he could do was stand there, watching.

Robert ran over to Stewart's prone body and Billy stared at his back with a rising anger. He might have turned away there and then but Robert's voice froze him.

"Billy! Billy – you've got to help."

By the time he turned round, Billy could see a small pool of blood on the stony path next to Stewart's head.

"Christ," he said, running over, "what the hell have I gone and done now?"

"He's got a nasty gash. Must have cracked his head on one of the boulders. It's not a pretty sight. But he'll survive."

"Serves him bloody right! Why did he have to start poking his nose into business that's none of his anyway, eh?"

"What matters now is stopping this bleeding. He'll need a stitch or two."

Billy watched while Robert put his arm under Stewart's head.

"Give me a hand will you, Billy. I can't carry him by myself you know. It's going to take two of us to get him to the ambulance."

"If he's so important to you, then you carry him," Billy said walking away towards the bridge.

He heard Robert call his name once and then he was gone.

25

Connie

"Where are you going now?" Harry asked, without lifting his head from the newspaper.

As soon as Connie noticed Harry hiding behind the paper, she knew it was time to go. She was so desperate to see Angela she'd been waiting for the right moment all day. She was in the hall getting her coat from the peg when she heard Harry speak.

"Martha said she'd lend me a blouse. For the party," she replied, trying to sound as convincing as possible. She waited for his response but when nothing came she added, "it's so pretty. Pearl buttons and lacy cuffs."

"Bit late isn't it? To be planning your wardrobe?"

"Don't be like that, Harry! She only offered it to me because she knew I didn't have anything special to wear at the moment and no coupons neither. It needed a bit of stitching and you know she's been so busy at work she's hardly a moment to herself." She paused. "She's got an electric iron too!"

"Should have tried Mend and Tear – they'd have done it in a jiff."

"And cost me!"

"'Course, she's a Quaker, isn't she?"

"What's that supposed to mean?"

"Can't see her doing union work with all that pacifism hanging round her neck."

"Why ever not? Doesn't stop her trying to make a difference, does it?"

Harry tutted and then sat back again.

"I'll be off then," Connie said.

"Is Alf coming tonight?"

"What? Alf Peters coming to your homecoming party?"

"Why not? I've seen him around quite a bit."

"Down The Lamb, you mean?"

"Sometimes. Lost one boy in France. Another in Italy. He needs company."

"Well I'm not sure I need his company. Can't think when I last saw him sober."

"Just thinking."

"I'll leave you to your thoughts while I go sort out my dress."

Connie's hand was on the door when she heard Harry's voice.

"Thought you said it was a blouse you was after."

"Bye," she called and pulled the door behind her. As she heard the lock's well-oiled click, she walked away with an energy that had been absent all day.

Weekends! Connie was beginning to dread them and the way they made it so hard for her to see Angela. She was shocked at how easy she found it to lie. For her it had become a world of fantasy which she took shelter in whenever she needed to. She seemed to be able to invent reasons and excuses on the spur of the moment if it meant that she would be able to see Angela. The more she needed Angela, the quicker she invented a story. Her life had become nothing more than a string of lies and deceit.

All the way up to Martha's she was wondering whether her life and Angela's could ever recover from this pretence which was supposed to protect her from Harry's anger.

"I can't do it anymore," she blurted as Martha opened the door to her, "I'm not going to."

"Hey, just a minute. Let's steady on a bit, shall we?" Martha said, taking Connie by the arm and leading her through to the parlour. "Come in and then we'll talk."

"Where's Billy?"

"Where he usually spends his free moments. Down – "

"… on his bloody patch?" Connie added.

"Too right! I mean he always used to be keen on his marrows and curly kale – to say nothing of his runner beans. But these days I just can't get him away from them. Even though he nearly got himself blown to bits there when he helped that young boy."

Connie was silent for a moment wondering if there could ever be a right moment to talk about Billy.

"It'll probably blow over, whatever it is," she said.

"That's what puzzles me about this whole thing, Connie. You see he's been acting sort of strange ever since he had that accident at the works. Preoccupied, that's what he is."

For a moment Connie could feel the pain again, hearing Robert's words as he told her about *seeing someone for the first time.* But here was her dearest friend feeling her husband was hiding from her. She couldn't bear to see the hurt.

"Like I say, it won't stay for long. Everything's changing now. Give it time."

"You're probably right, Connie. But it doesn't stop me thinking."

"Well, think about what the next government is going to do to make it a better life for poor sods like you and me and… Oh my God! Angela! I haven't even–"

"Don't worry, Connie. She's fine."

"What do you mean she's fine? Where is she?" Connie asked, getting up from the chair and moving to the door.

"Out!"

"What?"

"Out, with Billy."

"What's going on, Martha?"

"Your little darling needs some fresh air like anybody else. Was Billy's idea, actually. But I thought it would do her a world of good. Well, it couldn't do her any harm could it?"

"What if people start talking? You know *'Hey that's Billy Hilton over there. Isn't it? What's he doing with a baby? Can't be his. Wonder who it belongs to?'*"

"Stop worrying, Connie! Anyone would think they hadn't seen a baby in a pram before."

"Not pushed by Billy, they haven't."

"That pram! I can tell you he's right proud of his handiwork. Told you about the evening we spent looking for ball-bearings on the kitchen when the tin spilt, didn't I? Buggers went everywhere."

Connie was trying not to laugh because she knew that she'd just as easily break down sobbing.

"It's alright, Connie, Angela's fine. You see."

"That's just it, isn't it? It's not fine for her, nothing's ordinary, and she can't do what you'd expect every child to be able to do. Lying in a pram as the world went on its way around her."

"Like I said."

"But Angela can't do that yet and I'm sick to death of having a baby and not being able to let her live like a baby."

She could see Martha looking at her.

"Oh, Martha, Harry's in a terrible state. He does nothing! Sits around, looks at the paper. Goes to the pub. Comes back. Goes to sleep it off. And the whole bloomin' thing starts again. He's got to know about Angela. I can't keep it back from him, can I?" She paused for a moment before continuing. "Why can't it be a homecoming for the two of them?"

"What? You mean take Angela back with you tonight?"

"He's got to find out soon, Martha."

"But it's a party for him, Connie! No, that's not fair. He won't know what's hit him."

"He'll survive! Anyway, two birds with one stone sort of thing, to my way of thinking."

"What's brought this on then?"

"Oh Martha, this isn't new. Every evening I leave here, I cry my way home and then have to put a face on for him. Every day I wonder how much longer I can bear to be apart from Angela. She belongs to me, Martha. She's part of me. I can't explain it. Imagine having the most precious magical present which you had to keep locked away in a box and you knew where it was but you could never see it. You can't live like that!"

Martha came across to Connie and put her arm around Connie's shoulders.

"No, you can't and you won't. But I think you need to think about your timing."

"OK. I have. Tomorrow. I can't live like this Martha and nor can you."

"Hey, don't you worry about us. We'll manage."

"Maybe you two need to do more than just manage at the moment."

"What do you mean?"

"I mean wherever Billy is, you need to reach him."

"God, I don't like the sound of that Connie, is there something you're not telling me?"

The rattle of the front door made both of them stare at each other, turn and almost with one breath, call out "Billy!" before moving towards the door as quickly as they could.

"What a reception we're getting, Angie! Just look at them! Martha and Connie! They can't wait to get their hands on you. Anyone would think we'd been to the bloody south pole and back. Hang on, Martha, I need to navigate this pram through the doorway carefully. Never was much clearance."

In her hurry, Martha had not only prevented Billy from lifting the pram over the step into the hall, but blocked Connie's path.

"How's our Angel, then?" Martha said, peering over into the pram when Billy had pulled it up to the parlour door.

Connie gazed at her but couldn't hold back any longer. With Billy at one end of the pram and Martha at the other, she squeezed between them, reached down for Angela and picked her out of the pram.

"Come here," she said, patting the baby's back, "come here."

There was a flush in Billy's cheeks as if the wind and sun had restored some of vitality that had been absent recently and his good-humoured manner helped to take the fear and shock out of Connie's voice.

"Did you see anyone, Billy? I mean did anyone see the baby?"

"Angie was lying in her pram – I built it for dreaming and comfort remember – on the edge of the allotment but she only had a couple of blackbirds and a magpie for company. Cawing and screeching they were too."

By now Connie was back in the parlour sitting down with her arms around the baby.

"You're a saint, Billy Hilton. I just get so scared sometimes."

"'Course you do," he said, "anyway, what brings you here? Aren't you expecting friends round tonight?"

"Yes, I know we are. Why did I ever suggest it? Oh yes, I remember. It was the bloody gossip talking about a celebration. Had to think of something to distract Harry and came up with the idea of a party. At the time it didn't sound too bad."

"It might still work out."

"Some chance! He'll probably be half-cut by the time anyone pitches up. But I just had to come over today to see her. You don't know what it's like missing her every second I'm not with her. It's not what's supposed to happen, is it?"

"We were talking about Connie returning with the baby," Martha said.

"It's got to happen at some point, hasn't it? Stands to reason," Billy added.

"But Connie's talking about going back with Angela a bit sooner than that, aren't you?"

Billy looked at Connie and then back at Martha.

"What? Today?" Billy didn't try to hide the astonishment in his voice.

"Not you as well, Billy," Connie said, shaking her head.

"That's the way I saw it too, Billy," Martha said.

"God, this whole thing is becoming my worst nightmare. I'm sorry. I can't! I just can't do it."

"Well, why don't you enjoy the party tonight and if you feel the time's right, bring the baby back tomorrow," Billy offered.

"It's going to end terrible. I can see it," Connie said.

"Now don't get like that," Martha said, "and as you're here you might as well enjoy the baby."

"That's –" Connie never finished what she had to say.

"Have you seen Robert around, Billy?" Martha asked.

Billy looked down at the floor before and shook his head.

"No. Why should I have?" he asked walking towards the kitchen.

"Don't get like that, Billy Hilton, even if you are talking about my brother."

Billy kept on walking until he reached the back door.

Connie let the silence reach her and hold her. For one moment she wasn't going to be able to stop herself speaking out there and then about Billy. She couldn't lose the image of Martha standing in front of her as she tried to reach Angela. Though she had a part of her that wanted to protect her oldest friend, she was beginning to wonder how long it was going to last.

But as Martha got up to follow Billy, she knew she didn't have the strength to do it. It made her wonder whether there would ever be a right time to share the painful truth that she had guessed. Secrets seemed to have their own way of destroying the very people that had created them. So caught up in these thoughts, it wasn't until she heard Martha speak that she noticed the tears falling onto Angela's shawl.

"You know, Connie, I used to think I could read Billy like a book. At the moment it might be written in Chinese for all the sense I can make of him."

Connie nodded.

"Like I said, if there's something up, he'll try and tell you when he's ready."

"I'm beginning to feel as though the rest of the world knows something I don't. Now I thought you all of people would let me know if there was something that I needed to be told."

"What's that supposed to mean?"

"Well after what we've been through," Martha said. "Connie, I'm only asking for some honesty between friends. Is that so much to ask? Isn't that what we deserve?"

Connie looked down at Angela sleeping and felt withered at the way everything which used to be so simple, had suddenly become entangled with misunderstandings. In her vague attempt to protect Billy, she had met nothing but Martha's suspicions. Whatever she said to Martha now was likely to be misconstrued.

"I can't do it! I'm sorry, Martha!"

"I see, it's alright for you to wash your hands of it and walk away, is it? After what we've done for you! Sorry, but we're clearly not talking about the same thing. Because I thought real friendship meant that you were there for each other when it mattered."

Connie closed her eyes for a moment.

"You can shut your eyes, Connie, but that's not going to make it go away."

It felt to Connie as though someone was pulling the curtains in front of her before she had finished making her speech. But with that blackness in front of her at that very moment, it only made her think of what she had to do next. With no leeway for manoeuvre, what had once appeared a heavy fog was clear for the first time.

"I'll be here in the morning," she said getting up with Angela and walking over to the pram, "and I'll be taking Angela with me."

"You don't have to, Connie? I mean Billy and I, we could–"

"No, Martha, I'm as sure as I can be about anything at the moment. It's funny. I seemed to know what I had to do during the war years. There wasn't much choice really, was there? But it's so different now."

"If that's what you want," Martha added.

"I just know I can't be here anymore, Martha. It's like living two lives. And I must leave you to yours." She paused. "But I still hope I'll see you later at the party."

Without waiting for an answer, Connie walked out of the house.

26

Connie

"Give us a hand will you, Harry. I can't carry this table on my own. Weighs a bloody ton."

By the time Connie returned from Martha's, she found it hard to see what Harry had been doing.

"Putting up the streamer, wasn't I?" he said.

It had been lent by one of the neighbours who'd kept it after the VE day celebrations, on the understanding no harm came to it. Now it stretched from the front door through to the back door, winding its way round light fittings on the way through.

"And what else? Harry we've got to get this whole place sorted out in the next hour!"

That's when they agreed to put a picnic table in the yard for bottles and glasses. She knew that if the neighbours and friends whom she'd invited all managed to arrive at the same time, they'd be stepping on each other's toes in the kitchen. The weather was good and Connie thought there was always something special about an outdoor celebration. Harry said he didn't mind provided the booze didn't run out.

"Well, it will if you start drinking it," she said. She hoped there was enough in her voice to warn him off, because there was precious little anyway. All those she invited had promised to bring a bottle of something with them. No one really expected parties like they saw in the films. These days, she thought, it wasn't even easy to get hold of a packet of fags, they were in such short supply. What sort of party was it without booze and fags?

"Don't see much evidence of your very special trip to see Martha. Where's the dress gone?"

As soon as Harry mentioned it, Connie tried to stop the flush spreading to her cheeks.

"Blouse! It's gone nowhere because it doesn't fit. Martha can't be more than a size ten at the moment. I'll have to find one of my own."

"Dare say you will."

"What about you?"

"It'll have to be the demob suit, won't it? Haven't got another jacket worth wearing!"

"Suit yourself!"

As soon as she said it, she started laughing and it didn't take long before they were both giggling away.

"Oh, that's a good one. Here," Harry said going up to Connie and putting his arm around her neck as affectionately as he could, "we need to get laughing together you and me, Connie. And get closer. I waited long enough, haven't I."

"If that means what I think it means Harry Morris, then the answer's no! We've got a dozen people coming tonight and I'm nowhere near ready. Let's get things ready and then maybe we could have our own celebratory drink before the guests arrive."

"Now you're talking sense," Harry said.

By eight o clock Connie felt happier. The house and yard began to have a festive feel that had been absent all day. But when Connie tiptoed down the stairs with beetroot juice on her lips and the seam of stockings pencilled down her legs, it wasn't the tinsel that Harry had managed to find in a box with other tired Christmas decorations hidden away on top of an old wardrobe which he had put on the mantelpiece, around the picture and in the hall that she found herself staring at. Because she had wanted to come down and make something of an entrance, Harry hadn't heard her. He wouldn't have expected her to see him in the mirror. But framed by tinsel, she could have sworn she saw Harry lifting a flask from his jacket pocket, taking a swig and then replacing it as quickly as he had removed it. It was all so sudden she tried at first telling herself that she must have made it up.

"It's party time," she said, feeling her nails biting into her hands and as she came into the room she did a pirouette before doing a mock curtsey.

"My, who's my gorgeous girl then?" Harry asked, doing his own bow in front of her.

"It's good to have you back, Harry," she said, taking his hands in hers.

"Here," he said, passing her a glass, "let's drink to you and me then."

"Stout alright?" he asked.

Taking the glass from Harry brought her close enough now to smell the whiskey on his breath.

But she took the glass from him anyway.

"Course it is. What else have we been drinking?"

"Nothing that isn't good for you."

"Cheers," she said weakly, lifting her glass to his and looking him in the eye, "to us."

But even as she said it, she couldn't stop herself shaking. It was the way she had grown accustomed to make things up, to lie and yet convince herself that there was really no other option. She tried to turn her back on Harry, but he caught her by the shoulder and pulled her round.

"Here," Harry said, "have you got the shivers or what?"

"Nah," Connie said, "it's nothing. Probably just a bit nervy. It's not every day we have parties, is it?"

If someone hadn't started knocking on the door then, Connie didn't know what she would have done. Holding himself straight, and checking that he looked the part in the mirror on his way to the front door, Harry had a smile as broad as a beam as he opened the door.

"Early," she heard Harry say, "'course you're not early. Not to my party, you can't be. Connie, mind? Why ever should she mind? It's my bloody party after all. Come on in, DD."

She should have guessed. Not content with the list that they had made up together, which they had pored over for ages, Harry had decided to make some of his own invitations.

Why couldn't he have told her?

"This is Connie. Doesn't she just look something tonight?"

Harry gave the man at his side a nudge in the ribs and a leering look.

"Stop that, Harry. Don't you want to introduce me to your guest? It would have been nice to know that the list was being extended."

"'Course, if you'd been around this afternoon, I'd have told you. Meet Duncan. We call him Drunken Duncan – DD – because he tries to spend as much time blotto as he can. Isn't that right DD?"

Duncan came forward towards Connie and offered her his hand.

"The pleasure is entirely mine at the moment. But I

hope that on acquaintance we shall be able to reverse that state of affairs."

"Cut out the toff stuff, DD. Come on and follow me. We've put as much as we've got outside," Harry said looking at DD's empty hands.

"Don't worry, old boy," DD said tapping his nose, "I am well versed in secreting the elixir in different parts of my habit and I shall divulge presently."

Connie watched them go out through the kitchen into the yard and for one awful moment she thought that she was going to cry. A knock at the front door saved her.

"Robert! Oh, thank God! I can't tell you how pleased I am to see you. Come in."

"Well," he said coming into the house, "if I'd known what sort of welcome to expect, I'd have come earlier. You did warn me."

"Don't be daft. I was talking about how we need each other. Then you frightened me. What you were doing wasn't going to help keep us together." She paused before adding. "You know you're always welcome here."

"Who were you expecting? The M.P.?"

"No! Much more sinister. One more cup-holder from The Lamb."

Robert laughed.

"What's the matter? Are they taking over the party or something?"

"I think I'll call them unexpected arrivals."

"Uninvited guests you mean?"

"Something like that."

"By you?"

"Don't worry, it's probably not worth the effort."

"Tell me," Robert asked, "is Martha here?"

Connie put out her hand and stopped him as they walked through the kitchen.

"No, Robert," she said, "Billy's not here either, yet."

He turned slowly until he was facing Connie. The first thing she could see in his face was alarm, but the longer he kept her gaze, the softer the edges of his mouth became.

"I just wondered," he said.

"'Course you did."

"I need to see him that's all."

"Bust-up, is it?"

Connie saw the hurt look on Robert's face.

"Oh, it's none of my business," she added.

"It's Stewart again. You remember me telling you."

"How could I forget it? It's not an everyday happening in Olthorp, is it?"

"He's been trying to blackmail me. He said that he'd tell Martha if I didn't pay up."

"What a nerve! I hope you didn't give in."

"Connie, it wasn't as easy as that. I needed to get him away from here. Things were turning nasty. Then they met yesterday down by the canal, quite by chance and Billy and Stewart started fighting. Needless to say, Stewart came off worse and needed a few stitches in his head for his troubles."

"Where is he now?"

"I put him on a train to Birmingham this morning."

"Birmingham?"

"He said he had friends there."

"You think he'll manage?"

"He's got ten quid in his pocket, so he bloody well should."

"Robert!"

"I couldn't see another way out of it."

"Hang on. That's someone at the door. Give me a minute, will you?" Connie asked.

"You're not worried what Harry will say if Martha and Billy don't come together?" he asked as Connie turned away.

"Robert, stop worrying! If I didn't think I could lie my way through that, then I wouldn't be here now, I can tell you."

27

Connie

Over the course of the next couple of hours, the house and yard began to fill with the guests whom Connie had invited. With them they brought along a motley collection of bottles, some saved up from weeks past, others picked up in the preceding week, which as planned they put onto the table outside the back door.

Connie had watched as Harry positioned himself by the table at the start of the evening. He'd said he wanted to make sure all refreshments brought were open to anyone. Some had struggled to find anything at all to bring but their omission was quickly excused and forgotten. Nevertheless, positioned as he was by the table holding the drinks, she could see that he still found it almost impossible to hand or pour a guest a glass of ale or stout or ginger beer without proposing a toast to life beyond the war, survivors, demob suits, Boche bashing.

"Martha," Connie said, spying the familiar length of Martha's dark locks, in the kitchen and walking towards her, "you made it."

"Making it was never in doubt, Connie. But it's a bit of a relay effort this evening. Thought I'd come first before the drink takes its toll."

"Be nice to have enough to have that sort of effect. Beggars can't be choosers though. Look, I'm sorry about this afternoon. I really didn't want to make you feel –"

"Harry!" cried Martha, "Welcome home," she said throwing her arms around him.

"Ta. It's a grand ol' party. People enjoying themselves now, aren't they? They don't need looking after. Here," he said looking over Martha's shoulder towards the others in the kitchen, "where's your Billy, then?"

"I can't stay long myself, Harry. Terrible migraine at the moment. But Billy – he'll be along in a while," Martha added.

"He's not jacked out of it, has he?"

"No, he got in late from his patch that's all. It's taken him a while to get used to it again. Memories aren't very good there, as you can imagine. I'm pleased he's gone at all."

"He's a good man, your Billy. I mean if it weren't for Billy then the two of us," he said slipping his arm around Connie's waist and giving her thigh a gentle slap as he walked through to the kitchen, "well, we wouldn't be here now would we?"

"Tch. Watch yourself, Harry," Connie said removing his hand. "What was you after anyway?"

"Nothing much," he said and walked away.

Connie watched Harry go through the kitchen, and then up the stairs. A few moments later she saw the light go on upstairs. It wasn't on for long.

"I can't trust him, Martha."

"What do you think he's up to?"

"He's got his own supply."

"From where?"

"God knows! You know he's been down the pub, fleecing some of the regulars."

"So I heard."

"Too bloody right. I even bumped into the landlord who's threatening to ban Harry from The Lamb because he reckons that if Harry does it again, someone's going to take it out on him. Not prepared to risk his license, is he?"

"Can't blame him."

"So what does Harry do? Moves down to the Queens Head and carries on there. See that guy there, at the bottom of the yard, the one wearing a hat," Connie said pointing.

"What about him?"

"That's Duncan, Harry's friend at the Queens Head. Harry calls him DD. Stands for Drunken Duncan. Now I know why."

"What are you going to do?"

"Oh, Martha, I dunno. What can I do? All I've been thinking about is bringing Angela home."

"Still tomorrow, right?"

"Oh God, I'm terrified but I can't wait for it to happen."

"You've waited Connie. It was always going to shock him, wasn't it?"

"And some!"

"Then when you bring Angela back to the house, maybe that's the time."

"What? To confront him about his drinking? I'm frightened of what he'll do when he sees the baby."

"You'll have to tell him that everything's changed. It's not just you anymore but the two of you. And it's not right having a child in the house with someone who can't control his drinking."

Her voice trailed away as she saw Robert approaching her.

"Hi Martha," Robert said

"Hullo, Robert."

"Billy not coming tonight?"

"Why is everyone suddenly interested in Billy?" she asked.

Connie could see Martha looking at her brother as if waiting for a reply when there was a sudden crashing sound from the bottom of the stairs followed by the sound of Harry swearing.

"Oh God!" Connie said, leaving the two of them together, "I knew this was going to happen."

As she turned out of the parlour, she almost walked into him. Harry was lying there, rubbing the top of his shoulder and cursing.

"Watch your mouth! There are guests here."

"Soles! They're like bloody glass. Slipped out from under me."

"Told you you should have scored them."

"Cracked me shoulder something rotten when I fell."

"You've not broken anything then?" Connie asked.

As soon as she said it, his hand reached for his jacket. She could tell that he was feeling for something in the inside pocket, but he started rubbing his ribs up and down in an exaggerated way, while complaining about the pain.

"That's not your shoulder, Harry," she said and walked back towards the kitchen before going out into the yard.

Billy

Though Billy had left the house as soon as Martha returned, even walking as quickly as he could along the towpath, the light had faded by the time he reached Connie's. Martha told him that a few had already tired of the party, tired of watching Harry dug in at the end of the yard with his friend

DD and not prepared to wait any longer for him to come and be sociable. Others he could now see were in huddles eking out their meagre alcohol rations, but trying to maintain the spirit that things were going to get better. There was talk of the new government, 'the Labour landslide', with some talking of Churchill receiving a slap in the face after his war efforts. 'Couldn't have done it without him' was a common comment often followed by 'The country needing a change.'

"Billy!"

It was Connie.

"I came as soon as I could."

"How is she?" Connie asked.

"Sleeping," he said.

Connie couldn't seem to stop herself going up to Billy, throwing her arms around his neck and kissing him.

"Billy, you're an angel. What would I have done without you? Come with me Billy, the others are out the back. If there's anything to drink, that's where you'll find it."

Billy held Connie by the arm and stopped her moving.

"Is," he started, "is –"

"Robert here?" she said, turning to face him.

Trust Connie. There was a part of him that felt as though some frightening weight had been lifted from his shoulders. The rest of him probably wore the look of an animal that's been chased and suddenly realises that it's run down a dead end leaving no way out.

"How did you know I was talking about him? It could have been anyone."

Connie came a bit closer to Billy and whispered.

"I told you about being careful."

"Christ, Connie, it's me that needs me to be in control. Maybe that's what I want, but the longer this lasts, the less

I know how to stop myself. If Martha – you haven't said anything to her, have you?"

"'Course I bleeding haven't! What do you take me for? She may be my best friend and all that but secrets are secrets."

"If anyone finds out, that's it."

"No, stop all that, Billy. I'm just pleased to see you here, because I guess you want to talk to Robert. Unfinished business and all that."

"You could say."

"Well, there's no use your standing there because the last time I saw him he was outside, near the brazier at the bottom of the yard."

28

Robert

There was a small shed towards the back of the yard. It looked to Robert as though it had been in a sorry state for some time, with one of the glass windows cracked and felt blowing from the roof. He was leaning against the doorway, watching and waiting. Harry and DD were in the shelter. Pieces of corrugated iron had been thrown to one side and in the hollow itself, there was enough room for the two of them to sit submerged and out of sight.

At one point, when Robert stood next to the brazier rubbing his hands, Harry had climbed out with a bottle in his hand.

"That you, Robert?" he asked, pronouncing each word with deliberate effort and staggering forwards towards the fire as he did so. "Grand party. Here," he said, grabbing hold of Robert and using him to stay on his feet, "come and join us. DD?" he asked trying to look over his shoulder, "DD, where the hell have you gone?"

Robert saw the bearded face of DD momentarily appear above the shelter before sliding out of view again.

"What you doing?" Harry asked, retreating back to the shelter. Then Robert saw Billy.

He was coming out of the kitchen. Just for a moment, Robert saw him as he had done only weeks ago. Like an image that was burned inside him which he couldn't add to or move or change in any way. Then, he had felt a frightening pull towards him which no strength of will could placate. Tonight he could only stand still and gaze. The closer Billy came, the tighter Robert clutched the bottle in his hand, and the more he felt like closing his eyes and let the waves of anticipation wriggle down his body.

There was little light at the end of the yard where Robert was standing. Even the burning brazier did little to dispel the shadows and gloom. He could see Billy was coming straight towards him, nodding at the few welcoming appeals from other visitors as he did so.

As Billy came nearer it was easier for Robert to make out the look of steely determination on his face. Looking straight at Robert, Billy walked up to Robert and without saying anything, pulled Robert towards him and hugged him.

With his back to them, Robert would never have known that there was anybody walking up the path had Harry not blurted out,

"I need to piss," and staggered past them on his way to the house and then presumably looking in their direction adding, "yeah, have a fondle. What did the old boy say? As old as the woman you feel! Christ, that's not you, is it Billy?"

Even as Robert tried to turn Billy so that Harry could only see Billy's back, he knew it was too late.

"Can't be! Not our Billy! Oh my word, if ol' Harry hasn't seen everything tonight. Another drink, DD," Harry shouted, stumbling forward towards the house, "need another. Otherwise, I'll think I'm dreaming."

Robert looked at Billy and held him by the forearms.

"Don't worry!" he said.

"What do you mean, don't bloody worry!" he said, breaking away from Robert, "Christ, we've really done it now, haven't we? Why did I have to go and do that now?"

"Because you wanted to, Billy."

"Yes, I did. All I've been thinking about is what that man, your old friend, did to you. Why should he be able to if I can't? That's what I want to know."

Robert looked at Billy and tried to catch his wary eyes that looked haunted at the moment. If Robert's world turning, Billy's was on the Big Dipper and Billy knew it wasn't stopping.

"Hey," Robert said, trying to pull Billy towards him, "come here."

But Billy had already turned away and was hurrying back towards the house.

Connie

"Looks like I've done it again," Robert said to Connie as she came out into the yard looking for him.

"Billy was in a bit of a hurry to leave. Can't say he looked very happy."

"That's one way of putting it!"

"What happened? Maybe I shouldn't ask?"

"Harry. He saw us… together, if you know what I mean?"

"Oh, Robert!"

"I can't believe it. Billy was so cross already because of what happened with Stewart down at the canal. I think tonight was his way of showing me how much it meant to him."

"You mean how much you mean to him."

"Aye. All spoilt by bad bloody timing."

"Don't fret before it's necessary. Who knows, Robert? In his pickled state, I can't see Harry remembering anything in the morning."

"I wish! But you know what Harry's like. Dog with a bone?"

"You think you've made a mistake, Robert. Just look over there at the pair of them over there – completely soused. It's enough to break my heart at the moment."

"He's not been back long, Connie. Maybe it's his way of dealing with what he's been through."

"Oh, stop being so bloody reasonable, Robert. He's got no right to act like that. Watch out, here they come."

Harry and DD were getting to their feet. But as they did so, she saw Harry fall against DD, causing him to totter backwards and crash into the canes that Billy had erected for the runner beans.

"Hey," shouted Connie, "watch out, will you? Some of us have to eat as well as drink, you know."

She was aware that the guests, who were close enough to her, quietened their voices, but she didn't care.

"Come on, DD," Harry said, getting hold of his friend's jacket and trying to pull him away from the frame, "looks like the end of the party here. This ain't no bloody good to me anymore, is it?"

He couldn't have thrown it hard but the sound of the bottle breaking against the back wall was enough to turn the heads of the guests.

As DD lurched forward, Harry put his arm through DD's and tried to guide him slowly down the yard towards the back door. As they weaved their way forward the few remaining guests parted to give them an easier route.

"He's a disgrace," Connie whispered to Robert as

she watched the pair stagger their way into the house, "I shouldn't have bothered."

"Why did you?"

"I didn't mean to. Mrs Gossip Granger saw me and Harry together and started talking about my 'celebration'. I was terrified. A party was the first thing I thought of."

"Quick thinking."

"Yeah, but now look at the trouble it's getting me into."

Connie could see Robert looking at her.

"What do you want to do?" he asked her.

"Bye," Connie waved to some guests as they left, and added, "sorry," as an afterthought.

"It's not for you to apologise," Robert said.

"Well, he's not going to, is he? Robert, if you really want to know, I don't want to stay here tonight. He scares me when he's like this."

It wasn't until she said it, that she felt her nails digging into the palms of her hands.

"What'll you do? Go to Martha's?"

"Oh God, I shouldn't. Haven't they done enough for me already?"

"If you like I could walk you there."

"Are you sure?"

"It's me, Connie. I'm the one that needs to go."

29

Billy

Billy hurried away from Connie's, kicking his feet as he went. He couldn't get rid of Harry's face with his look of surprise and shock. And he shook his head as he remembered the wonderful spirit he had felt inside him when he arrived, knowing that he would be seeing Robert, talking to him, being together with him for a few minutes. But all that was behind him now and he was only left with Harry's mocking words in his ears.

There was no one about and the lamps threw a calm glow across hard edges of the streets. There were occasional lights which could be seen behind flimsy parlour curtains, but he knew they'd be in darkness within the hour.

Some part of him wanted to be there, behind those curtains, tied to a world that had an evenness that his own couldn't accept. By the time he stood outside his house, he thought of the time he'd been there, standing and listening to Angela's cries, unable to move for the strangeness and magic of this new life that had arrived when everything else was coming to an end. He remembered thinking at the time that the event must have a special significance, that the baby must be blessed in some way.

Oh how those thoughts had come to haunt him in the weeks since. The baby had allowed some of the pieces on the board to be moved and that had given them a chance which they might never otherwise have had. But if Robert did mean something to him, why couldn't he show him? Running away was only going to make it more difficult to reach him. He was no closer to understanding what he should do when he turned the key in the lock.

The lights were off and the house was quiet which probably meant that Martha was in bed and Angela sleeping. Probably just as well, he thought. The last thing he wanted now was Martha quizzing him about Harry and Connie and Robert and how he had found them all. It could wait until the morning. But the more he thought about the party, the less he felt like sleeping. He didn't know how long he had been sitting there, his arms behind his head, and feet stretched out before him before he noticed Martha by the door, at the foot of the stairs.

"Are you not coming to bed?" she asked.

"Yeah, in a minute," he said, hoping that he would not have to explain his reasons.

"Anything the matter, Billy? You look terrible."

"No, I've had it for tonight, though. Harry – he's a pisshead. Dunno why Connie bothers."

"None of us is perfect."

"No, but most of us try."

"Talking of trying, Billy," she said, holding out her hand to him, "isn't it time we tried."

Billy swallowed and pointed his finger upstairs.

"Angela's off with the fairies. She won't disturb us," Martha said.

As Martha winked at him, he could feel only shivers on his back as he remembered the last time they had tried it. But before he had time to say anything there was a knock at the front door.

"Who the bloody hell is that now?" Martha asked walking towards the front door.

Without hesitating Billy jumped up and was standing behind Martha as she opened the door.

"Connie!" Martha exclaimed opening the door, "What…? Oh my God, what's happened? No, don't stand there. Come inside the pair of you."

As soon as Billy heard, he felt a flicker of anticipation which he let grow and pulse inside him. Without hesitating he jumped up and joined Martha in the hallway.

"I'm really sorry about this, Martha," Connie said walking into the house, "I promise you this wasn't supposed to happen. Sorry, Billy."

Billy waited until Connie had passed him before stepping towards the door. He was right! Robert was waiting on the pavement and as soon as he saw Billy at the door, he smiled.

"Billy," Robert said, putting his foot on the step, "I needed to see you."

"Get Robert in here and close the door will you, Billy," Martha shouted, "let's keep some warmth in the house."

Billy stepped out of the way to let Robert pass but as he did so, Robert's hand reached out for his own and squeezed it.

"It's OK," Robert whispered and moved into the parlour.

"Well," said Martha, "are you going to tell us what happened or do we have to force it out of you?"

"I'm sorry, Martha."

"And you can stop apologising too."

Connie let out a sigh and put her head back in the chair. Billy couldn't listen. Part of him was still reeling at the thought of Harry talking about what he'd seen. It was little comfort convincing himself that Harry wouldn't be able to remember in the morning because Billy wasn't worried about the morning. Oh no, he was terrified of now! In his current state, there was no guessing what Harry might blather to anyone within listening distance. And as far as Billy was concerned, the night was still very young. The only thing he knew for certain was that Harry would wrap up the story to make it sound even more shocking than it was already. For a moment, Billy remembered what Martha had said and felt a guilty hope that the landlord may have carried out his threat.

"I think you did the right thing," he heard Martha say, "men in that state are a menace to themselves let alone anybody else."

"I've never been more frightened in my own home, ever," Connie replied.

"It was lucky for you that Robert hadn't left. I wouldn't want to think of you walking back on your own in the dead of night. It's not fair. Thanks, Robert," Martha added.

Billy saw Robert smiling and nodding at her.

"Come on, Connie, it's time for some shuteye. I was nearly asleep half an hour ago! Anyway, we can't do anymore tonight, can we?" Martha said.

As Connie got to her feet, she hesitated.

"I'd be happy on the sofa here."

"Don't be daft, Connie. You're back in your old room. Alright?"

"Thanks. I really appreciate –"

Martha never let her finish.

"Like we agreed, Billy, alright?" Martha said going out of the parlour and onto the stairs.

"'Course," he said, "be up in a minute."

He waited to hear the bedroom door close before he did anything.

"What are we going to do?" he asked, getting out of his chair and moving towards Robert.

"We can't 'do' anything, Billy," Robert replied, standing up and moving closer to him.

"What if Harry talks? Christ, why am I such a bloody fool! I should have known this would happen."

There was something about Robert in moments of crisis like this that Billy loved. It was as if nothing was going to rock him and he stood there with an impish grin stretched across his face. Without him, Billy wondered what he would do. They looked at each other, gorging on this freedom to stare and let each other's eyes stroke their faces.

"I need to go Billy," Robert said, "but this is what I would have done if we'd been able to stay."

When Billy went upstairs a few minutes later, Martha was already in bed. He could see her nightie had been tossed onto the floor beside the bed.

"Come on, Billy," she said, patting the bed beside her, "didn't anyone tell you that you shouldn't keep a woman waiting?"

"I'm coming," he said. But as he undid the laces of his shoes and fumbled with the buttons of his shirt, all he could think about was the touch of Robert's fingers and the warmth of those arms around him.

"Here get yourself under the sheet and hold me will you?"

Billy's body gave a shudder.

"What is it?"

"Nothing," he said, "probably tired that's all."

"You can make as much noise as you like as far as I care," Martha said, rolling Billy onto his back.

But the only sound to come from him that night was the silent heaving of his chest, as he lay there afterwards, struggling with the fear that he would never be able to do it again.

Connie

That evening when Connie went upstairs to see Angela, it was the first time since she'd been staying there that she knew she would not have to leave her. She had looked at the dark curls against the pillow and listened to the soft whimpers that Angela made. By the time she fell asleep, with the tears dried on her face, slithers of light had edged their way into the room.

She didn't know how long she slept before Angela's cries and whimpers woke her. But she had never felt so happy to hear them.

"Yes, my angel," she crooned, leaning over and picking the baby out of the basket, "I'm here."

By the time Connie had got the bottle in Angela's mouth, having taken the chill off it by placing it in a pan of boiling water, she thought Angela's cries must have woken everyone in the house. She couldn't have known that her being here again with Angela was like a turned-off switch for both of them. Though Martha was probably dead to the world, by the look on Billy's face, he had heard the cries throughout the night.

"Morning, Connie," he said as he came into the kitchen.

"Oh, Billy, I didn't mean to wake you," Connie said looking at the dark rings under his eyes.

"You didn't."

"Are you OK, Billy? You look terrible."

"Couldn't sleep."

"Oh, I'm sorry. That must have been – "

"Angela? No. Never heard her."

"Well? Do you want to tell me about it or do I have to guess?"

She looked at Billy who stood there shaking his head.

"It's me and Martha. I don't see how…"

"What? How you two can stay together?"

"Connie," he said, "I don't. I really don't know."

"It'll be easier when we've gone, you wait. We'll be out of your hair soon."

Billy shook his head.

"I'm sorry you're going in a funny sort of way. I've got used to her."

"I know Billy, it looks like that. But it's been too long already."

"You'll be off then?"

"Just as soon as we're ready."

"Do you want me to come with you?" Billy asked, with his head turned on its side to face her.

Connie looked at him and smiled.

"D'you know Billy, I don't know what I'd have done without you both. But that part has come to an end. Now it's my turn. And Billy, thanks for everything," she said going up to him and throwing her arms around him before adding as a whisper, "and good luck."

Connie's stride had gained its usual purposefulness as she walked home. She wasn't prepared to waver on street corners worried who she might meet with Angela. In a strange way, the longer she walked with Angela at her side, the better she felt.

Carrying Angela now at her side in the basket, she stopped every few minutes because she found the handle cutting her wrists. As she walked, she practised what she was going to say to Harry when she returned. It wouldn't be reproachful – she had passed that stage. Neither would it be defensive as in we-can-all-make-mistakes. No, the more she thought about it the more she had to present Angela as a fact of her life. If Harry decided that he couldn't accept it then Connie was now ready to face the consequences by herself, uncomfortable and lonely as she knew them to be.

As her front door came into view, she found herself clutching the basket even more tightly. Approaching the doorstep she put the basket on the pavement as she took the key from her purse and watched her shaking hand put it in the lock.

"It's me," she shouted, trying to sound matter-of-fact about it but the warble in her voice gave it away. She closed the door behind her.

Waiting there, she felt as though she wanted to stop time, so frightened of what might happen next. The silence of the house gave no clues. Walking slowly into the parlour she put the basket onto the table. With a quick glance towards the kitchen, she saw the debris left over from the party. Plates, glasses and bottles were still strewn over the surfaces, as she had left them.

Leaving the basket, she went upstairs. Harry was a heavy sleeper and after a night like that, there was no way of guessing how long he would sleep. Even so, she found herself climbing the stairs as quietly as she could, avoiding the squeaky board in the middle of the rise. The few steps to the front bedroom seemed to take forever and by the time she stood at the door listening for Harry's snoring or at least heavy breathing, she could only hear the beating in her own chest.

Taking the handle of the door, she inched it open. The bed lay behind the door against the front wall and she had to open it wide enough to be able to peer round it. The counterpane had belonged to her mother and as soon as she saw its unruffled edge she knew that there was no one in the bed. She pushed the door open and walked into the room.

The flannelette shirt hung over the back of the chair where she had left it before changing for the party. The dressing table showed the hurry that she had been in to get ready with the face cream and eyebrow pencil lying like discarded ornaments. Other than that, there was no sign that anyone had been near the bedroom since she left it the evening before. With the back of her legs against the side of the bed she let herself fall backwards onto the quilted counterpane. It must have been the way that she had been sick to death of what might happen when she returned to the house with Angela that caused it. Tears started to roll down her face and had it not been for the sound of kids playing with a wheel which they were whacking down the street with sticks, she might have revelled in that state for longer still.

But she was at home now with her baby – a situation which she had been dreaming of ever since Angela was born – and she needed to find a way of letting the two of them be here and stay here. That's all she thought. She's my child, and this is my house. She let these thoughts pull her to her feet and lead her around the house, all the time picturing the changes that would be necessary.

By the time she heard the door rattling it was already midday and the house had been transformed from the state she had found it in when she came back earlier.

She froze, her hands in the water, washing up the remains of a pot that had been used as an ashtray.

"You back yet?" she heard him shout. "Connie," he started again, "are you, are you there?"

"Yes," she said as calmly as she could, wiping her hands on her pinafore and then as quickly as she could, rushing through to the back room where Angela's basket lay on the table. Harry had got there first. Holding up one hand for support, he was leaning against the window at an angle and staring down at Angela.

"Well, well, well," he said dragging out each word and lowering his head as if needing to focus on the sight in front of him, "who's a pretty baby then?" Connie saw Harry slide his hand down the pane and then hold it above the basket. He was moving his fingers up and down as if he was waving at the baby.

"Don't touch her," she screamed.

"Now, now," he said backing off a little, "looking after her, are we? Now I think about it, DD said something about Moira Pyke breeding again. Bloody tart. Pretty thing, ain't she? Can't see Moira in her though."

The next moment Harry took a step backwards and as he did so, he lost balance and only kept his feet by holding onto the table. For one moment, Connie thought he was going to pull the basket off the table with him and sprung forward to stop it from moving.

"Watch out," she said.

There was a sharpness in her tongue which she hadn't heard before. Whether Harry heard it she couldn't tell because as she glowered at him, he started laughing.

"What's so funny, then?" she asked, never expecting a serious answer to her question.

"Just thinking."

"Well that would be new," she said.

"Tch, tch, tch," he started, "no need for your cattiness. Maybe that's what you need."

"What?" she asked.

"A baby."

Connie looked at him and saw him trying to wrestle with the possibilities he had just unearthed. The seriousness of his face made her jaw drop.

"It would be grand, Connie. You, me and the baby. Only one mind, or maybe two. What do you think?"

Of all the possible reactions Connie had toyed with, this one she could never ever have dreamed up.

"Harry," she said, all the time trying to run through the various possible openings she had been thinking of to broach the subject.

"Oh, I know, I know, I know what you're going to say. But this time," he said with deliberate slowness, "it would be different."

"It's not that, Harry."

"What? You mean you don't want to give me a chance? Just one more chance?"

"It's not about chances, Harry."

"Christ, why did you marry me if you didn't want babies? There," he said straightening himself and pulling his shoulders back, "I've said it. Let's you and me start a family? You'd be a great mother, Connie."

Harry must have seen the utter confusion in Connie's face.

"You don't have to hurry your decision, mind. It's if, not when, that matters," he said, "but I'll leave you to think about it," before he turned on himself and guided his unsteady way out to the yard.

30

Martha

Martha awoke to a cloudless sky.

All she could think about was getting out to the hills with Billy. Perhaps they could take a snack with them and try and heal some of the distance that seemed to be blocked between them. But after Connie had gone, she came downstairs to find him asleep on the sofa.

"What's up with you?" she asked, walking past his outstretched legs and going into the kitchen.

"Uh," he said putting his hand through his hair, "I woke up when I heard Connie leaving."

"How was she?"

"Pretty calm, I think," he said, stifling a yawn, "but I can't really believe it."

"There's nothing else she can do now, is there? I mean either Harry accepts Angela or he doesn't."

"I don't think life's ever that simple. But for her sake, I hope you're right."

"So do I," Martha said, before adding, "Billy, I've got a plan. Thought we could go to the dales. Take a picnic with us, lie back and… and dream."

"What's brought all this on?" he asked.

Martha came over to Billy, pushed him back a little so that she could sit on the sofa, and took his hand and placed it on her stomach.

As Billy's hand rested on Martha, she could see his eyes moving restlessly, unable to settle, frightened. He couldn't look at her.

"Take it away then," she said, lifting his hand away from her. "I can see there's no point talking to you at the moment."

Billy groaned.

"It's true though, isn't it? You're miles away. I can tell it in your eyes, Billy."

"I was still thinking about Connie," he said.

"Oh yeah? What?"

"I'm frightened for her, that's all."

"She's tougher than you think."

"Maybe, but Harry can get out of control with the drink. He's got a mean streak somewhere."

"You can't change the past, Billy. They're married, remember, for better or worse. God, haven't we tried to make it as easy as we can for them over Angela? Don't forget that after she was born, we had no privacy and had to get used to Connie and all the fuss and the mess and the boiling nappies. To say nothing of getting Angela to sleep when she woke in the middle of the night and decided that bottled milk wasn't good enough for her."

Billy nodded.

"Then after a break Angela was back here every night, wasn't she, needing to be fed, changed and then waking us with her croup. Hasn't done much for you and me and our ideas for the future has it, Billy? Or don't those really bother you at the moment?"

"I still want to see if she's alright."

"Oh, go on then, suit yourself. I'm out of this house today before I do something I'll regret."

Martha knew that something was happening with her body. She had been as regular as anyone and now that she was several weeks late, she was beginning to let her belief in her pregnancy grow. She was so excited she'd wanted to share it with Billy today, out here on the hills with him where there was a warmth in the air, the rich smell of summer and hay making – a sense of new life. But she couldn't hold herself back. And what did she get for it? One glance at him with that haunted look that had crept on him and shadowed him recently was enough to convince her that she'd have to find another time to share her news with him.

So, without him she took the bus and then followed the familiar path up along the dell before it turned away and weaved its way through dense bracken up towards the ridge. Even though there was no one about, she didn't feel alone: lying back against a slab of rock, she listened to the wind and the occasional cries of birds and watched the high clouds chase each other across an otherwise empty sky.

Resting her hands on her stomach, she allowed herself to wallow while picturing her unborn child in her imagination. She'd have straight hair, not the mass of curls that she had struggled to keep shaped and tidy during the lean years of using soap to wash her own and asking friends to cut it at regular intervals. She'd even done it herself once but had been so shocked at the results she swore that she'd never be tempted again. She could see her with beautiful shoulder length hair, which she'd tie back in a ponytail when she was at school. She thought there'd have to be another child too, and wondered how much persuasion Billy would need.

She couldn't remember how long she stayed there, drifting in and out of her daydreams and smiling at the prospect of the days to come.

Even when she got back home, she felt she could forgive Billy for his lack of interest this morning because she wanted so much to share the news with someone. Yes, she could have made a mistake but her whole body seemed to be willing this transformation to take place and she didn't want it to stop.

"I'm back," she said, throwing her bag down in the hall and going through to the parlour. "Billy?" she called, loud enough to be heard at any part of the house.

As she moved from room to room, the silence seemed to follow her. Perhaps it had an edge to her that day because of how she was feeling about the preciousness of life. Then she remembered what Billy had said to her about Connie and how concerned he was. Without waiting, she picked up her bag and left the house.

Billy

Billy looked around him and for the first time in his own home, surrounded by memories of places he and Martha had been together, holidays and dreams they had shared, he felt a stranger. Like Connie he had started leading his own double life, and he was beginning to wonder which was the more real.

As soon as Billy left the house, all he could think about was finding Robert. Running now, he went back to Robert's lodgings, but he wasn't there. Neither was the ambulance. No one else had seen him that morning. He tried the allotment, because he knew that if Robert wanted to find him, on Sundays it was as good a place as any to start. There were only two people there, digging and raking over their patch. Thinking that Robert might have been there already,

Billy asked each of them in turn if they had seen somebody of Robert's description. Not as tall as me, he started, wavy hair, blue eyes, high cheekbones. He thought there was no limit to the picture that he could have described. Because talking about Robert made him real in his mind, he had to pull himself away from the allotment.

Where are you, Robert, he kept shouting to himself as he turned away from the allotment and followed the canal back towards town. One or two people he passed looked at him and shook their heads and walked on. All the way into town he couldn't get Robert out of his mind. Alongside the water he was thinking of the fight he'd had with Stewart and how Robert had been ready to take him off to hospital to get the gash seen to. Images of Robert seemed to follow him: the way he'd turn to Billy with that lopsided smile spreading across his face; the way he'd shake his head sometimes before speaking; or the way he'd hold out his hand to Billy like an offering.

"Robert!" he shouted as loud as he could before leaving the towpath and joining the road again. He looked both ways and covered his face with his hands. The Lamb couldn't have been more than a street or two away from here, he thought, and if Robert wasn't there, maybe he might stop for a drink anyway to dull some of the constant throbbing he felt.

It was still early for the regulars at The Lamb and as Billy approached it, he could see a number of people waiting outside for the pub to open. It wasn't until the landlord unlocked the door and the few made their way inside that Billy noticed Harry amongst them. What's he doing here, he thought? Has Connie spoken to him? Maybe that's why he is here, Billy reasoned. Maybe if Billy spoke to him, it would make things easier for Connie. He followed Harry into the bar of The Lamb. By the time Billy had bought himself a bottle of stout, he could see Harry sitting by himself towards the back of the room. He moved away from the bar.

"Well, I didn't expect to see you here, Billy."

"Me neither. Wish I could say the same for you, Harry."

"Knock it off will you, I've got enough on my mind at the moment," he said.

Billy couldn't quite believe what Harry had just said and as he put his glass down on the table and sat down next to Harry, the words were out before he could stop himself.

"Sure you have. Look if there's anything else that Martha and me can do to help, you just have to say."

Billy was looking at Harry. He thought Harry had a quizzical look on his face as if struggling to follow what Billy was saying. But it didn't take Harry long.

"No, we'll get over this little patch by ourselves, Billy. But thanks all the same. We'd hardly spent any time together and then I got myself shut away in a camp for too long. It was always going to be a shock coming back. You expect things haven't changed and that life can carry on as before. But it's not like that now, is it? I mean we fought for freedom, didn't we?"

"You did, Harry."

"Freedom means you're not tied to anything, doesn't it? That you make your own decisions."

Billy gulped. Harry had gone to war for freedom, hadn't he? Now the freedom he fought for had suddenly been snatched away from him with the present that Connie had just brought him.

"How do you feel now?"

"To be honest with you, Billy, I'm just trying to clear my 'ead from last night. I mean grand party an' all but I think I mixed a few too many at the end if you know what I mean."

"What about this morning?"

"What about it?"

"I mean Connie. Connie and the babe."

"Fast asleep it was. Another one of Moira Pyke's, so I hear."

Billy stared at Harry.

"Who told you that?"

"Why it must have been DD. Last night at the party. Told me she was the local tart and that she'd just had another bastard delivered."

"So what's the baby doing at Connie's then," Billy asked, trying to mask his exasperation.

"You know my Connie. She'd lend anyone a hand if they were desperate."

"Connie's looking after Moira's baby?" Billy asked, unwilling to lower the growing tone of incredulity in his voice. "Is that what you she told you or is that what you think?"

Harry hesitated for a moment.

"Well, stands to reason, doesn't it? Someone's gotta look after it. Think DD said something about Moira having hurt her shoulder."

"What!" cried Billy. "You mean Connie never told you?"

"Told me what? Look, I wasn't there more than a few moments."

Billy sat back in his chair cradling the glass in his hands and looking at the patterns made by the beer, as if expecting that from somewhere he would be given a lead about what he could say to Harry.

"Here," Harry started, "let me get you another."

"No Harry, I don't want another thanks."

"Right, I'll just get my own then," he said getting to his feet.

"Harry," Billy said, more as a way of stopping this runaway train hurtling along a line where the points had been switched, "things are not what they seem. I think you need to go back and talk to Connie."

"Oh, I'll be back just as soon as I'm ready."

But Harry got halfway to the bar before turning round slowly and facing Billy.

"How come you know so much about it?" Harry paused. "And what things aren't what they seem to be then, eh, Billy?"

He looked at Harry and saw the slightest uncertainty cross Harry's face, like a shadow.

"It's not for me to say, Harry. You need to talk to Connie."

"Stop teasing me, Billy. Spit out what you know, will you."

But Billy couldn't say anything. He feared he must have already levered the lid from the top of the poisonous can. That was as much as he was going to do. All he could do was wait for Harry's reaction. And it didn't take long.

For a moment, Harry stood there without moving. Whether Harry had suddenly seen a connection that the drink had earlier denied him, Billy didn't know. But he watched Harry putting the pieces together in his mind because as the empty glass dropped from Harry's hand, it seemed to fall so slowly before smashing on the stone flagged floor.

"I don't bloody believe it!" was all Billy heard, before Harry turned and left him there with the broken glass at his feet and the other drinkers staring in silence.

"Now look what you've done, Billy Hilton! You bloody fool!" he swore to himself as he ran out of The Lamb, wondering what on earth he could tell Connie and what good it would do her. So preoccupied with his meeting with Harry, he didn't hear the van hooting at him until it pulled alongside him.

"Billy! What the hell are you doing here?"

"Robert! You bloody frightened me, you did. Where have you been? Spent all morning looking for you."

"Liar!"

"Well, long enough I can tell you."

"Sorry, but I was on my way back from an accident down out by the mill and–"

Billy never let him finish.

"Robert, Robert, you've got to help me. I need to get to Connie's before Harry."

"Get in Billy and tell me what's going on will you?"

"It's Harry. He knows. He's put the picture together. I need to get to Connie to warn her."

"I'll go and tell Connie." Robert said, "You can go back to the pub and stall Harry."

By the time the ambulance moved off, Billy was back at the pub, desperately hoping that Harry hadn't already gone off looking for Connie.

31

Robert

Robert parked the ambulance outside number 34 and was just getting out of it when Connie opened the front door.

"Robert," she shouted with a warble in her voice that made him hurry over to her, "Oh Robert," she said holding onto his jacket, "what have I done?"

"Connie, listen. I bumped into Billy. He's been in the pub with Harry. He told me that they had got talking. I mean you didn't tell Harry anything, did you?"

"Christ, I never had the time. One moment he comes in taking me by surprise, the next he's drooling over the baby, saying it must be Moira's – some idea that his drinking mate DD fed him. Why?"

Robert's silence made Connie uneasy.

"What's happened?" she asked.

His face must have told her the answer.

"No! Billy hasn't told Harry, has he?"

"No," he said, "he hasn't, but he's still probably said enough to make Harry suspicious."

"Oh God!"

"You can't blame Billy, Connie. From what Harry said, he thought you must already have spoken to Harry and that Harry was only in the pub to drown his sorrows."

"Well, he's a walking sorrow at the moment. So, what exactly does Harry know?"

"Billy thinks Harry has guessed the truth."

As soon as Robert had spoken, Connie's whole body crumbled into his.

"There," he said putting his arms around her, "the first thing we need to do is get you and the baby out of here until Harry's had a chance to cool down."

"And what?" she cried pulling away from him, "wait for Harry to hunt me down? Sorry, Robert, this is my story and the sooner I put him in the picture, the sooner it will end."

"But Connie, there's no knowing what he'll do."

"Whatever it is, it's not going to go away without me, is it?"

"Let me take Angela then."

"Where to?"

"Anywhere but here. It's not safe."

"Maybe you could take her back to yours?"

"Fine! Harry's never been there."

"Oh, Robert," Connie screamed as she left him on the street to go back into the house, "you can't let him harm her. I'll kill him."

Robert went inside and watched while Connie picked out the few items that Angela couldn't do without and stuffed them into a bag.

"Here," she said giving the bag to him, "put this in the ambulance and I'll fetch Angela."

Billy

By the time Billy got back to The Lamb, Harry was at the bar thumping his fist on the counter.

"What do you mean?" Harry asked the landlord.

"I'm not serving you. That's what I mean."

"Why the bloody hell not? I pay for my drinks, don't I?"

"Yeah, but not with your money, is it? I've warned you about fleecing my regulars of their hard-earned pennies, haven't I?"

"They could have won! Just a simple bet that's all it was."

"And how many times have you lost? You and your bloody tricks!"

"Well, I've done here anyway," said Harry turning his back on the landlord, and walking towards the door, "because there's another small matter I've to attend to."

"Where are you going, Harry?" Billy asked as he caught up with him just outside the door of the pub.

"Where the bloody hell do you think I'm going? To find out if it's true. If she'll admit it."

"What?"

"Christ, don't start that again, Billy," Harry said stubbing his finger into Billy's chest, "bet you've known about it all along."

All the way back to the house, Billy stayed a little ahead of Harry. Listening to him muttering about lies and deceit, about everybody knowing and him being the laughing stock of Olthorp, made Billy pray that Robert had got to Connie in time to get her out of the house. Harry needed the time to cool down.

But as they turned into Hestor Terrace, Billy saw the ambulance. A couple of seconds later, Connie came out of her house carrying the basket in her hand. He watched her go round to the open back of the ambulance where he could see the doors were open. The next thing Billy knew the doors had been slammed shut and Robert was coming from the back of the van and getting in behind the wheel of the ambulance. Billy heard the engine of the ambulance turning over and then saw it gradually pick up speed as it came down the road towards them

"Bugger me," Harry said, "she's trying to take the bastard away."

That's when Harry ran out straight into the middle of the street.

"Stop, Harry," Billy shouted and ran forward to catch up with him.

Hearing the sound of the ambulance get louder as it picked up speed going down the street towards them, he remembered it like a slow-motion picture. One moment he was in the middle of the road grappling with Harry, trying to drag him to safety. The next moment he heard the screech of brakes and then looked up to see Robert driving, turning the wheel frantically, trying to pull the ambulance to the left to miss the two figures standing in its path. A glance to his right and he saw the ambulance ride up the pavement before the front of the van hit the lamppost with a sickening scrunch.

Of the three onlookers, it was Billy who was the first to move. Within seconds he was pulling at the driver's side door trying to open it. Inside he could see Robert's body slumped forward, his head resting against the wheel. But the impact of the lamp post had crushed the hinges of the door so that it was impossible to open.

"Robert," he was shouting again and again, banging on the window in desperation. He ran around the front of the van and tried the other door, but it was locked. That's when he smelt petrol.

"Help me, Harry," he shouted.

Billy hadn't seen Harry run to the back of the ambulance to open its double doors. Inside there were stretchers strapped against the side of the van. But the basket was there, tied by a loop of the hessian cord that had been passed through the handles of the basket and secured so that the basket wouldn't be dislodged.

But just at that moment, the baby started crying.

For one moment, Harry just stared at the basket but when the baby's crying got louder and louder, his hand went inside his coat and pulled out a knife and started to cut through the rope, pulling it taut with one hand and hacking at it with his other shaking hand.

"We've got to get Robert out, Harry. The door's jammed and I can smell petrol."

"I'm getting the baby out. Give me a second, will you, I'm nearly through."

As soon as Harry said it, the knife cut through the cord and the basket came loose from the side of the van.

"Here," Harry said, passing the basket to Billy at the back of the van. "Careful now," he said.

"We need to get Robert out, Harry," Billy said holding out his hand to take hold of the basket.

"Oh my God, oh my God, where's Angela?" Connie cried reaching the back of the ambulance.

"Angela?" he heard Harry mutter.

"She's alright," said Billy, giving her the basket.

Billy went inside to the grill screen that divided the front seat from the back of the van. Looking through he could see Robert's inert body slumped over the wheel. Next to the stretcher, there was a fire extinguisher, buckled to the side wall. Undoing the rusty clips, he wrenched the extinguisher and started to hammer it against the grill. At first it showed little sign of giving. Perhaps it was seeing Robert from another angle or it may have been the way that Robert's head was lolling, but Billy began to crash into the grill wildly with as much force as he could. As soon as he'd cleared a wide enough gap, he lunged forward to get hold of Robert's body and then pulled as hard as he could to lever him so that the top half of his body was through the gap.

"I've got him," Harry said taking hold of Robert's head and shoulders.

Though Robert was not a large man, there was little room for clearance and Billy was terrified that they'd injure him further trying to get him out. With Harry at the front of Robert's body and Billy feeding the legs and feet through the gap, it wasn't long before they had him stretched out at the back of the van. That's when he saw the deep gash on Robert's forehead and the blood trickling down his face.

"It's OK, Robert, you're safe now," Billy said holding onto his arm.

"Get him on a stretcher," Harry shouted.

Billy undid one of the stretchers from the side panel and laid it on the floor and together they lifted him onto the canvas.

"Now, let's get him out of here." Harry said. "This van's going nowhere."

It wasn't until they had the stretcher out of the van and resting on the pavement that he heard one of the onlookers who had come out of their houses at the sound of the crash say,

"Poor bugger! He's not in much of a state, is he? Test his pulse!"

As soon as Billy heard it, a part of him knew. He froze, unable to do anything that would make the nightmarish possibility become any more real. Then standing back, he could only watch as Harry came forward and put two fingers against the artery of Robert's neck.

Billy watched as Harry slowly turned his head to face him and then shook it, first one way and then the other.

Billy covered his face with one hand and started thumping the inside of the ambulance with the other. It wasn't until he felt someone's arm, Connie's, restraining his and pulling him away that he turned towards her and let her hold his silent howling body as tightly as she could.

Martha

All she could think about as she hurried over to Connie's was telling Billy the news. She didn't think Connie would mind if she dragged Billy away. Now, her mind was so taken up with seeing him and being with him that it took her a moment to take in the scene that confronted her as she turned into Hestor Terrace. Halfway up the street, jammed against a lamppost, with its front end buckled, she could see the ambulance that Robert drove.

"Oh my God," she shouted as she ran up the street towards it, "no, no," she kept on repeating. As she walked towards it she could see there was no one in it.

"Robert," she shouted. "Robert."

That's when Billy came out of the house onto the pavement.

"Billy!" she screamed at him. "Where is he? Where's Robert?"

But Billy looked paralysed and just stood there, waiting for her to get closer to him. As she did she could see a look on his face that she knew would haunt her forever. His face was ashen and his eyes red.

"No, no, Billy, tell me Robert's alright."

"Martha," he said, holding out his arms to her, unable to stop the tears running down his cheeks, "I'm so sorry. He was trying to save me."

"Don't say that!" she said, pushing past Billy and going into the house. "Where is he?"

"Upstairs," Billy murmured.

By the time Martha burst into the room, Connie and Harry were still there, sitting on the bed holding each other's hands.

"Oh God," she said, throwing herself down on Robert and stroking his hair, as her whole body starting to shake and heave with the despair of her sobbing.

Billy

"We've left Martha with Robert," Connie said as she came downstairs with Harry.

He nodded.

"It was my fault, Billy," Harry said, grabbing hold of Billy's sleeve as he walked past.

"Come on, Harry. Not now, eh?" Connie said, pulling him into the parlour.

Connie tutted and went back into the parlour.

Harry told them that an ambulance was on its way.

"We'll tell you when it arrives," Connie said.

Billy muttered his thanks and went up to the bedroom.

For a moment, it was just the two of them.

"It's only me," Billy said coming into the room. As quietly as he could, he sat down on the floor with his head against the bed, leaving Martha collapsed next to Robert. The only sound he could hear was her rasping breath and the only image he could see was the raw slash against the slightly blue tinge on Robert's face, as he lay there stretched out on the canvas stretcher.

The siren of the ambulance pierced the heavy air in the bedroom and as soon as Martha heard it she pulled herself slowly back from Robert, then kissed him and got unsteadily to her feet. Touching Billy on the shoulder as she moved away from the bed, she left the room and closed the door.

Billy pulled himself onto the bed and sat there looking at Robert. Now that he was alone with him, he felt the silence like stab wounds. He tried to speak.

"I'm sorry… I never said… but I did love you," he said and kissed him and then just watched his tears falling down onto Robert's face.

By the time he got to the bottom of the stairs, he moved out of the way to let the ambulance crew through. He could hear Harry in the parlour trying to explain to a constable what had happened.

"Yes, he was driving fast. But I'd seen him put the baby in the back of the van and I wasn't having him take it away. That's why I stood in the road. To try and stop him."

"Well, you did that an' all, I'll say," said the constable.

"Look, I didn't mean it to happen that way. If I'd been on my own he might not have swerved," Harry said.

"What do you mean?"

"Billy was there with me?"

"Billy who?"

"Billy Hilton, that's me," he said, coming forward.

"So the two of you were in the road, trying to stop him driving and he had to swerve to get out of your way."

"That's right. You see Billy here was a friend of Robert's, that's why he missed us. That's right, isn't it, Billy?"

Billy could hear no malice in Harry's voice, no sniggering.

Harry went on,

"I'd drunk too much, officer. Billy here was only trying to stop me and get me out of the road."

"Right, I'm going to need you both down the station to give a statement."

Harry looked across the room towards Connie and she responded by nodding her head.

"I'll go with you, officer," Harry said. "I think Martha here needs Billy to stay with her."

The constable looked at Harry with his heavy eyebrows that locked in the middle of his forehead.

"Martha?" the constable asked.

"Robert's sister."

"The sister of the deceased?" the constable offered.

"That's right," Harry agreed.

"Well, he'll be back just as soon as I've taken a statement or two. You two are coming with me down the station and we'll let the ambulance crew take over here, shall we?"

Billy didn't want to watch them as they brought Robert down on another stretcher and put it into their ambulance, but before the crew had taken Robert's body away, they asked if any relative or next of kin wanted to accompany the body. Martha's head seemed to give an involuntary lurch forward but then change to a painful slow shake. That's when she turned to face Billy.

"You can take the body," he told them.

By the time they returned from the station with neither able to find the words to help each other, a stunned silence had spread around Connie's house. Billy walked through to the kitchen to see if Connie was there. He saw her busying herself with Angela, making up a bottle of milk.

"We're not far away, Connie," Billy said.

"I won't forget," she replied.

Billy went through to the parlour. Now the end of this heartrending day was in sight, he knew he couldn't leave without trying to speak to Harry. Lodging himself in the frame of the door, Billy watched as Harry turned around to face him. But the look he then gave Billy belonged to someone whose very will to live seemed threatened with every passing moment. He'd never seen Harry look so tired – as if his body couldn't find a way to support the weight of his actions anymore.

Harry tried to say something but Billy couldn't hear.

"Say that again, Harry," Billy said.

Harry came forward with his hands clenched together. When he muttered something, Billy again interrupted him.

"I can't hear you," Billy said.

"You loved him, didn't you?" Harry asked, looking up at Billy.

It was such a simple thing to say but even so Billy wondered whether he had heard correctly. But the tired grieving lines on Harry's face had gone past the lying stage and now he could see his mouth twitching, caught between the shame and the intimacy of his words.

There was nothing Billy could do to stop himself. He ran out of the house without any idea of where he was going. All he knew was that he couldn't stay there a moment longer.

32

Connie

Nothing could stop Connie now that Angela had really come home. With Angela under the same roof as her, Connie had already moved the pieces of khaki that she used for nappies into the back room. The cream was in the bathroom where she'd change her. There was an old board which was wide enough to put across the tub and drape a towel over too. She thought she might use the back bedroom by putting a towel over the chest of drawers.

It wasn't difficult to find somewhere to put the bottle and the spare teat that she'd been given. She'd never seen Harry in the kitchen before, not cleaning and scrubbing as he'd been doing before Martha and Billy left. The place was cleaner than she'd seen it for ages and for once she found herself smiling as she put on the pan to boil some water for Angela's bottle.

There were leftovers, mince and tatties, and Connie was getting ready to heat them up when she heard the front door rattle.

"Is that you, Harry?" she shouted, putting the dish down on the counter, next to the empty soap bowl and dreading the sarcasm that she had grown so used to.

"True, it's me," he said, taking off his jacket and placing it carefully over the back of the chair.

"Well, what did they say, down at the station?"

For too long Harry didn't respond and it made Connie fear the worst.

"Oh my God, they're not going to charge you, are they?"

"I told them to."

"What! Charge you with murder?"

"No. Accidental death."

"Harry," she pleaded, "whatever for?"

"Because it was my fault, wasn't it?"

"Well, maybe–"

"There's no maybes about it, Connie. I was still pissed. If I hadn't stood there in the middle of the road, Robert wouldn't have swerved the van. That's what I told them. That I regretted everything I did."

"Do you?"

"How can you ask me that? I know I've been a long way down but…"

"What did they say?"

"Said they believed me."

"Which part?"

"That I didn't mean it to happen."

"What will they do now?"

"It's been logged that's all."

"Which means what?"

"If they find me drunk and disorderly in the neighbourhood, they'll string me up by the balls, that's what."

Connie looked at Harry warily, trying to pick a way through the maze of what she was hearing. One minute contrite, the next cocky as hell. She knew that Harry was hot and cold all over, but for a moment she couldn't decide whether any of this was real. For once she thought he looked sober, tired and frail too, with his thin face scored by heavy lines of too much alcohol.

"Why didn't you tell me?" he asked.

"How could I? You would have killed me!"

"Is that what you think?"

"Because you wouldn't have believed it was a mistake, Harry."

"What? To jump into bed with the first GI in town, who's offering you chocolates and stockings."

Connie took a sudden intake of breath.

"Oh yes, I saw them upstairs at the back of the drawer. Thought I'd miss them, did you? A mistake? Bloody convenient, I'd say."

"I didn't want to say it, Harry, but I thought you were dead. I hadn't heard anything. Missing in action was the only thing I heard."

"And if I'm dead, it doesn't matter what you do. Is that it?"

"I'd had too much to drink. We got carried away."

"I'll say you did."

"You're a fine one to talk about! This is the first time I've heard you half-sober since you got back. How many pubs have you been chucked out of now? Three? Harry the fleece, that's what they're calling you. And they don't want you back, either. I suppose you know that."

Harry stood there silent, shaking his head before asking, "What's she called?"

Connie took a moment to follow what Harry was talking about.

"Angela. Angela Morris."

Harry looked around for a moment as if searching for confirmation.

"It's a nice name."

"Well, it's the only one she's got."

"Can I see her?"

"'Course you bloody can. When she wakes."

"You know that's why I did it?"

"What?"

"Tried to stop Robert driving away."

"Tell me."

"The baby."

"What about it?"

"I only wanted to see the baby."

"Well, you were standing there in the middle of the road, weren't you? Waving your arms about like a clown. No one could have had any idea. What did you think Robert –?" Her hands came up to her face.

"Here. Come here." Harry said, moving closer to Connie and putting his arms around her. "I'll stand by that baby girl, now, Connie. You know that, don't you? I've no choice."

"I won't let you forget that."

"You won't have to. Every time I see her, I'll be seeing Robert as well. I won't let him die in vain, Connie. I promise. I've seen too many who did."

33

Billy

The wind had picked up and the marram grass along the path waved in front of them like spirits. They were walking a little apart as if the space around each of them had become their own private grieving grounds. Even if the wind had not been blowing in their faces, their eyes would have been streaming. Slowly Billy was trying to release some of the sickening throb of grief that had been strangling him in the days since Robert's death. It had helped to go back to Robert's room and see it as he had left it, full of that sense of life and spirit and spontaneity that had made him live, as Robert said, for freedom.

That's when he found the diary. He hadn't gone to find it. The room was in such a state it was lucky he found it at all. It was lying on the low table beside his bed and then Billy remembered Robert talking about how he would try and write his diary last thing at night. He told Billy it was his way of clearing his head before falling asleep. Picking it up, Billy could feel the grainy black cover, and he had tried to think of Robert doing the same thing. He remembered Robert's soft hands, with those long fingers. He opened it. Inside had been written: *The diary of Robert Chalmers 1945.*

Turning the pages and seeing Robert's writing, the attempted poems, the diary entries, the scribbles and sketches made Billy realise that this was the last part of Robert that he would ever see. If he kept it, it would stay with him as a reminder, like some fixed thread to a place that Robert had believed in.

Now walking up the knoll, he was trying so hard to remember something from the diary that he didn't feel it at first when Martha started tugging at his sleeve. He let himself stop and wait for Martha to come up and stand closer to him than she had all afternoon. His head was still lowered when he felt her hands on his face.

"Stand still for a moment, Billy Hilton, and look at me," she said.

He forced himself to move his head so that he could see her eyes. His own were still so close to tears that it took him a little while to blink them dry enough to see her.

"Say it once," she said slowly, her whole body heaving with the effort, "and I'll never ask you to say it again."

Martha was looking at Billy, with her dark eyes, that looked so full of pain, and with her arms still cradling his head, waiting.

"But I want to…" Billy started, "I never went looking for it. And I fought it, but then I couldn't stop it."

Holding his head quite still he moved his body closer to her so that Martha's face filled his whole vision.

"There was something about him, Martha." Billy paused.

"I know."

"He started smiling at me even before there was anything between us. As though he was looking for something to hold onto. That only I could give him. I couldn't understand it then. Things were changing too fast and I felt like running away. And then when I stopped being frightened and learnt to love him, it was… too late."

Billy could feel his tears as he looked for Martha's eyes again, which flickered for a moment and then closed. As they did, she took her arms from his head and put them around his body.

"Hold me," she said, before she collapsed into his broad embrace in an outburst of sobbing.

They stood there, wrapped in each other's arms, without talking, and he could feel her body shaking, as she searched for ways to make sense of her life without Robert.

Then pulling herself away from Billy, she took his hand and placed it on the front of her smock.

"I was up here the other day, wishing I could have told you, wishing you were ready for it. Wishing you could hear."

Billy looked up at her face.

"There's someone else to love now, Billy."

But he held his hand there on Martha, almost waiting for a sign.

"Are you sure?" he asked.

"I'm about six weeks bloody late, Billy! I've never been late before in my life. I did try and tell you, remember, but I couldn't find you then."

Billy shook his head.

"What's the matter? Don't you want one?" Martha asked when she saw the look on his face.

"It's not that! It's just too much after what's just happened. I need time to take it in."

"I thought you'd be pleased! I've been waiting for days to tell you."

"Oh, I am," Billy said, catching hold of Martha's hand and pulling her towards him, "but I can't lose his face – Robert's – just lying there."

"Now, don't start me again, Billy," she said, putting her hand up to her face.

"Do you know something?" he asked.

"What's that?"

"Robert – he would have been so pleased for us, for the… three of us. But he was always so wary of you, the radical part of you. He thought you were anti-everything sometimes, including families. He didn't see you signing up to a bourgeois lifestyle!"

"You talk like I intimidated him. Me! Intimidate Robert? Come on, Billy! It was him that always had the answers to everything. He made me feel clueless sometimes."

"But he admired you for the way you stood up for yourself. He'd be so proud of you now."

"And you too, Billy."

"I can't forget him."

"You don't have to. Maybe," she said resting his hand across her stomach again, "if it's another Robert."

"It will be," Billy said.

They walked without talking for a moment until Billy said,

"I found his diary,"

It took her a moment to answer, "And?"

"Do you want it?" he asked.

Martha was silent and for a while all Billy could hear was his heart beating and the sound of a train somewhere distant.

"No," Martha said, "you keep it and then we won't lose him again. Because he'll stay with you, Billy, won't he?"

Billy was nodding but he suddenly remembered the words Robert had scribbled in his diary –

'My heart, my heart

So full of the reach of love.'

He turned towards Martha.

"I think Robert will stay with all of us," he said and holding Martha's hand he helped her down the grassy slope before they reached the path again.

* * *